BLOOD OF THE BOURGEOISIE

BLOOD
OF THE
BOURGEOISIE

MICHAEL
R. SULLIVAN

"The bourgeoisie is the class of modern capitalists, owners of the means of social production and employers of wage labor."

KARL MARX

"The bourgeoisie no longer wears top hats and monocles; it wears Patagonia vests and talks about innovation."

ANONYMOUS

"The bourgeoisie was never naturally the enemy of the working man. It was the state that set them against each other by pitting one group's privileges against another's burdens."

HANS-HERMANN HOPPE

"The bourgeoisie no longer hoards land—it hoards information."

EDWARD SNOWDEN

"The bourgeoisie will not let itself be disarmed, neither by words nor by votes. Only violence can destroy it."

JEAN-PAUL SARTRE

CHAPTER 1

————

The glimmer of the morning sun off the Hudson
River reminded Cal of the moment he watched
Max die. He saw the final flicker of realization
in the man's eyes, the waves of disgust as Max gazed
into the face of his killer.

And I deserved every bit of it.

Cal shook the thought from his mind and looked
out over the waters.

Fourth of July weekend.

New York City.

This place would soon fill with tourists and locals,
all coming to watch the fireworks light up the night
sky. But right now, most of the city was still asleep.
Cal took a drink of his coffee. On a typical morning,
he'd sip it from behind his computer screen while an-
alyzing laundered financial transactions.

Not today.

The sun's rays were beginning to light up the east-
ern sky, casting a golden hue over the bay. The Statue
of Liberty stood tall in the distance. The longer he'd

lived in this city, the more it faded into the background. He wondered what Americans of the past would think about the country she looked over today.

Would they still think of us as the land of the free and the home of the brave?

Cal ran his fingers through his beard. He still wasn't used to leaving his house unshaven. It felt wrong. The military was behind him, but the instinct to start each day with a blade lingered somewhere in his bones.

In a previous life, I would've shaved before meeting her.

He wished he had turned her away, but she'd been so persistent. She had the kind of charming smile that was impossible to reject, no matter how much Cal detested journalists.

"Captain Lamarck?" said a soft voice from behind him. He turned to see a young woman in a dark dress. Her sun-kissed skin looked like it had recently seen more sunshine than New York's dreary skies had to offer. Her smooth brown hair framed her bright smile.

"Just Cal," he said. "That title ended the day I resigned."

"Sofia," she said, extending her hand. Each of her nails was polished with a classic white French tip.

"You're late."

"I'm sorry," she said. "It's been a crazy couple of days."

She flashed a smile that Cal imagined convinced most men to say yes to her.

I have to resist that charm. Reporters like her have twisted my words before.

Cal started walking.

She followed.

"Why do you people still want to interview me?"

"I can't speak for other reporters," Sofia said as she clicked her pen. "But my instincts tell me there is more to the story."

"I think that's a lie," Cal said. "You people just want to hear about the moment I killed Max."

She didn't respond. She didn't need to. He saw the answer in her brown eyes.

"I didn't come here for another clickbait headline," she said as they passed by the trees and shrubbery lining the edges of the park. "I came here to understand the man who brought down Max Aldrich."

Cal didn't respond.

The two of them walked toward the older buildings in the financial district. They crossed the street and passed a building with small gargoyles on its corners.

"Previous journalists may have painted you in a bad light," she continued. "I promise you I won't."

"Why should I believe that?"

They walked past the ornately carved statues of a museum and into Bowling Green Square. The lush green grass and manicured hedges stood in sharp contrast to the towering buildings surrounding them. Today would be a long day if he had to endure her constant questions. He looked ahead toward their destination, wondering why it had been chosen.

He began to cross the street.

"Wait," she said, grabbing his wrist. "I've fought with my editor all week for this opportunity. She's looking for any excuse to get me fired. This is my last chance."

"That's not my problem."

"I pitched her a story about resilience. A story about a man whose family escaped from war-torn Yugoslavia.

A man who emerged from those struggles to lead one of the most decorated digital forensics teams in military history."

"What about the man who shamefully resigned?" Cal asked. "Will that man be included in your story of resilience?"

"If you'll let me," she said. "Just let me tag along for the rest of the day. You'll be paid handsomely."

"I don't need your money."

"I will only publish what you approve."

"I assure you, it isn't as exciting as you've been led to believe."

"Twenty-four hours, Cal. That's all I'm asking. Let me tell your story."

"One day," Cal said over the sounds of traffic. "And I'm going to have to give precedence to my current case."

"One day," she repeated.

He nodded in agreement.

"Where should we begin?" she asked.

"That is completely up to—"

Her words were cut short by a crashing sound from the square.

CHAPTER 2

Sofia watched people run past. It transported her back to her memories of reporting in war-torn countries.

The screams.

The panic.

The darkness she'd lived through.

Allowing fear to control you is a surefire way to miss a great story.

And a great story now stood directly in front of her.

Sofia glanced at Cal's face, studying his demeanor as chaos erupted in front of them. The fatigue in his eyes vanished.

She'd only just met him, but he seemed different from what she expected. Despite hunching over a computer for most of his day job, he still had the rigid posture typical of someone who had served in the military. But he looked more disheveled than she'd seen during his interviews with scraggly facial hair and dark circles under his eyes.

There was warmth in his eyes.

Despite his attempts to brush her off, she sensed kindness.

During her career as a journalist, she'd been around military types before. Endless discipline. Cool under pressure. She'd gotten better at being brave when faced with life-threatening situations, but people like Cal seemed to *enjoy* it.

He ran toward the commotion, like he was compelled to help those in danger.

She followed.

Bowling Green Square was a small green pocket inside the towering metropolis of New York City. The tops of the buildings were beginning to catch the early morning light. People sprinted past them, faces white with terror.

Cal didn't look back at her. He didn't care.

At least not yet.

They came upon the cause of the turmoil. A giant bronze beast stood between the cross streets, the beacon of the United States' financial dominance.

The Bull of Bowling Green.

The giant charging bull, symbolizing Wall Street's financial power, was normally a tourist magnet. But not today. Upon each of its horns hung mutilated corpses. Two men. Each skewered through the abdomen and arching backwards, their limbs dangling. Blood dripped over the head of the bull, spilling down onto the concrete below.

"You aren't going to go near it, are you?" Sofia asked as Cal approached.

He looked back at her with a calculating gaze, his eyes narrowing as he assessed the situation.

"I think this is why I'm here," he stated cautiously.

"You don't know?"

"I was only given a time and place."

Sofia stepped over a fallen wall, aluminum framing wrapped in black vinyl, toppled like dominoes around the statue. They had likely been set up to block the view until the right moment. The tension wires that once held them upright now lay tangled at their feet like cut marionette strings.

The last thing Sofia wanted to do was get closer to the large volume of blood pooling beneath the bull. The metallic smell alone was enough to make her lightheaded.

Just breathe.

If she truly wanted to win Cal over, she had to show him she could handle anything.

"Damn," Cal said as they stepped to the front of the bull and saw each of the men. Something had been carved into their chests, just above the bronze horn that pierced their stomachs.

Twelve words. Each with small trails of blood weaving like scarlet spiderwebs over their skin.

"What is it?" Sofia asked.

"Seed phrases," Cal said, his voice barely a whisper.

"Should I know what that means?"

"You should if you're planning to write a story about me," Cal said as he glanced at her. "This has to be why they want to hire me."

"You are correct, Cal," said a deep voice behind them.

CHAPTER 3

NINE YEARS EARLIER

Nahla looked down at the twelve words on the page, unsure what her uncle wanted her to say. "I don't understand how this helps us."

"Diversification," Uncle Hashim stated. "Many people I know have been stopped at the border. Even with the right credentials, the Sudanese government grows more restrictive each day. If they search us and find any money, they will take it from us… or worse."

"Have you told Tariq?" Nahla asked.

Hashim gazed out the window at the dusty streets of Khartoum. This city had been their home for years. The call to prayer echoed in the background, a reminder of the life they were leaving behind.

It didn't feel like home. Nothing in this country felt like home anymore.

"You know Tariq," Hashim said. "That boy is always excited about learning some new technology. He helped me set it up, but he's nervous about breaking the law. Working for al-Bashir is getting to him. We need to get out of here before he succumbs to their corruption and lies."

"I fear we have limited time, Uncle."

Tears began to well up in Hashim's eyes. She had to look away. She couldn't bear to see him cry. He'd seen his country collapse in a way she could never fully understand. In his younger years, Hashim still had hope. That hope was now dead.

"The officers on the border are becoming more savvy by the day," he said. "Do you trust me?"

She nodded, but what she felt was much different from trust.

Hashim and Tariq were the only family she had left. He took her in after her childhood home burned to the ground. He was her final shred of hope.

"I want you to memorize them," he said, sliding the strange list of words across the table.

"Can't this wait?" she asked. "I'm exhausted. My fingers are still sore from molding all your gold into clothes hangers."

He smiled at her. A pained smile, but that was the most joy she saw from him these days.

"I'm sorry, Nahla," he said. "This is important. Earlier today, someone else I know was caught and—"

He trailed off, but she knew how that sentence would end.

I'm not blind, Uncle. I know how many of your friends have been killed.

No matter how old she got or how much darkness she'd seen, he still tried to protect her from it.

He acted like she hadn't seen her parents murdered in front of her.

He reached across the table, cupping her hands in his own.

"We are so close to being rid of this place for good. Please, do this one last thing for me."

She looked down again at the list of words. All twelve of them in American English. Another reminder of the country they'd soon be in, a place where voices were not quelled by an oppressive government.

In some ways, I already feel like an American.

Hashim paid for their education with the hope that one day they'd become US citizens. Tariq spent most of his time in the tech labs at the American University in Cairo before returning to Sudan to work under Omar al-Bashir. Nahla, meanwhile, attended Khartoum International Community School. She was surrounded by the children of diplomats and foreign executives, but she never felt like one of them.

What she loved about America wasn't the success stories of Silicon Valley or the glamour of Hollywood. It was the revolutionary spirit. While her classmates focused on Ivy League exams, she stayed glued to books about the Founding Fathers.

They fought for freedom in the face of tyranny, a legacy of liberty that still echoed through the world.

Nahla wanted to do the same.

She wanted to stay and fight for Sudan, putting her life on the line like those men once did for their own country. This was where she was born, and now Hashim wanted to run away from their problems.

The words of Thomas Paine ran through her head.

'These are the times that try men's souls.'

But Hashim was an economist, not a fighter. He showed his love by educating her about the world and by paying for her fancy education, but he was no revolutionary. He was the sort of man who kept silent during danger, the sort of man who prioritized safety over bravery. So when he asked her to break the law, she immediately knew things were getting serious.

"I'll do it," she said as she adjusted the hem of her thobe. "What are they?"

"It's called a seed phrase. It's a way to store money in your mind. As long as you remember these words, you'll be able to access our money after we cross the border."

She tried to hide her skepticism. She trusted him. For now, that was enough.

Nahla stared at the paper, unsure how it could help them as much as the dollars and gold they had saved for their escape.

"We leave tomorrow," he said. "The guard on duty in the morning is an old friend. It might be our last opportunity to cross."

She smiled, watching him get excited for the first time in months. The optimistic look on his face was out of place, but she enjoyed it.

For a moment, Nahla let herself think that their luck might finally be changing.

Then she heard the fist pounding on the door.

CHAPTER 4

———

A grey man approached.

Cal did a double-take.

He wore a grey pinstriped suit that looked as if it had cost tens of thousands of dollars. His hair was slicked back, with a well-trimmed beard all a similar tone of grey.

Cal's eyes instinctively scanned for bulges in the jacket. No obvious weapons, no printing. The man had a grizzled look about him. His pale eyes looked like they'd seen the same kind of darkness as the men Cal used to serve with.

"Harold?" Cal asked.

"It's a pleasure to meet you," Harold said, extending a hand. The scent of cigar smoke drifted from his suit. His grip was firm. Practiced.

"The circumstances are worse than you led me to believe," Cal said.

"I'm afraid so," Harold said as he caught Sofia's eye. "And who might this be?"

"Sofia," she said, extending her hand. "I'm writing a story about Cal."

"This was not in the terms we agreed to regarding your employment," Harold stated, his eyes narrowing.

"Who said I was accepting the terms of your employment?" Cal asked.

"I assumed your attendance here today was an acceptance of our offer?" Harold asked, raising an eyebrow.

"Your crime scene is twenty-seven blocks from my doorstep, and you offered me an exorbitant amount of money. I had to check it out."

"You find yourself in a position to gain favor from some of the wealthiest people in this city," Harold said. "I'm surprised you haven't accepted the case more enthusiastically."

"It's hard to imagine anything that I desire less than the favor of the hyper-wealthy. I'm a self-made man. I intend on keeping it that way."

"Being self-made is a fantasy for the powerless. Every empire stands on the shoulders of those who came before."

"And if I don't desire to create an empire?"

"Then you'll spend your life bowing to those of us who do," Harold said as he stepped back. A small line of blood was dripping from the bodies running near his meticulously polished grey shoes.

"How did you know the bodies would be here?" Cal asked.

"We'll get to that," Harold said as he began to examine the bodies more closely. "Do either of you recognize these men?"

Cal looked at Sofia. Her complexion had gone pale as she stared at the corpses. She shook her head.

Cal tried to ignore the horns piercing the men's stomachs as he analyzed their bodies. He'd seen gruesome deaths during his first deployment, but nothing quite so theatrical.

"I don't think so," Cal said.

"These are the Valhner brothers," Harold said. "Two of the wealthiest men in New York City."

"That means nothing to me."

"That building bears their name," Harold said as he pointed to one of the skyscrapers in the distance.

"Not exactly the sort of people I care about."

"Doesn't your work center around money?"

"I'm more interested in improving our money systems to reduce the gap between the elites and the rest of us," Cal said. "I don't worship at the altar of the penthouse class."

The corner of Sofia's mouth turned up into a smile as she scribbled some notes on her notepad.

Maybe it won't be so bad to have her around after all. I'm not sure if I can stomach being alone with Harold all day.

What did Harold want from him? He wasn't a crime scene detective. His only urge was to open a laptop, investigate the wallets associated with the seed phrases, and look through their transactions.

Regardless, Cal examined the bodies more closely.

The two men looked as though they'd been tortured. The man closest to him was missing an ear, the other a couple of fingers. Both of their genitals had been sawed off. Blood spilled out of the bottom of their torsos and over the back of the giant bronze beast.

"What more can you tell us about them?" Cal asked as he used his phone to take a picture of the words carved into the men's chests.

"They were a previous client of mine," Harold said. "They acquired their wealth from defense contracting."

"What exactly did you do for them?"

"Confidentiality is the cornerstone of my profession. Surely you are familiar with the concept."

"You've hired me to investigate. Now isn't the time for keeping secrets."

"My world is laced in secrecy," Harold said as he met Cal's eyes. "I'm not even sure I can trust you yet, let alone the journalist you've decided to invite into my affairs."

"How did you even know these bodies would be here? Can you tell me that?"

"The Valhner brothers received death threats and ransom demands frequently," Harold began. "They didn't take them very seriously. None of my employers do."

"Seems like they should have."

"We are reevaluating those threats now," Harold said. "Yesterday evening, we were given a time and a place. That's when I decided to hire you."

"I've still not committed to anything."

Harold looked at Cal. There was more than darkness in those eyes. There was certainty. They held the kind of old-world entitlement that the financial district of New York City was founded upon.

"You will," Harold said.

CHAPTER 5

———

Sofia noticed a shift in Harold's personality. The pompous facade fell away and behind it was something dark. His eyes became sharp and calculating.

"I think the more you learn about what's going on, the more you will want to be involved," Harold said to Cal.

Sofia jotted down some notes, mostly for show. It served as a reminder of her role, and she liked having something to do with her hands to keep her distracted. Every time she looked at the bodies of the Valhner brothers, her heart raced.

Get your shit together.

"If they were tortured and killed here, there would be larger pools of blood," Harold said, his keen eyes studying the bodies.

The metallic scent of blood mixing with the morning air made Sofia's stomach turn.

"Each of the holes was made after they were already dead," Harold said. "Their bodies were transported here."

"Are you a detective?" Cal asked.

"Sometimes," Harold said as he stepped over one of the temporary walls. There was a confidence in his posture, like he'd done this before.

"Why did you hire Cal?" Sofia asked.

"The ransom was demanded in Bitcoin, and it's no secret that Cal is an expert. His last case made it clear that he was willing to do whatever it takes to complete the job, even if it meant getting his hands dirty."

"Are you referring to what happened with Max Aldrich?" Sofia asked.

"The criminal justice system often doesn't act as decisively as it should," Harold stated. "I was pleasantly surprised to hear that Max died before some lawyer was able to get him off on a technicality."

Any warmth in Cal's face was gone, leaving only tension and regret.

His posture stiffened.

She wanted to probe deeper, but her journalistic instincts told her to be patient. Her plan would be cut short if Harold didn't allow her to tag along.

Police sirens grew nearer, piercing the early morning calm.

"What's with the twelve words again?" she whispered to Cal, hoping to distract him from thinking about Max. Harold continued investigating the tension wires attached to the collapsed walls.

"Each set of words is a seed phrase for a Bitcoin wallet."

"But what does that mean?"

"It's like a password," Cal began, slipping into the practiced cadence of someone who's explained this a hundred times before. "A password so complex that you don't even need a username. There is a lot of cryptography involved, but put simply, those twelve words allow complete access and control over a chunk of bitcoin."

The sirens grew closer.

"I'll need to use my computer and investigate each of the two seed phrases," Cal said. "It's strange. They gave us the full private keys instead of just a single address. We have full transparency. This has to be some kind of message."

"On that, we agree," Harold said. "Two of the richest men in New York City, their bodies speared over the symbol of financial power in the United States."

"While using the next evolution of financial tech," Cal said.

Sofia noticed Harold's eyes narrowing. Cal was too focused on examining the bodies to realize he'd struck a nerve with Harold.

"Why are younger generations so determined to make things more complex with new technology?" Harold said.

Cal cast a tight-lipped smile toward Sofia.

Perhaps that's my way in with him.

She shared the same sentiment as Harold. The work Cal did was so far over her head. But that didn't matter. The more Harold disagreed with Cal, the more it gave her an opportunity to support him.

"I think you're onto something," she said to Cal. "There is so much symbolism here."

The flashing lights of police cars reflected off the towering glass buildings as the vehicles parked. Two officers got out of the car and approached them, their faces grim.

"The three of you need to step away from the scene immediately."

"Hello, officers," Harold said, laying on the charm. The sudden shift in his personality was jarring. Sofia had come to know these types during her career. The kind willing to wear whatever face was necessary to reach their goals. "I was the one who tipped you off. I've personally spoken with the chief, and he authorized our presence here."

"We'll require your statements," the officer said.

"Unfortunately," Harold said, handing them a business card. "We don't have time for that. We have another crime scene to get to."

CHAPTER 6

———

NINE YEARS EARLIER

"Hashim!" a voice bellowed outside the door.
Soldiers.
Hashim's eyes connected with Nahla's. She watched the hope inside them die.

A fist pounded on the door.

"As decreed by President Omar al-Bashir, Sudan is under emergency economic law. All private gold is property of the state."

Hashim launched to his feet and grabbed the list of words he'd set in front of her.

He raced to his office.

Nahla followed.

Not now. Not like this.

Frantically, he began to pull out drawers, searching for something.

The pounding on the door echoed through their modest house. The air was thick with dust. Dirt and sand found their way into every home during Khartoum's dry season.

"Uncle?" she asked, her voice barely above a whisper. "How did they find us?"

He ignored her, but she had a feeling she already knew the answer.

Hashim found what he was looking for. He pulled a small metal capsule from his desk, opened it, rolled up the piece of parchment with the seed phrase, and thrust it into her hand.

"Swallow it. Now."

She did, forcing the large metal pill into the back of her throat. Cold and dry, it slowly moved down her esophagus, taking a few swallows to get it down. For a moment, she thought her stomach would reject it. She focused on her breathing, willing her body to hold it down.

The front door burst open.

Boots stomped across the wooden floors, their heavy thuds mirroring the pounding of her heartbeat. The soldiers flooded the room, bringing with them the stench of sweat and gunpowder.

"Protect it with your life," Hashim said, grasping her hands, his voice shaking with urgency. "It'll be more than enough for you and Tariq to get out of here, to get a new life. Get away from—"

A military man rounded the corner, his uniform crisp and intimidating.

"Hashim," said the thick-bodied officer, behind him, sneering military grunts gripped their weapons. "You're accused of harboring state property. Surrender it immediately, or it will be taken by force."

Hashim stared back, too afraid to respond. Nahla had seen enough military raids to know that any word could end in cruelty. It was best to shut up and take your blows. To beg for forgiveness.

The burly man kneeled and stared into Hashim's eyes, only inches between their faces. "I hate people like you. Fearful little cockroaches that would rather escape their country than fight for freedom."

"Is it really freedom that you fight for?" Hashim questioned. "Is that what the opposition would say as you butcher their women and children?"

You chose this moment to be brave?

The large man sneered. He stepped back and rammed the butt of his gun into Hashim's face. Hashim's nose burst, blood painting the floor.

"Who's she?" he said, staring directly at Nahla.

"A maid," Hashim said. "She's just leaving."

The man cocked his head to the side and looked at her.

"Your face looks far too regal to be poor," the general said. He lifted her chin and examined her face. "What's your name?"

Nahla wasn't physically able to speak. She did everything in her power to keep the metal capsule in her stomach.

"What's her name, boy?" the burly man asked.

That's when she saw him. Tariq. Standing behind the rest of the soldiers, his face was pale, his eyes wide with fear. He refused to meet her eyes.

No. No. No.

"What have you done, boy?" Hashim bellowed.

Tariq just stood there, his gaze fixed to the ground. He mumbled her name under his breath.

"Nahla," the general whispered into her ear. His breath reeked of cigarettes. "Your uncle thinks he knows what freedom is. He thinks I care what my enemies scream as they leave this world."

He stood up, addressing the room.

"You know what the only thing I hate more than the insurgents?" the broad-faced man asked the room, slowly running his knuckles down the front of her thobe.

"What's that, sir?" one of the military men asked. Hashim looked cold and angry. He vibrated with rage while one of the men forced him onto his knees.

"Rats that want to escape this country. We are building a new empire, and vermin like you want to flee with our riches."

He slapped the back of his hand across Nahla's face. The ring on his middle finger collided with her cheekbone, causing blinding pain as she crumpled to the ground. The taste of blood flooded her mouth. She gagged, almost spilling the contents of her stomach. She steadied herself, focusing all her energy on keeping the metal capsule down.

The man grabbed Nahla by her hair, pressing the cold blade of a knife to her throat.

"You tell us where the gold is immediately, or the skinny bitch gets her throat slit."

"Clothes hangers," Tariq shouted from behind the soldiers. "They were fashioning the gold bullion into clothes hangers."

One of the soldiers jumped into action, running into the closet and beginning to throw their clothing onto the floor.

Nahla watched in disgust as so much of what they had been working for over the past years was taken away. For a moment, she wished the man would kill her.

He pulled the knife away, shoving her to the ground once more.

"I can smell their fear," the wide-faced man continued, now hulking over Hashim. "I know you want to weasel away with all our hard-earned wealth."

Hashim didn't bow his head. He stood there unyielding, accepting his fate.

"Confiscate the gold," the large man said. "Then book him. We've got a prison cell with his name on it."

"How dare you go to these vile pigs, Tariq?" Hashim bellowed as they placed him in handcuffs. "Have I taught you nothing?"

Tariq looked up, finding his father's eyes. Nahla saw at that moment that he was just as afraid as she was. She saw the deep regret in his eyes. She saw the weak, scared boy Tariq had always been.

Nahla watched the rage boil over in the large man. In an instant, he was back across the room.

"Tariq has learned not to be a lying rat like his father," the large soldier said. For the first time, a wide smile appeared on his face. "He loves his country. That's something a weak man like you could never understand."

"Omar al-Bashir sits in his mansion and drinks fine wine while he has his thugs shake down families and harass little girls."

"What did you call me?"

"I said you were a—"

The soldier drove his knife into Hashim's chest.

Time froze.

Particles of dust hung in the air between them as Nahla's mind raced over how she might have prevented this. She could feel the terrible image seared into her memory. The blood slowly soaked through her uncle's shirt.

"No," Tariq yelled, attempting to sprint toward his father. The soldiers grabbed his arms, pulling him back.

Hashim's face went white.

The soldier grabbed the back of Hashim's head, pulling his body into the blade, shoving the weapon deeper into his heart and lungs. Their faces were inches apart as the soldier watched Hashim realize that his life was ending.

Nahla closed her eyes, but the sound of the blade plunging into Hashim's lungs replayed over and over in her mind. Her soul fractured in that moment. The man who brought hope back into her life collapsed onto the dusty floor.

A deep guttural noise erupted out of her.

"Shut your mouth, bitch, or I'll come back here tonight and make you wish you had as quick a death as your uncle."

Nahla fell to her knees, her uncle's blood flowing toward her, mingling with the dust and dirt on the floor. Nahla saw the tears streaming down Tariq's face. Her only comfort was knowing he must be feeling the same pain.

The soldiers left with the gold, their boots shuffled on the wooden floor, the sound echoing through the silent house.

Nahla couldn't hold it in.

She threw up.

The metal capsule spilled onto the floor.

She grabbed it, holding it for a moment in the palm of her hand.

The only piece of what Hashim left for her.

My final chance at freedom.

CHAPTER 7

C al sat in a plush leather chair, watching Sofia chat with the bartender. Harold's cigar smoke wafted through the dimly lit space. Soft classical music echoed across the polished marble floor as one of Harold's crew members played a grand piano.

All while the plane flew over the Atlantic Ocean.

Harold's private jet was a modern marvel of engineering. The cabin felt surprisingly luxurious, despite everything being bolted to the ground. If not for the clouds outside the window, Cal might've thought he was in a high-end hotel.

But there was something else on his mind.

Something that drove him to the edge of his seat.

This doesn't make any sense.

The first time he looked at his computer screen, he assumed it was a mistake. He did it again, rebooting from the minimal Linux distro on his encrypted flash drive and entering the seed phrase once more. Same result. He even connected to a variety of Bitcoin nodes to verify that nothing was wrong with his personal one.

This can't be right.

It was immediately apparent why he was called here. He understood why so many rich and powerful people were interested in his work. Unfortunately, he was now certain that he was out of his depth.

Harold returned from speaking with the pilot, his polished grey shoes clacking across the marbled flooring. He sat across from Cal.

"I told you," Harold said.

"You told me what exactly?"

"You'd take the case," Harold continued. "If not for the prestige, for the luxury. My employers and I will spare no expense to ensure that we have everything we desire to accomplish the task at hand. Was it the jet that finally persuaded you? The open bar?"

"Neither."

"Some people like to pretend they are above wealth and amenities," Harold said. "But these things are fundamental human desires."

Cal ignored him. Instead, he focused on the numbers on his screen that seemed impossible.

He triple-checked.

Sofia took a seat alongside him. He still wasn't sure about bringing her, but it was better than being alone with Harold.

She must be ecstatic about having lucked into this new story.

"Are you going to tell me you don't find this plane comfortable?" Harold asked.

"I'm more concerned about how many more dead bodies you have for us," Cal said.

"Hopefully only one," Harold said. "But my employers

hope we can get enough information to stop whoever is behind this."

"What do your employers do?" Sofia asked.

"Entrepreneurs, politicians, and everywhere in between," Harold began.

"And what do they employ you to do?" Cal asked.

Harold leaned back and crossed his legs. The smoke from his cigar drifted up and around the cabin.

"I solve problems, Cal," he said. "Yesterday, it was helping a young prince prepare a speech on the international stage. Today, it's investigating the actions of a potential terrorist organization."

"So you're a fix-it man?" Sofia asked. "Just for rich people."

"There is a skill that seems lost on the younger generations of today," Harold said. "The art of getting things done, regardless of what problems lie in front of you. That's my specialty. I eliminate obstacles, no matter what gets in the way."

"Even laws?" Sofia asked.

Cal noticed that questions flowed out of her naturally, and the responses were recorded automatically as though her pen was an extension of her hand. It didn't matter that she was here to interview Cal. She seemed genuinely curious and couldn't turn it off.

"Yes, even laws," Harold replied, with a tight-lipped smile. "Speaking of which…"

Harold reached into his bag, pulling out a heavily modified handgun.

"We're following dangerous people, Cal," Harold said. "I want to make sure you are adequately prepared."

"A Sig M18," Cal said as he looked at the familiar firearm.

"I know the M17 is standard issue," Harold stated. "But I thought you might want something more compact to carry today."

Cal took the gun and cleared it. Mag out. Slide racked. Chamber clear. He ran the slide again, feeling the balance in his grip. He racked it once more and then checked the trigger break. The familiar movement came back to him naturally. The muscle memory was so deeply ingrained, it felt like his hands were operating independently of the rest of him.

The DLC-coated slide and African blackwood grip made it a flawless blend of luxury and function. In his military days, he would have killed for the opportunity to carry something like this.

"Filled with Federal HST," Harold said, as he handed Cal a few loaded magazines.

"Your team did their research," Cal said. "But I don't want it."

"I get it," Harold said. "You military guys have a thing for your personal firearm. I thought it might further convince you to take the case. I assumed it's nicer than whatever you've got. It's the best money can—"

"I'm not carrying," Cal said.

"What?"

"It's a beautiful gun, but I don't carry anymore."

"Suit yourself," Harold said.

Sofia looked at him curiously before writing down something else in her notebook. He wondered if she would include this in her story. He imagined what she might write about him not wanting to carry a gun after what happened with Max.

She wouldn't be wrong.

Cal looked out the window again, the expansive blue water spanning out over the east side of the plane. He could feel the angle of the plane changing as they began their descent. In front of him, the computer completed its final check.

Same result.

"Didn't the Valhner brothers have security teams?" Cal asked.

"We didn't take the threats seriously at first," Harold said. "Ultra-high-net-worth individuals with a *history* like theirs receive threats constantly."

"And exactly what kind of *history* is that?" Sofia asked with a bitterness in her voice. It seemed he wasn't the only one getting put off by Harold's unscrupulous background.

"Defense contracting."

"Or put more clearly," Cal began, thinking back to his military days. "Profiting off of forever wars. Can't imagine why anyone would wish violence upon men like that."

He caught the corner of Sofia's mouth turn up into a smile again, but she did her best to hide it and continue to write down notes.

"We have reason to believe a large team of people is involved," Harold continued, ignoring their snide comments. "Maybe even a terrorist organization."

"A terrorist organization with a statement to make," Cal said. "Spearing two bodies over the symbol of capitalism isn't exactly a subtle message."

"That's some groundbreaking analysis, Cal," Harold said, his voice laced with sarcasm. "I now see why you are the best."

"Their use of Bitcoin only drives that symbolism home," Cal continued. "Bitcoin itself is a direct threat to the manipulative financial powers of the elite class."

"As a card-carrying member of that elite class, I don't find it so threatening," Harold said with a look of skepticism.

"You sound like the kings and bishops who once tried to ban the printing press," Cal said. "Back then, wealthy people decided what the masses were allowed to believe. The printing press ripped that control away. You could burn a book, but you couldn't kill an idea once it spread. In the same way books decentralized knowledge, Bitcoin decentralizes money."

"I require your skill set, Cal," Harold said. "But lessons about a technology I will never use are unnecessary."

No surprises here. The people most open-minded toward Bitcoin are usually the ones crushed by the existing system, not the ones controlling it.

From Harold's vantage point, the financial system probably seemed fine. Why question a machine designed to serve you?

Most rich CEOs never bothered to understand Bitcoin because it didn't affect them. Investors lined up to hand them free money during capital raises. Politicians, on the other hand, couldn't fathom why the people they governed would turn to Bitcoin. When you control the money printer, you can't imagine a world without it. The technology's first adopters weren't Silicon Valley billionaires or DC politicians. They were freedom-loving individuals upset by government bail-outs and inflation.

People like Harold didn't care that Bitcoin was the culmination of 50 years of rigorous cryptographic research. They didn't know that engineers had been attempting to develop forms of digital money for thirty years before the Bitcoin protocol was discovered.

He doesn't care, because he doesn't need to care. The current monetary system keeps him in power.

"What have you found so far?" Harold asked.

"Why don't you look for yourself?" Cal asked as he turned his computer screen toward Harold and Sofia.

"What are we looking at here?" Sofia asked.

"This is where the entire net worth of the Valhner brothers disappeared to," Cal said. "This is the full transaction history for these two wallets."

"This was exactly our employer's concern when they mentioned Bitcoin in their ransom demands," Harold said. "The technology was basically designed for money laundering. We want you to track down the transactions so we can return the funds."

"Bitcoin was designed to be a form of money people like your employers couldn't control," Cal stated. "Which I assume is why you are so intimidated by it."

Harold glared at him as the plane continued its descent.

It reminded Cal of the way Colonel Blackwell looked at him during their takedown of Max Aldrich. The look of a man who desperately needed his knowledge, but couldn't care less about understanding the technology.

I'm nothing but a means to an end for him.

"I had to use advanced programs and algorithms to track Max's financial trail," he continued. "This time I don't have to. They don't have the money."

"That's impossible," Harold said, ashing his cigar. "All the brothers' assets were liquidated over the last few days. That's the entire point of this thing. Why else target the wealthy?"

"About that," Cal said, pulling up one of the news headlines that broke a few minutes before.

Thousands of individuals report receiving large sums of Bitcoin from a random donor.

"I've verified it on the timechain myself. I've checked. I've rechecked. They didn't steal it for themselves. They took all the Valhner brothers' money and transferred it to random people around the world."

CHAPTER 8

———

Sofia exited the town car into the humid Miami air. The three of them stood in front of a massive Venetian-style mansion.

Vizcaya Gardens.

They walked down the cobblestone path beneath the lush tree-lined entrance. The tall trees formed a natural canopy overhead, their leaves rustling softly in the warm breeze. As they passed the empty ticket counter, Sofia imagined what this place would normally look like. She could almost see the crowds of tourists exploring the museum and strolling through the gardens.

Today, a more somber mood hung over the estate.

The magnificent Vizcaya Museum came into view. It resembled an Italian villa. The facade featured intricate stonework and elegant arches. A beautiful archway and a set of grand stairs framed the museum entrance.

Sofia was nervous they were about to stumble across another body.

Will this crime scene be as violent as the last?

"This place normally operates as a museum," Harold said as they entered the immaculate estate. "But Rafael rented it out for a private Fourth of July celebration."

"You can rent a museum?" Cal asked.

"You can rent anything with enough money," Harold said.

"What kind of other weird stuff do you rich people rent?" Cal asked.

Harold glared at him.

"Do you know anything about the history of this place?" Sofia asked.

"It was built by a Chicago industrialist who made his fortune selling agricultural machinery in the early 1900s. He modeled it after Renaissance-era estates, even importing pieces of actual European palaces to build it. He used to host parties here for aristocrats."

"I'm sensing a trend," Cal said. "Another murdered rich person and another location synonymous with wealth gained at the expense of others."

The marble flooring and ornately carved woodwork transported Sofia back to her past. She'd spent a summer in Venice during her time in university. The art on the walls reminded her so much of the ones she used to look at while contemplating the direction of her life.

Sofia watched Cal walk in front of an intricate tapestry as they entered the Tea Room. She wondered what thoughts were running through his mind. The entire time on the plane, his head was buried in his computer, leaving her no time to ask questions.

Be patient. He'll open up to me eventually.

She smelled the body before she saw it.

BLOOD OF THE BOURGEOISIE | **43**

Lying there, sprawled out across the marbled floor, was an old man. His face was smashed so hard that Sofia couldn't recognize the features. Sunlight from the gigantic glass doors poured over his body, baking the blood in the Florida heat.

Across his shirtless torso were twelve words carved into his chest.

"Repeated blunt force trauma," Harold stated as he immediately shifted into focus and crouched down beside the body. "Cause of death was fractures to his skull."

"The murder weapon is over there," said one of the officers. He pointed to one of the solid metal rope stands that would have been used to hold up a queue. The bottom of it was covered in blood and hair.

"Victim is male," Harold continued. "We can't make out his face or hair, but the age spots and grey chest hair indicate he was mid-sixties. Body has been sitting here since late last night. Roughly sometime between one and four in the morning."

Cal pulled out his laptop, inserted a flash drive, and booted it up. Sofia caught a glimpse of the screen. There was no desktop or applications, just a black terminal window with lines of scrolling code. He typed the words carved into the man's chest into his machine.

Sofia pulled out her notepad, more to distract herself than to seriously take notes.

Her stomach turned.

She took a deep breath to calm herself, but it only pulled the stench of sun-baked blood deeper into her lungs. The estate had no air conditioning, and she could feel her legs growing weak. She waited until Cal was focused on the body, then she slipped outside to get a breath of fresh air.

What the hell have I gotten myself into?

CHAPTER 9

NINE YEARS EARLIER

Nahla looked back across the sands of Sudan as she waited in line to cross the border. The vast expanse of desert stretched endlessly behind her. The scorching sun cast long shadows over the familiar landscape. This was the country where she played football with her friends and learned how to sing with her mother.

The country where everyone she loved was buried.

You let this place consume your soul, Tariq. Why could you not have been braver?

Everyone with a fighting spirit lost their lives at the hands of evil men who ruled this country. As she stood awaiting her turn to leave, she realized everything that had once tied her to this place was gone.

Her new country awaited her.

The United States of America. The kind of place where a woman like me can experience freedom.

"Please, no!" a man shouted from behind her as a guard ripped open his bag and rummaged through his belongings. "I have nothing."

Nahla held onto her backpack more tightly while the sun beat down on them.

Just look straight ahead. Blend in. Be forgettable.

She kept her eyes forward and slunk her head.

"You next," the guard said to the old man in front of her.

The man stumbled forward and dumped out the contents of his bag. Clothing scattered across the sand. A few pieces of bread, a small bottle of water.

"I have nothing," he said. "The rest of my family is in Alexandria."

The guard squinted as he examined his belongings. Such a small amount of food for the long journey that stood in front of them. Without more, she was certain the old man wouldn't survive.

"Such a long way to go all by yourself," the guard said.

The old man said nothing.

The guard stepped around him, eyeing him like an animal he might slaughter if it suited him.

"Take off your shirt," the guard commanded.

Nahla watched as the man's shoulders slumped in defeat. Slowly, he peeled off his clothing, tattered rags that barely covered his body. Tucked into his pants were stacks of Egyptian pounds, held together by rubber bands.

"Please," the old man begged. "They aren't even worth anything anymore."

Nahla's blood boiled.

Hashim had told her and Tariq about the devaluation. The Egyptian Central Bank printed enormous amounts of its currency to build luxurious buildings for the country's politicians. They had far-reaching plans to build monolithic new government buildings that would match the grandeur of the pyramids, all funded by stealing wealth away from the average citizen through inflation.

True freedom can only be found in the richest countries in the world. Countries where the government doesn't inflate the currency.

Nahla readied herself for violence. She'd heard of men killed for carrying far less money across the border. The soldier stepped forward, slowly fingering the gun on his belt.

But he never drew it.

Instead, the guard gestured for the man to remain silent. Methodically, the soldier pulled the bills from the man's pants and placed them into his own pockets.

"I'm begging you," the man said. "I won't make it to Alexandria without that money."

The guard said nothing. He simply drew his gun and placed it up to the man's face as he grabbed stack after stack of the money.

"Move," the guard said, tossing the shirt back at the man.

The old man shuffled his feet forward through the sand, his head hung low, sobbing with each step closer to the border crossing. He would make it over the border, but at what cost? Could he even survive the journey?

Could she?

It took everything in her power not to react.

The military men who had taken over her country were nothing more than thugs. No better than the insurgents they were fighting against. All the same. The men who poisoned Tariq's mind and killed Uncle Hashim were part of a larger system. All stemming from the head of the snake.

Omar al-Bashir.

Nahla would have sacrificed all her freedoms for two minutes inside a room with the president and a knife.

"Next," the guard yelled.

She stepped forward. Her feet throbbed in pain from standing for so many hours. She didn't let it show. She stared off into the horizon, willing her mind to think only about what happened next. The sun bore down on her, unrelenting, as the heat waves shimmered in the distance.

"Open your bag."

Slowly, she removed the backpack from her shoulders and placed it on the ground in front of her. Unzipping the leather pouch in the back and spilling all her possessions into the dirt. It looked so meager laid out before her. She didn't even have photos to remember her family or any part of her life. All she had was a pile of clothes, most of them covered in dust from the long journey to the border.

The guard began to rummage through her belongings. Pawing through her clothes with his dirty hands, not caring that she'd have to wear them now with dirt and sand ground into the fabric.

He looked through her shirts.

He picked up her underwear.

The guard's gaze slid back to her. She stared straight ahead, avoiding eye contact at all costs. She could feel his eyes slide over her breasts.

"You look like a rich bitch. This can't be all you have. Take off your hijab."

"Everything I own is in that bag," she said, growing more nervous. "Don't make me do this."

"Skin like that costs money," the soldier said, raising the barrel of his gun.

Just do as he says. This will all be over soon.

She began unwrapping, pulling out the pins that held her hijab in place. Slowly, she let the fabric fall into the sand and dirt.

She looked over the crowd. Their eyes now focused completely on her. Her hair was fully exposed in the midday sun. The soldier wanted her to feel vulnerable, but it had the opposite effect. She felt powerful, like the same kind of freedom she would soon have in America.

She was so close to her end goal. All she had to do was make it one hundred more feet, and she would be free of this country.

"Why did you stop?" the soldier said. "Remove your thobe."

Her heart sank.

Slowly, she let the cloth fall onto the ground.

Standing there, in front of the entire crowd, more exposed than she'd ever been in her life, the sun against her abdomen felt intrusive. The soldier's eyes violated her body, probing without her consent. His eyes didn't view her as a human, but something disposable for his pleasure.

If only you could see the strength that I carry within me.

Something broke inside her.

The rage and anger that had been building up boiled over. She felt a full-body urge to kill him. To take his gun and shoot him in the head. Who cared if it cost her life? Watching one of these men die might be enough to make it all worth it.

No. Even that wasn't good enough. This weak skeleton of a man would soon be replaced by another. No matter if she fulfilled her fantasy of listening to the final gurgles of air leave his body, it wouldn't solve the problems that affected this country.

A slow gust of wind blew across the desert. She shivered as it passed her bare skin.

No.

Survival was all that mattered now.

She made a promise to herself right in that moment. As she stood naked in front of her fellow compatriots, she swore she would carry the fight with her.

I will return.

One day, she would stamp out the rot that plagued her country.

"Carry on," the soldier said, finally getting rid of his lustful urges.

He found nothing.

She *had* nothing.

The only thing she carried from Hashim existed inside her mind. The last chance to hold onto her family's legacy. Everything her parents had worked for, everything they had inherited, everything passed down.

The only hope that remained.

The wealth of generations was embedded in her brain.

She pulled back on her thobe, sand sticking to her skin in the midday heat. Slowly, haphazardly, she threw her hijab around her hair.

Twelve words.

It was everything she had. She swore to herself she would make it count. Not merely for survival, but vengeance.

She thought of Omar al-Bashir and the men like him who subjected the people she loved to humiliation and violence. Men who stole freedoms away from the country they claimed to love.

I'm going to burn you to the fucking ground.

CHAPTER 10

———

Cal pored over his laptop screen in the lavish Tea Room of the Vizcaya manor, trying his best not to let the smell of blood baking in the Miami sun get to him.

A pattern emerged.

This wallet showed a massive influx of bitcoin over the last few days. Then, exactly eleven hours ago, thousands of transactions poured out of the wallet.

It followed the same profile as the Valhner brothers. Random, small Bitcoin addresses, no known large holders, no exchanges. Just thousands of donations to small users of the Bitcoin network.

Bitcoin miners must be pleased with the fees they paid to get these transactions through quickly.

"His name was Rafael," said Harold, as he continued searching the premises. "He was found dead by his staff this morning."

"Did you work for him too?" Cal asked.

"We were acquaintances," Harold said. "Some of our employers pleaded with him not to host the party last night."

"You keep calling them *our* employers," Cal said. "I don't work for these people."

"Why are you still here then?"

"Curiosity."

"I don't believe that."

"And I don't need you to," Cal said. "Believe it or not, some people are motivated by things other than money."

Harold glared at him.

"If the people you work for warned him," Cal asked. "Why still hold the party?"

"Rafael dealt with death threats frequently."

"Why am I beginning to sense a trend among friends of yours?"

"Rafael ran one of the largest shipping fleets in the world," Harold continued. "He was responsible for the majority of transportation in the Gulf of Mexico, but some of his methods were... controversial."

"You work for assholes," Cal stated. "That's the trend."

"Something isn't sitting right with me," Harold said, completely ignoring Cal's comment. "This crime scene is more violent and erratic than the last."

Cal looked down at the body, his head smashed to a pulp.

How many times did his attacker slam the metal stand into his head?

"There is a common saying in homicide," Harold said. "If a man is stabbed once, it's a murder. If he's stabbed thirty times, it's a marital dispute."

"Did he have a wife?"

"They haven't seen her since last night," Harold said. "The Valhner brothers were done cold. Methodical. If someone bashed his head in with this much gusto, I suspect a previous relationship. Even the password phrase—"

"Seed phrase," Cal corrected.

"Whatever it is, it was carved into his chest erratically," Harold said. "I suspect this was a very different sort of person than what we saw in New York."

Cal looked out the beautiful glass archways toward the turquoise waters of Biscayne Bay. Sofia stood alongside the yacht. She looked exhausted.

A pang of guilt reverberated through him.

Dammit.

He'd seen violence so often during his years of service that he forgot how much of a toll it could take on people less accustomed to it. He hadn't considered how poorly she might have been handling it. This wasn't what she signed up for. As conflicted as he was about being interviewed, he should still check in with her. He owed her that much.

"I'll be right back," he said to Harold.

He walked out of the gigantic glass doors. The brilliant blue waters of Biscayne Bay stretched out to meet the horizon. The smell of the floral garden was a stark contrast to the stagnant blood.

A massive yacht floated in the bay.

As he approached, he was able to make out the name written in cursive letters across the side: *The Castillo Tax.* Cal might have been more enamored with its luxury had he not just stepped off the richest private jet he'd ever seen.

"It was too much in there," Sofia said as he approached. "And I wanted to give an update to my editor."

"I understand," he said, taking another deep breath of the floral garden and ocean breeze.

"Do you *really* understand, though?" she asked. "I did my homework. You've seen much worse things during your career."

"That doesn't make it any less terrible," he said. "You just get better at forcing yourself to get through it."

A silence hung in the air for a moment.

"This place reminds me of why I started writing," she said.

"I'm not familiar with how journalism works," Cal said. "But I think I'm supposed to be the one divulging information about *my* past."

She flashed her bright smile as she took a couple of steps closer toward the water. She placed her hand on one of the wooden poles rising up out of the water. It was painted in blue and white.

"These are called pali de casada," she said. "You see them all over Venetian waterways. They're used to tie up gondolas."

Cal watched her eyes get lost as she touched it. Her dark brown hair moved in the gentle breeze off the water. Even with beautiful floral gardens in the background, he couldn't stop his eyes from being drawn to her.

"I went to Venice searching for something," she began. "I was at a complete loss for what to do with my life. I figured getting back to my family history could help me think through my future…"

Cal smiled and nodded, but he couldn't help thinking about how different her life sounded from his. European vacations. Soul-searching. Following her passions.

Must be nice.

"Journalism was invented in Venice," she continued. "Notizie scritte they called it. It was the first time in history that the average person could understand events happening globally. It made the world feel more open and transparent for everyone."

Listening to the Italian words on her lips felt like it added to the picture of Sofia.

"My career has brought me all over the world," she said. "I've seen beautiful countryside, and I've had experiences I wish I could forget. But I certainly didn't expect it to bring me here today."

"Is this what you do?" Cal asked.

She gave him a confused look.

"Open up to people, hoping that they'll respond with their own life story?"

"Sometimes," she said with a smirk. "Is it working?"

"A little," Cal said. "I wanted more than anything to study computer science and cryptography at a university, but my family didn't have the money. The military seemed like the only escape from a life of poverty. I still haven't had time to find myself."

"You seem as though you might have found yourself. You seem quite passionate about what you do for a living."

"If so, it certainly wasn't from European vacations."

"Weren't you born in Europe?"

"Fleeing Yugoslavia with my family is very different from spending a summer in Italy."

There was some more movement on the yacht in front of them. The sound of voices drifted over the water, mingling with the gentle lapping of the waves against the dock.

Interesting.

"I'm in no hurry to get back inside the mansion," he said.

"I'm not sure if I can handle going back in there," Sofia said. "Is there anything else worth investigating in the gardens?"

"I've got a different idea."

"What's that?"

"I think it's time we start doing some real investigating."

CHAPTER 11

———

Sofia followed Cal onto the yacht. The polished teak of the deck gleamed under the midday sun, a testament to the meticulous care given to every inch of the vessel. They walked past the hot tub, the smell of chlorine mingling with the saltiness of the sea breeze.

If it weren't for the putrid smell of dead bodies and stressing about my boss, I might be able to enjoy this.

Cal moved up the steps with the efficiency of a well-trained soldier. Based on his technical role in the military, she expected him to have a rigid posture, but the way he carried himself told a different story. He proceeded with caution. Taking note of his surroundings and checking each door and exit they passed.

She'd seen lavish boats and mansions while reporting on political leaders, but this yacht outdid them all. She felt underdressed. Had she known where today was heading, she might've worn more extravagant jewelry. Then again, most of the wealthy people she'd met today were already dead.

The walls were adorned with intricate wood paneling and artwork. One specific painting caught her eye. It was a portrait of Rafael Castillo, his face barely recognizable compared to what she'd seen inside the mansion.

"These people are unbelievably out of touch," Cal said as they neared the galley.

They began hearing sounds of conversation.

"...they'll be gone in a few hours," said a broad-chested man standing over a cutting board. His shirt sleeves looked as though they couldn't physically stretch any further to make room for his biceps. He was slicing tomatoes and making sandwiches while the rest of the staff stood around.

"You said that a few hours ago," said another. All of them were dressed in the same uniform. A white polo and navy blue slacks that looked to Sofia like they would be uncomfortably hot in the Miami heat.

"What are you in such a rush for?" the big man asked. "I'd rather hang out looking at a beautiful mansion in Miami than sitting on a big cargo ship in the middle of the ocean."

The conversation came to an abrupt stop when they entered the room.

The big man with the knife stopped and looked at them. One of the workers took her feet off the table and sat up straighter. Another put his cap back on and adjusted his hair.

"No need to put on a face for us," Cal said, wearing a big smile, so much more disarming than the disgruntled face he'd first shown her alongside the Hudson.

They relaxed slightly, but the silence still hung in the air.

"Who are you?" asked the big man, his tone suspicious.

"Cal Lamarck, and this is my partner Sofia."

"I'm your *partner* now?" Sofia whispered.

"Just go with it," Cal said with a shrug.

"You told me you hated reporters," she whispered. "And now we are *partners*. You're warming up to me after all."

Cal rolled his eyes.

"Are you cops?" asked one of the people around the room, a hint of fear in his voice.

"No, but they hired me to help with the investigation."

"You look like a cop," one of them said.

"It's that military posture," Sofia said to him. "If you stood any straighter, they'd put you in a recruitment poster."

Cal glared at her before continuing.

"I need to know exactly what each of you saw and heard last night."

Too forward, Cal.

Their eyes darted around the room, avoiding eye contact with both of them. A few of them cast cautious looks toward the big man making food.

Sofia placed her hand on Cal's shoulder, catching his gaze and gesturing for him to let her take the lead.

If you want to get information out of people, you have to get them talking first.

"What is your name?" she asked the big man.

"Mike," he replied curtly before going back to cutting tomatoes.

"How long have you been docked here, Mike?"

"Couple days."

She flashed him a wide smile and fervently pretended to write things in her notebook. Like he'd given her something useful and good. Most of the edges of her notepads were filled with doodles, but something about someone taking notes always seemed to keep people talking. It made them feel important.

I don't need to build rapport with the whole room. Just him.

"I can't imagine how difficult this must be for you," she said. "You lost your employer, and now you are stuck in the middle of an investigation."

There were a few nods and a couple of mumbled agreements.

"How long have you been working for Mr. Castillo?" Sofia asked.

A few different answers overtook the room. Spanning from months to years, the average tenure of a yacht crewman seemed short.

"Why do you care so much?" Mike asked, his eyes moving from suspicion to curiosity.

"This wasn't our first murder of the day," Sofia stated, her voice steady.

She watched more interest grow across the crew members' faces.

A little bit of intrigue could help grease the wheels of the conversation.

Now each of them was curious about the information *she* could offer *them.* If they played ball and gave her what she needed, perhaps they could learn more about the crime scene they'd just come from.

"Where were you docked before Miami?" she asked.

"We just got back from Saint Martin," Mike said. "Rafael had business back home in Mexico after that."

"Do you have any idea what it was?"

"None."

"Does he normally travel this often?"

"Mr. Castillo frequently had meetings that took him in different directions," Mike said. "He always used to say that his business spanned the entire ocean, so he needed to as well."

"Which means you all must have traveled all over the ocean as well."

Mike nodded.

"It must be hard not having a home base."

"We manage."

"Do you know who he was meeting with while he was here?"

"The moment Mr. Castillo steps foot off the yacht is the moment I stop paying attention," Mike said as his knife sliced through some meat. "We take that time to get away from Rafael and carry on with our own lives. How much longer will the investigation take?"

"The police were nearly done with the body," Cal said. "You should be released shortly."

There were a few relieved nods, but Sofia could still sense tension in the air. She imagined how uncertain each of their futures would be now. All of them would need to find new jobs and change their way of life entirely.

Or was there something more?

Sofia looked out through the windows of the yacht, over the gardens and manicured green lawns of the estate.

"How did Mr. Castillo come to afford lavish parties and a gigantic yacht?" Cal asked.

"He owns... owned a shipping empire," Mike said. "He would always tell you a story about how he'd dreamed of sailing oceans as a boy and that he turned that dream into a successful business."

"Was that story true?"

"Half-true," Mike said with a smile.

"And the other half?"

"He gambled his entire family's investments on a down-and-out shipping company that he built up into RC Enterprises. Then, because of some *suspiciously* fortunate trade regulations, he became the only person allowed to ship to many different Central American ports."

"Is that widely known?"

Some faces turned into smiles, and there were a couple of audible laughs.

"My family back home nearly disowned me when they heard I was working for him," Mike said. "He is constantly in the news in Panama. He profited from political corruption."

"Are there any specific individuals he upset?"

More laughter. That was good. Laughter always opened people up. Sofia reflected their mood with a large smile.

"Did you see the name of the boat you are currently on?" Mike asked.

She shook her head.

"In Mexico, there is a joke about what people call the 'Castillo Tax.' Every phone, computer, or imported electronic device is more expensive because of him. He was able to create a monopoly on the shipping industry in the region because of his alleged government bribes."

"He's dead now, Mike," said one of the other staff members. "We don't have to pretend like we didn't know about his bribes."

Mike smiled before continuing.

"Instead of changing his ways, he decided to flaunt his wealth even further and name his yacht after their suffering."

"Sounds like a real piece of shit," Sofia said, her voice laced with genuine disdain. A few more postures loosened.

"You must have had a view into his personal life," Cal asked, cutting in. "The police seem to think that his wife killed him. What do you think?"

"No idea," Mike said as he crossed his arms, his demeanor immediately shifting toward a guarded hostility.

Shit, Cal, that was too blunt. They were beginning to warm up to me.

Sofia watched the rest of the crew also grow tense. No longer making eye contact with either of them. They knew something, but they were a unified front about it.

"Where is she now?" Cal asked.

Mike shrugged.

Cal began pacing around the galley of the yacht, approaching the storage cabinets on the far side of the galley. With his back turned to the crew, he didn't see their posture stiffen as he approached. It was like a jolt ran through Mike's body as he immediately went into high alert.

"The more I think about it, the more I disagree with Harold," Cal continued. "I don't think Rafael Castillo's wife killed him."

Mike stopped cutting food. His attention was now focused exclusively on Cal.

"Cal," Sofia said, trying to get his attention or catch his eyes as innocently as possible without alarming him. He didn't listen. He was too wrapped up in the thought, oblivious to how unwelcoming each of the crew members was becoming.

We need to leave.

"That metal rope stand was too heavy for a small woman to pick up and slam into him with the force required to do that kind of damage to his skull," Cal continued. "I think it had to be someone much stronger."

Mike moved across the room toward Cal. The fake smile on his face disappeared. The knife was still gripped tightly in his hand.

"What did you come here to say?" Mike asked.

Cal seemed unfazed by the aggressive display.

"It's just curious," Cal replied. "That's all."

Mike stepped into Cal's space, his voice low.

"Curiosity may make a man clever, but it also makes him forget to watch his back."

CHAPTER 12

———

EIGHT YEARS EARLIER

The road to Egypt had been arduous. Months of sleeping on floors, riding in truck beds, and eating scraps of food from the kindness of strangers. She ran her fingers over the bones of her ribcage, each protrusion a testament to the pain she'd endured over these months on the road.

One thousand miles from home.

Can I even call Khartoum home anymore?

Home was a concept that had been shattered, a hazy idea she hoped might still exist somewhere in her future.

Right now, she had nothing.

No one.

Nowhere to go.

Physically, she had little energy left, but fortunately, the task at hand required only her mental power. Nahla had said the words in her mind over and over again as she walked each step to her freedom.

She sat in the same alleyway she had called home for the last two nights. The space between the dumpster and the decaying brick wall was a stark contrast to the comfortable life she'd known in Khartoum. The streets here were lined with litter, the remnants of past lives and forgotten dreams. The air was thick with the scent of hopelessness.

Nahla had no food or shelter. The only thing she had was a phone, acquired through means so desperate she never wanted to think about them again.

She turned it on. Its light illuminated her face and cast shadows on the surrounding walls. She looked around the alleyway, hoping the light would not make her a target in this unfamiliar city. Fortunately, there was no one around.

This last leg of her journey had to be done alone.

Is that the way I am now? Trusting no one?

She thought of Tariq's face as the soldiers dragged Hashim's body out of the house. She wished they had killed him, too, the weak excuse for a man willing to turn in his own father.

How is it that we come from the same family?

Was it the coddled life he lived, raised on Hashim's money, or his complete lack of social instincts?

While Nahla watched her parents die, Tariq sat in air-conditioned rooms, tinkering with computers. He would never have the kind of grit and resolve she did. Hashim failed to teach him how to have a backbone.

It cost him his life.

These twelve words were the final piece of her past. All her family fought to save during the seventy-five years of war and genocide in Sudan was wrapped up in this new technology that she barely understood.

She would understand it, though, no matter how hard it was or what was required. Hashim believed in her, and she would not let him down. She spent hours on the phone over the past few days. She wanted to learn everything she could about the new technology. It all came down to this.

Wealthier people used hardware wallets or complex multi-custodian configurations to protect their private keys. She didn't have enough money, so a cheap phone with a factory reset would have to do.

Methodically, she began to enter the words into her phone.

1—liberty

2—party

Each of the words had been repeated thousands of times in her head. Each syllable felt like it was a part of her.

3—boat

4—airport

She'd carried them with her so far. Past borders. Past checkpoints and soldiers. All the wealth that remained of her family was stored in the synapses of her brain.

The small amount of gold her father earned from his long days in the mines was given to Hashim after his death. The value moved into this confusing technology that still seemed so intangible.

5—dress

6—dance

She'd found a hotel that accepted bitcoin, but she didn't let herself dwell on the idea. Too much hope would only lead to disappointment.

She'd learned that the price was volatile, but that was something she was accustomed to. The currencies of Sudan and Egypt were devalued by the government every day. Would this be any different? Had the bitcoin Hashim left her lost its value too, just like the currencies of her country? If she did find it, would it be enough?

7—*liar*

8—*crash*

Even after all her research, it still seemed too good to be true. If this technology truly worked the way she was led to believe, wouldn't everyone on the planet adopt it?

It seemed to solve many of the problems faced by women in developing nations. In places like Afghanistan, females weren't even allowed to open their own bank accounts. Egypt and Sudan weren't much better. Many banks needed a male guardian for important transactions. They wouldn't approve loans, withdrawals, or property purchases without permission from a father or husband.

Even when a woman had full rights to her money, banks could freeze or restrict her account under the guise of "protection," forcing her to seek approval from the very men who controlled her life.

If this actually works, the world will never be the same.

"'There can be no freedom without financial freedom,'" Nahla said under her breath, repeating one of the phrases Hashim used to say.

9—*sea*

10—*horn*

A gust of wind rattled the tin roof of the structure she'd leaned against. But the cold of the early evening felt distant to her as she hung on each word.

She heard movement at the far end of the alley. She looked up.

Am I compromised? Did I do something wrong?

A man tripped over a bottle. The tumbling glass echoed down the alleyway as it came to a stop in front of her feet.

She hid the phone beneath her shirt, turning off the screen and obscuring it from view.

He continued closer. As she saw him up close, she realized how physically imposing he was. There was no way she could stop him if he wanted to harass her.

If he wanted to violate her.

She closed her eyes, pretending to sleep even though her heart raced in her chest. With every step he took, she wished for him to pass by. The stench of alcohol and urine filled her nostrils. She forced herself not to gag or make any kind of indication that she was awake.

The smell faded.

The man passed.

He continued to another spot where he would likely find his own place to sleep for the night.

She exhaled as his smell grew distant. She turned the screen back on and continued the task at hand.

11—razor

Her heart raced.

This was it. She was afraid to finish. If the money wasn't there… she didn't even want to consider it.

She spoke aloud to herself, hoping the sound of her voice might help to quell her fears.

"'We cannot ensure success,'" Nahla said, reciting her favorite line John Adams once wrote in a letter to his wife. "'But we can deserve it.'"

She entered the final word.

12—prison

She checked and double-checked. Finally, she clicked the button to confirm the words. There was a brief pause. Her entire life hung on the loading spinner of her phone.

Each rotation felt like an eternity.

The moment the numbers were displayed on the screen, she burst into tears.

It was there.

All of it.

Enough money for her to sleep indoors. Enough to escape to America and start a new life. Maybe even enough to make some kind of difference in the world.

She collapsed onto the ground, staring up at the deep blue evening sky. She let the sobs overtake her. The sliver of hope she'd clung to through every mile of her journey was still alive.

Thank you, Uncle.

CHAPTER 13

———

Cal stepped off the yacht and onto the green grass of Vizcaya.

In the distance of the gardens, he saw Harold looking down at something in his hand. Cal was grateful they didn't have to go back into the foyer with Rafael's body.

"Where are you going?" Sofia said as she placed a hand on his shoulder. The heat was starting to make her cheeks flush. The olive tone of her skin, glowing in the Miami sun, looked perfectly at home against the backdrop of the Italian villa. He could understand how she found herself while in Venice. The aura of this estate seemed like it was an extension of her.

"To speak with Harold," Cal said. "I want to tell him what happened with the yacht crew. They're clearly involved."

"No shit," she said. "But you're just going to proceed ahead? Mike threatened to kill you."

"And?"

"And I thought that might deter you," Sofia continued.

"If anything, Mike's aggression shows me we're on the right path."

Cal continued walking toward Harold.

"Stop for a minute," she said.

He did.

"Why are we here?" she asked.

"Some people say it's to serve God's purpose, some think it's to find love, and others think it's all a nihilistic accident. I don't think anybody knows for sure."

"You know what I mean," she said, trying to hide her smirk. "You don't like Harold. You don't like the people Harold works for. Mike just threatened your life, and *still* you are planning to continue. Why?"

"I thought you did your homework on me?"

"My research may have been lacking some details," she said. "For example, I didn't realize you were such a smartass."

"That's in my top three most desirable traits, right between technological brilliance and modesty."

"Why are you here?" she asked again. "I don't care how intriguing these murders are, it's not worth sacrificing your life for a bunch of rich snobs. We could be in danger."

"I understand that this is more than you bargained for, but I am going to continue with this investigation," Cal said. "I'll gladly pay for your flight back to New York. I didn't know I'd be putting you in danger when you asked to interview me."

"I'm a journalist," she continued. "I follow a story until its conclusion, no matter where it takes me. I want to understand why *you* are still here?"

He looked off in the distance.

"Bitcoin is more than my career path," he said. "It's a movement, one I believe has the power to change humanity."

"Are you willing to risk your life for some *technology*?"

"Money is the lifeblood of civilization," Cal said. "It's the foundation of trade, cooperation, and stability. When economies thrive, nations work together. When they collapse, war follows. Broken money breeds conflict. Bitcoin is a technologically superior form of capital, resistant to government control."

She gave him an unsure gaze as she took some notes on her notepad.

She doesn't understand. How could she?

Americans had never lived through true economic devastation. The reality Cal's family endured felt like fiction to them. Never had they woken up to find their wages worthless. Never had they lined up for hours to buy food that doubled in price by nightfall. Never had they watched their cities turn to battlegrounds as people fought over the last scraps of what once was.

People who had never seen a currency collapse couldn't understand its violence.

I must seem crazy to her.

Harold stood atop one of the carved stone staircases, looking across the manicured gardens. Party decorations from the night before still hung forgotten over the trees.

"Did you find anything?" Cal asked.

Harold looked over his shoulder, glancing at the police officers in the background to ensure he wasn't being watched.

"There was a phone in the foyer," he stated, pulling it from his pocket.

"Did you steal that from the crime scene?" Cal asked, connecting with Sofia's eyes. Her face seemed as skeptical as he felt.

"I solve problems, Cal," Harold said. "Sometimes that requires working outside the law. My employers provide us with unparalleled legal protection."

"And will you expect me to operate outside the law?" Cal asked.

"If it becomes necessary, yes," Harold said. "I can assure that you will be granted full immunity for anything that we do during this case."

"How can you possibly promise that?" Sofia asked.

"Someone is targeting some of the richest people in the world," Harold said. "You can't really be that naive about power dynamics, can you?"

"I'm not blind," Sofia shot back. "But blatantly ignoring the law?"

"People like you pretend that the world functions because of laws," Harold said to Sofia. "But in truth, people only follow incentives. My employers hold the single most powerful incentive in the world. Money."

Sofia's brown eyes flashed with disdain for a brief second, but she held her tongue.

"Did you find anything useful on it?" Cal asked.

"It appears to be Rafael's burner phone," Harold explained. "Pretty standard for the people I work with. The most recent conversation reads: 'Dial up security for the party. These threats are growing more serious.'"

"Hindsight is 20/20 on that one," Cal said.

"Rafael goes on to ask some questions about a masquerade ball taking place in Washington, DC. Seems as though some of my employers will be in attendance. Rafael was quite concerned about it."

"Is there a time and a place?"

"Tonight. The Watergate Hotel."

"That fits," Sofia said. "Another location associated with wealth and American history."

Cal expected Harold to make a snide comment about how Sofia wasn't technically involved in the case yet.

It didn't come.

Something passed over Harold's face, his gaze growing dark and distant.

"Harold, is something wrong?" Cal asked.

"Jonathan..." Harold said.

"Who?" Cal asked.

"He's... a senator. A former client," Harold said. "Whoever Rafael was texting with appeared very worried about him. They haven't heard from him in a couple of days, even though he was supposed to be planning the masquerade."

"Sofia is right," Cal said. "This can't be a coincidence."

Harold nodded.

A bout of commotion came from the back of the estate. A police officer sprinted across the sprawling green grass of the estate.

Then Cal saw why.

The Castillo Tax was no longer docked. The crew was beginning to take it out to sea.

They're fleeing from the scene of the crime.

CHAPTER 14

———

S ofia played with the stem of her wine glass as she watched the bartender toss a splash of Campari, sweet vermouth, and gin into a glass. With a trained hand, he added ice and stirred until the liquid was chilled. She watched the jet's wing cut through wisps of clouds over the bartender's shoulder, the horizon a blend of oranges and purples as the sun began its descent.

She took a sip of wine then checked her phone, anticipating another angry conversation with her boss.

You can be upset with me all you want, but you'll be grateful for the story I have.

"How is the Barolo?" the bartender asked. He had a thick beard and a smile that was a little bit kinder than his eyes. He tossed an orange twist into the Negroni glass before handing it off.

"Delicious," she said. She threw back the last of her glass, hoping it would help with her nerves. "I'll take another one of those along with Cal's drink."

The low lights and the rich scent of leather upholstery were disorienting. It felt like she was in a high-end bar in the city, not a plane shooting through the sky at hundreds of miles per hour. The gentle piano playing in the background was a nice touch, even if it was a bit over the top.

She thought about how disconnected these people were from the happenings in the real world. How much money did they have to waste if they were willing to hire someone to play piano for them on an airplane? She enjoyed music as much as the next person, but she'd never seen a more wasteful use of money in her journalistic career, even when interviewing political leaders.

Sofia grabbed the two drinks, made her way to the rear of the plane, and knocked on Cal's door. He opened it, only a towel wrapped around his waist, his beard covered in shaving cream.

She let out an involuntary snort of a laugh, shocked by the shirtless man greeting her at the door.

This is why you can't be pounding wine on an airplane. Get your shit together.

"I'm sorry, I didn't mean to interrupt," she said, trying her best not to let her eyes linger on his chest. The warmth of the wine was making that task more challenging. "I was hoping we could continue with our interview."

"I'm in the middle of something," he said, gesturing to the shaving cream that covered his face.

"It'll be quick," she said. "I've brought you a little something to sweeten the deal."

"What's that?"

"I'm enjoying the luxuries of the plane," she said. "When's the next time you'll get to fly in a private jet stocked with hundred-thousand-dollar bottles of liquor?"

She thrust the glass forward.

"What is it?"

"A Negroni," she said. "Made with the most expensive gin I've ever seen. This was one of my favorite drinks during my time in Italy."

"Come in," he said, grabbing the glass.

She stepped into his room. It was small, but slightly larger than the one she had on the other side of the plane. More than any of the luxurious furnishings, though, she was struck by the smell of his shaving cream. A deep and musky scent filled the air. She let the smell consume her for a moment.

"It seems that we had similar ideas," Cal said.

"What do you mean?"

"You decided to enjoy the luxuries of the plane's bar," he said. "I decided to take advantage of a different kind of luxury."

She continued following him as he moved into the bathroom. He took a sip of the Negroni and then set it down next to the mirror.

"And what luxury is that?" Sofia asked.

He grabbed the straight razor and handed it to her.

"Its blade is coated in iridium," he said. "It claims to be one of the sharpest razors in the world."

"How do you know that?" she asked as she turned it over in her hands, feeling the weight of it. It was a beautifully crafted piece.

"Hand-carved from a 700-year-old oak tree," Cal read from a fancy box sitting beside the bathroom mirror. "This meteor-forged iridium blade is perfect for showing poor people that you're able to spend more money on frivolous items than they make in a year."

"Seriously?"

"I may have made up that last bit."

She laughed.

"It was sitting here forgotten," he said. "I used to collect straight razors when I was stationed abroad, back when I was required to shave every day. This is the most beautiful one I've handled. I'd love to have something like this in my collection."

"You should take it with you," she said. "Harold wants you to mingle with all of these wealthy people. Having some expensive belongings would help you to fit in."

"I found multiple Rolexes in the dresser, too," Cal said.

"Wear one," Sofia said. "It'll help you look the part for the party."

"I'm not sure if I'd feel comfortable—"

"This is my second glass of wine, Cal. It happens to be the same age as me and apparently costs thousands of dollars. We need to understand how the super-rich think and act if they want us to catch who is targeting them."

"I suppose they can add it to my tab as payment for the job," Cal said as he looked over the razor in his hands.

"Just chalk it up to research," she said as she held out her glass. He clinked it. His deep blue eyes connected with hers.

"Please," she said, taking a long sip of her wine. "Show me how this thing works."

He turned back to the mirror, reaching over his head and pulling his skin taut. He placed the blade against his skin and began to pull it through the facial hair. There was something soothing in the low drag of steel through coarse whiskers.

"So what kind of questions do you have for me?"

He's relaxed. Time to shoot my shot.

"Did you want to kill Max?"

He slowly scraped off the white lather, bringing the blade down to a towel and cleaning it off with his hand.

"The military has given its statement on that matter. The record couldn't be clearer."

"I don't give a fuck about the record."

He stopped for a moment and looked at her. Reading her. She couldn't help but wonder who he saw.

"Do you remember what I told you this morning?" Sofia asked.

"Honestly, I was barely listening to you when we first met."

"I want to see the man behind the headlines. I want to tell your story. If you haven't noticed yet, I don't have my notepad with me. I've already got one hell of a story for my editor. I'm curious. Every interview I watched of you, I saw a sadness behind your eyes that no one had ever asked you about. You respected Max, didn't you?"

He held her gaze for a long moment. She felt a flash of that same sadness within them, thinking for a moment that she was about to be given the same set of rehearsed military lies.

"I regret what happened every day," he said. "Society hated him. A part of me understands why. He created one of the largest hubs for free drug trade over the internet, and the news painted him as some kind of villain... but he never saw himself that way."

He continued pulling the metal across his skin. The rhythmic rasp of the blade scraping through his stubble was hypnotic.

"How would he have seen himself?"

"I read through a lot of his personal communications during the investigation. He had a deep belief in the ideas of freedom and privacy. He thought of himself as a modern-day revolutionary, fighting against the tyranny of the government by providing a free and open market that anybody could use."

"And what do you think?"

"A lot of people died because of his actions," Cal said. "They gained access to drugs they wouldn't have been able to normally. Some overdosed, but he never once hurt anyone. He was peaceful. He believed that consenting adults should be able to do whatever they wanted with their own bodies."

Another wave of warmth ran through Sofia's body. She'd forgotten how much she loved this part of the job. Her intuition and ability to get people to open up were her greatest strengths.

"Did you mean to kill him?"

"Armed and dangerous," he said. "That's what they told me. They said he attempted to kill the arresting officer when he blew past the SWAT teams and sprinted toward me. Colonel Blackwell ordered me to shoot... I listened."

He grabbed the Negroni and took a long sip.

Sofia let the silence hang between them for a moment.

"Afterward, I learned Max was unarmed and that he never hurt anyone. He was simply trying to escape. Because I followed my orders, I killed a man whose only desire was to make the world a freer place."

He looked at himself in the mirror for a moment, his eyes locked on his own reflection. She watched him transform in front of her. He became the clean-shaven man she'd seen in interviews. While at the same time, she felt like she finally understood the tortured tension beneath his eyes.

"And now everyone in the military thinks I'm some hero."

She reached out, placing a hand on his bare shoulder. She hoped he could sense how much she wanted to comfort him with her touch. His skin was warm from the steam of the room, his muscles tense.

"I should be in prison for what I did," he continued. "But because I followed Colonel Blackwell's commands, it was completely ignored. The system wanted Max dead."

"I'm so sorry, Cal."

"I don't care if we catch up with whoever has been doing this. I don't care if Harold commands me. I'll never kill someone again."

A quiet pause lingered between them before he placed his hand on his cheekbone and pulled his skin taut to get a better angle with the blade. The edge of the razor glided over his wet skin.

A rumble of turbulence shook the plane.

Cal's hand slipped.

A bead of blood formed underneath Cal's neck. Sofia watched it run down his warm skin. Past his collarbone, down into the hair of his muscular chest.

"Damn," he said, immediately dabbing the cut with a towel to stop the bleeding.

Sofia felt the moment leave. She'd questioned him about that challenging time in his past enough for the time being. He'd graciously given her more honesty than she could have expected. It was unfair to ask for more intimate details about his past unless she first offered up some vulnerabilities of her own.

His imploring blue eyes made her want to do just that. She resisted the pull.

"Can I grab you a bandage?" she asked.

"In my bag, under the desk."

She reached down to grab one of them, seeing his computer still planted on the table, running some kind of computation. She looked at the screen, still not fully grasping the kind of work that he was doing.

She handed him the bandage. He placed it over the cut.

"What did you find out from exploring that Bitcoin wallet? Do you think it was the yacht crew that did this?"

He finished up the last few points of his shave. His hand moved more carefully than before.

"The transactions appear to have been done in the same way as the Valhner brothers," he stated. "Thousands of donations to random existing addresses on the Bitcoin network. But I think this confirms that there is a larger organization at play. Even if the crew is involved, I believe someone more technical was pulling the strings."

"They didn't seem like killers," she said. "They seemed so kind."

"Appearances can be deceiving," he said, looking deeply into her eyes. "You never know who someone truly is until you see them under pressure."

She felt her phone vibrate in her pocket.

Shit. Now? Right when I finally got him to start opening up to me.

"It's my editor," she said. "I've got to take this."

"Of course."

He splashed on some aftershave and finished the last of the Negroni.

He smiled at her in the mirror, his face was clean and smooth. As she left the room, she felt their plane begin to descend into Washington, DC.

CHAPTER 15

SEVEN YEARS EARLIER

Nahla closed her eyes and swallowed hard. She'd thought about this moment every day for the last year and a half. It was time to fulfill the promises she'd sworn to her uncle.

I've come so far from the girl in the alleyway.

The United Nations Building in New York City was an imposing structure. The towering glass and steel facade glinted in the morning sun, symbolizing power, peace, and prosperity. It was a place where the world's leaders came together to discuss the most pressing issues.

Today, she hoped they would listen to her.

This is for you, Hashim.

"Distinguished members of the United Nations and the General Assembly, I stand before you today with a plea for help."

Nahla scanned the assembly. The room teemed with delegates, their expressions a blend of skepticism and curiosity. Then, she found her. Senator Rosewall. The woman who championed the legislation that funneled money to al-Bashir's soldiers. She sat perched above the crowd, draped in an elegant green dress, completely disinterested.

It was, in no small part, her fault that Hashim was dead. All the while, her wealth had ballooned by millions through her business dealings in Africa.

"Many of the people in Sudan blame our economic hardships on Omar al-Bashir. I agree that he is a terrible man and at fault for the Darfurian genocide, but he does not bear the blame for all the problems of Africa."

There was still movement around the room, people talking and shuffling papers. Nahla had finally gotten to a place where she could speak to them, but they weren't even interested.

I have to make them listen.

"Many Africans would blame their hardship on things like colonialism and slavery. Many Americans would claim that Africans are lazy or that we fight each other constantly."

Nahla looked up at the congregation.

"Both parties are wrong. The blame sits on those of you in this room."

The shuffling stopped.

She had their attention.

"Africa is the poorest region in the world today because it is the most over-regulated. It is the hardest place in the world to do business, and because of that, no new technologies or innovations come through our borders."

Nahla felt a pang of sadness. She wished that Hashim were by her side. He was the one who educated her in the problems that plagued her country.

These ideas were his. I wish he were here to voice them.

"The people of Sudan fell prey to the economic lies of trade relationships and commerce between countries. But what kind of trade is it when our own money is controlled by foreign powers? Fourteen African countries use currencies pegged to the euro. The power-hungry elites at the European Central Bank dictate the value of our money, and yet you call us independent. These are lies. These are stories you tell yourselves to feel warm and fuzzy while pretending that you're helping us poor Africans. You sit in your climate-controlled chambers, in your pompous positions of morality, oblivious to the realities of the countries you legislate. You are sentimental tyrants, destroying people's lives under the guise of kindness."

Nahla looked up.

She was met with many angry gazes as her words echoed off the wooden walls of the chamber.

"Since Sudan *globalized*, the distance between the poor of my country and the elite has grown exponentially. We live in the most resource-rich and fertile lands in the world, yet we are the poorest. How can this be?"

The eyes of the diplomats avoided her.

"It was not always this way. Mansa Musa was the wealthiest man in human history. He was African. His stockpiles of gold dwarfed the fortunes of your countries. Your nations wrote the textbooks, so history forgot him. You erased our legacy and replaced it with pity."

Nahla let their silence resonate.

She let them feel it.

They deserve this guilt.

"We are told to export the things the wealthy countries need. Luxury goods and raw materials. Ivory, gold, and oil to fuel your yachts. We are told that we are becoming a part of the international community. These are lies. We sell our souls to bureaucratic devils. Instead of growing the food our people need, we create luxuries for the wealthy. Instead of local free markets, we import endless regulations that keep my people poor."

Nahla felt her heart pounding and her vision constricted. She fought to remain focused. If not for her, these people would never hear these words. The world might never change.

"You call this cooperation, but my uncle had a different word for it: *exploitation*."

Senator Rosewall had a sneer on her face as her advisor whispered something into her ear.

"Warlords across Africa accept loans from the IMF and World Bank. Organizations based in this very city have helped dictators build mansions and fund weapons of war. This leaves generations of people indebted. My people. Multinational corporations come to Africa bringing the promise of jobs. In reality, they pillage the resources that once made our lands plentiful. Instead of Africans investing in their own infrastructure, they are fed lies about being part of the global economy."

She looked into the smug eyes of the crowd.

"Even as I speak, warlords sit in this very room, listening to my words. Their actions are allowed because they cooperate with your cause. The continent of Africa has been economically raped by global superpowers. I am here today to open your eyes to end this misguided madness."

Senator Rosewall finished speaking with one of her advisors and finally decided to address Nahla.

"The accusations you are making today must not be done lightly, young lady. The world is not black and white," Senator Rosewall said. "Economic intervention is a necessary part of a collaborative global economy. I assure you that the United States has no interest in exploiting the people of Sudan. This panel helps to facilitate poverty reduction initiatives and utilizes our influence to promote equitable outcomes through global sustainability measures."

"'We have too many high-sounding words, and too few actions that correspond with them,'" Nahla said, quoting the great Abigail Adams. She wondered if the people in the room would even understand the reference.

This committee is nothing like the America I once dreamt of escaping to.

"What is that supposed to mean?" Senator Rosewall asked.

"When I was a young girl, your words of economic intervention filled me with hope. I thought your fancy suits and elite college degrees held the answer to our problems. But I've watched politicians from your countries profit off the labor of my people. For my late uncle's entire life, he watched *you* profit while terrible men drove our country into despair."

Senator Rosewall's face grew grim as she spoke again.

"Today, we have *gifted* you with the opportunity to speak in front of the General Assembly. Rather than make wild accusations and spread conspiracy theories, I would encourage you to use this time to present real evidence. Since you are here to spread propaganda, I'm formally asking you to leave."

The rage welled up inside of her.

Even if Senator Rosewall won't listen to my words, perhaps a representative from another country will.

"My uncle was labeled an anti-government rebel because he helped people exchange currencies outside the purview of the state powers. He helped people escape from the slow death of starvation that their government forced upon them via currency debasement. Hashim was a hero. The soldiers your cancerous bureaucracy helped to fund slaughtered him like a pig. All he was trying to do was give life jackets to people who were drowning."

She looked around the room.

Not a single welcoming gaze.

Surrounded by hundreds of people from hundreds of different countries, she'd never felt more alone in her entire life.

"Just because it makes you uncomfortable that your system is broken doesn't make my words wrong," Nahla continued. "You sleep in your mansions while the people of my country starve."

Senator Rosewall whispered into the ear of one of the security guards before addressing Nahla again.

"We have dedicated intelligence agencies responsible for investigating such matters," Senator Rosewall continued. "I encourage you to present your evidence to the appropriate authorities."

"Appropriate authorities?" Nahla said. "What else do you propose that I do? Will you ignore—"

An arm grabbed her shoulder from behind, guiding her away from the podium. A security guard escorted her out of the room.

"I have a right to be here!"

"I will not have my name slandered without any proof," Senator Rosewall said.

Then I will find proof.

CHAPTER 16

———

C al looked out the window as the plane's wheels touched the tarmac. His stomach lurched forward, suddenly feeling the Negroni's effect on him.

Cal used Bitcoin transactions to paint a narrative around the person using them. His job was to judge, but he was having a hard time judging Sofia.

He thought reporters from news corporations were all the same. They all asked the same questions. They all wanted the same answers. But there was something different in her soft brown eyes. There was genuine curiosity. Intensity.

She's trying to get me comfortable, so I'll tell her more about myself than I should.

The cold air hit his face, a strong contrast to the humidity of Miami. He didn't mind. He pulled the breath deep into his lungs and walked down the steps of the plane.

It was strange to think he'd already flown the length of the Atlantic coast twice, and the day wasn't even over.

The airstrip was quiet, the hum of the plane's engines fading into the background. These private hangars reminded him of the ones he trained in during his military service. In the distance, he could see the Capitol building, the white dome standing out against the darkening blue sky. He wondered if their path would cross with any of the politicians who called that place their office.

Harold walked off the plane, his face pale and exhausted.

"Have you found anything?" Cal asked.

"I've been trying to get in touch with Jonathan, but he's not answering," Harold said, looking visibly upset. "I fear the worst."

"I'm sorry," Sofia said. "Were the two of you close?"

"Yes, the two of us were... we used to be quite close."

Sofia looked like she wanted to ask for more details, but didn't press any further.

"We have a time and a place," Sofia said. "Are we going to go straight there?"

"We need to proceed with caution," Harold stated. There was a certainty in his voice, a kind of commanding tone that implored both of them to fall in line with his suggestion. Cal wondered if that was just the way Harold was or if it was a habit cultivated over the years spent with the rich and powerful.

"Why wait?" Sofia asked. "Couldn't your friend's life be in danger?"

"You forget yourself, Sofia," Harold said. "This is not your decision."

Cal watched a fire grow in Sofia's eyes. He was impressed she kept her mouth shut.

"This is my world," Harold continued. "We can't just go in guns blazing. This is a delicate situation."

"So what will you have us do?" Cal asked.

"*I* am going to get in touch with contacts that are attending," Harold said. "But *you* have a different problem."

Harold strutted to the town car that had pulled up to the plane, casting a familiar wave to the driver.

"What problem is that?"

"Your attire," Harold said. "Go buy yourself something decent. I'd like to be able to introduce you without people assuming you're a valet."

CHAPTER 17

———

"How is this one?" Cal asked, stepping out of the dressing room.

Sofia thought the jet-black suit seemed like the sort of thing a person would wear to a prom.

"That's not it."

"Seriously?"

"Try on another one."

"I'd rather be locked in a hot room with Rafael Castillo's corpse than go back into that changing room again," he said. His tone was growing more annoyed with each additional outfit. "Doesn't this suit make me look like a rich asshole?"

"You've always looked like an asshole… but that one doesn't make you look rich."

"Ouch," Cal said, rolling his eyes and going back into the changing room.

Like most of the places they'd been in the last day, the boutique had a luxurious, old-money aesthetic. Every detail felt deliberately curated.

"Harold knows something he isn't telling us," Sofia said, watching the top of Cal's head in the changing room as he removed the previous suit jacket. "And I think he's downplaying his relationship with Jonathan. He seems truly concerned."

"Are you saying that Harold has emotions?" Cal asked with a smirk. "That seems unlikely."

A couple walked in off the street and entered the boutique. They both held themselves with an air of arrogance, a reminder of the kind of people they would soon be surrounded by at the party.

"I've interviewed people like him before," Sofia said. "Men obsessed with controlling every aspect of their existence. People like that aren't usually good at dealing with loss and uncertainty."

"So you think Jonathan is dead?"

"We've seen three bodies so far. Would it surprise you if there was another?"

"I can understand why he's so nervous," Cal said. "This is his world. If we can't figure out who is doing this, then people he's close to are going to die."

"Do you think all of them deserve saving?"

"I don't let myself think like that," Cal said.

"I just don't get it," Sofia said. "Why are you so intent on helping these people?"

Cal glared at her over the dressing room door.

"What's with all these questions? You're worse than the therapist the military stuck me with after Max."

"I'm a reporter, Cal. This is what I do. If you'd like, though, you could lie down on a couch while I ask you about your childhood traumas."

Cal rolled his eyes.

"Why do *you* think I'm so intent on saving these people then, Ms. Therapist?"

She paused for a moment while one of the staff members cleaned up some of Cal's rejected suits.

"I see the way your eyes light up when there's a problem to solve," Sofia said. "At first, I thought it was about solving a puzzle, but after our conversation on the plane… I'm not so sure."

"What is it then?"

"I think that your guilt for killing Max is eating at you. I think you want to do everything in your power to save lives to repent for the one that you took."

There was a long pause as she watched the top of his head as he buttoned up the front of his shirt.

"Well, if this whole journalist thing doesn't work out for you, I think you could have a lucrative career in therapy."

Cal stepped out of the dressing room.

The suit looked fantastic. An evening blue that seemed to have been made specifically to complement his muscular physique. It brought out his cold, blue eyes, which seemed to see right through her.

Why is it that I sometimes feel like I'm the one being investigated?

Even the details were striking. The cuff links perfectly matched the gold Rolex Cal had taken from Harold's plane. His clean-shaven jawline made him look like a completely different man from the one she'd first met.

"That's the one," she said, taking in this new man standing in front of her.

"I look like a pompous, rich jerk."

A wealthy-looking man was looking at the same suit from across the store and cast him a judgmental gaze.

"The only thing that might look better is if you wore a tie."

"Absolutely not," Cal said, observing himself in the mirror. "If I get into an altercation and someone grabs it, it's a death sentence."

"Didn't you refuse to carry a firearm?" Sofia asked. "I thought you had no intention of harming anyone for Harold."

"I did and I won't," Cal stated. "Just because I refuse to harm anyone on Harold's behalf doesn't mean I'm blind to the realities of the world. We have no idea what we are walking into. I have to be prepared."

She attempted to hide the flash of nervousness that bubbled up beneath her sternum. Cal was beginning to warm up to her, but she couldn't let him see that weakness.

"Your turn," Cal said to her. "What are you going to wear?"

She gave him a smirk as she walked toward the changing room.

"Harold gave you his credit card, right?"

Cal nodded.

"Then I'm picking out the most expensive dress in this entire place."

CHAPTER 18

SEVEN YEARS EARLIER

Nahla walked through the same dusty streets she'd escaped from, back into a world she had sworn never to return to.

She remembered how trapped she felt as a young girl when she lived in this city. She remembered her dreams of escaping to the United States.

A young woman said hello to her in Arabic as she walked past a street vendor selling cheap white jalabiya robes and schoolgirl veils, their fabric fluttering in the dusty heat. Immediately, a forgotten part of herself re-emerged. She wasn't sure if she'd forgotten about it or if she'd subconsciously pushed it down deep within her.

The streets were filled with the familiar smells of her youth, but there was one distinctive difference. Her. The despair that once consumed her was absent. Hashim succeeded in that sense. His words rang through her mind.

'*Only through understanding the world can one attain true freedom.*'

She turned a corner, past two kids kicking a football. They didn't even look up at her. Her worries of no longer being able to fit in on the streets here vanished.

She walked through one of the more dangerous parts of the city, passing an alley where she had once been mugged. For a brief moment, the fear returned, the memory of how terrified she used to be carrying the meager wages she had worked so hard to earn.

No longer.

She now had more wealth than that young girl could have imagined. All held in those same twelve words in her mind. It had been over two years since she received the bitcoin from Hashim, and its value had appreciated exponentially during that time. She considered trading her bitcoin for dollars to fund her new life in America, but she wasn't a US citizen. She met none of the identification requirements that most banks required, and she had no credit history.

So she held it.

She acted as her own bank, free from the controls of any single government.

The price was volatile, but the more it appreciated in value, the more she learned about it. The more she learned, the more she enjoyed the unique kind of economic freedom only Bitcoin could provide.

I lived my entire life with no control over my economic reality. I will never give that freedom up again.

When she arrived in Khartoum, she was able to get in touch with a money exchanger who once worked with Hashim. He accepted a small chunk of her bitcoin in exchange for a sufficient amount of Sudanese pounds to fund her travels.

She reached her destination at the end of the street, not sure if she was in the correct location.

At first, she thought it looked abandoned. If it weren't for the battered sign that said **COMPUTER REPAIRS,** she'd have assumed it was abandoned.

She knocked on the door.

He opened it.

Tariq's face was gaunt. It looked as though each year had aged him a decade. Beneath the layers of hardship, she could still see the face of the boy she had grown up alongside.

He stepped back, his eyes wide with shock. Instinctively, he put up his hands to protect himself.

"I'm not going to hurt you," Nahla said, showing him the palms of her hands.

"Then why are you here?"

"Unfinished business."

His eyes bore through her. The whites of them were more yellow and muted than she'd remembered, the hope he once had absent. He cautiously gestured for her to enter his home.

Garbage overflowed on his kitchen table, and the dust of the streets outside lingered in the air here too. The only thing that looked organized in the entire house was the workbench covered with computers.

"You shouldn't be here," he said.

"Where I should and shouldn't be is not of your concern."

"I can still see the hate in your eyes as clearly as I did the day the soldiers killed my father. It should have been me who died that day."

She said nothing.

There was no use arguing with the truth.

"I'd hoped that you were able to find a better life. That you'd finally been able to escape to America."

"I was," she stated. "And I did."

"Then why are you back?"

"The world is not fair."

"Did you really need to travel to the West to learn that lesson?"

"For our entire childhood, Hashim spoke of the freedom that could be found in the USA. It's true. But how can I live comfortably in America when I know the travesties still happening to people in Sudan?"

He studied her face, a shadow of the man she'd once known.

No matter how much I resent him, no matter how much I want to seek revenge, I must not. I need his help.

"I still hold onto that sliver of hope Hashim instilled in us," Nahla continued. "If I can find evidence of al-Bashir's wrongdoings, if I can *prove* that other countries are profiting from Sudan's continual downfall, perhaps we can truly make a difference in the world."

"Things have changed since you were here, Nahla. Al-Bashir has only grown more paranoid. What exactly are you proposing?"

"I'm proposing that we get close to him. I'm proposing that we find a way to prove that he is receiving financial aid from wealthy countries. I want to prove people like Senator Rosewall are indirectly profiting from the mistreatment of the Sudanese people."

"That's a death sentence."

She stared at him. Looking at the weak, spineless man her cousin had become. She didn't respect him, but without his help, this would be nearly impossible.

"It was all your fault," Nahla said, staring into his cautious eyes.

"You think I don't know that?"

"I think you need reminding," Nahla continued. "I think you've lost the plot. I think you are living in a quiet hell and that you hate yourself."

There was a quick snarl on his face, but she didn't need to see it to know that her words struck a deep chord.

"I'm here with a chance at redemption. I'm here to offer you a second chance, a way out of this place."

He straightened up a bit as she watched the idea pass over him. She sensed his interest, even if he was doing his best to hide it.

"Hashim would have wanted us to do everything in our power to bring al-Bashir down," she said. "He resented the global systems that profited from Sudan's slow collapse. What if we can do something to fix it?"

She watched him thinking it through. Even though his face now had a beard, even though it had been years, she could sense his thoughts shifting.

"Why would you even want me?"

"'Liberty once lost is lost forever.'"

"It's good to see you are still quoting John Adams, but can you speak plainly? I have no time for games."

"Sudan is on the verge of being lost. No matter our past, no matter our differences, we have to do what is right for this country. We have to do what Hashim would have wanted."

Tariq looked at his feet, appearing downtrodden and beaten.

"I know you are capable of more than this," she said as she gestured around the room. "You've always understood technology better than I have, and you have the right connections to get me into al-Bashir's mansion. I cannot do this without you."

He finally met her eyes. His gaze was still tortured, but there was a flicker of something else inside it.

She stepped closer.

"What do you say?"

CHAPTER 19

———

C al ran his fingers over the freshly shaven skin of his face while he looked at himself in the mirror. He hated how much he looked like Harold, a man focused more on his external appearance than his character.

He toyed with the iridium straight razor in his pocket. It was one of the two souvenirs he'd taken from the plane. The other was the gold Rolex Submariner on his wrist. Cal wasn't usually one to wear a watch, but he had to admit that it paired well with the suit.

It feels like I'm living a lie. This isn't me.

The more time they spent around these sorts of people, the more he felt like an outcast. Sofia, on the other hand, seemed to fit right in. Luxury suited her.

"Why are you brooding out there?" she asked, poking her head around the corner of the changing room.

"I'm not *brooding*. I'm thinking of what we are getting ourselves into."

"I've interviewed hundreds of people, Cal," she said. "I've seen reformed criminals who looked less regretful than you do right now."

He couldn't help but let the corner of his mouth turn into a smile.

"I found Bitcoin because I believed it could take power away from people like them," he said. His gaze shifted to the streets of downtown Washington, DC. Businessmen and politicians hurried past. Their tailored suits bore a striking resemblance to his own. "Now I'm helping track down whoever killed the Valhner brothers. Two men who profited from international war."

"Do you truly believe that?"

"What?"

"That Bitcoin can take power away from the politicians," she said. "That seems a bit idealistic."

"Don't you care that politicians can freeze the assets of people who disagree with them? Don't you care about everything in the world getting more expensive every year?"

"Of course I care," she responded. "Having your bank accounts closed by a politician is terrible, but you speak about Bitcoin like it has the ability to bring about world peace."

"It's not just bank account closures," Cal stated. "Currency debasement is a cancer. I believe Bitcoin can help people escape from it."

"I'm not sure that I can see where you are coming from," Sofia said as she zipped up the back of her dress. "Prices go up, but I still find a way to afford the things I need."

"I'm sure you do."

"And I don't know a single person who's lost access to their bank accounts."

"That's quite the privileged perspective."

"You barely know me. How can you call me *privileged*?"

"You are blind to these problems because you grew up in a developed economy," Cal said. "My parents lost their entire savings during the hyperinflation in Yugoslavia. I saw firsthand how economic struggles transformed into class struggles. I watched as financial desperation ripped children away from their screaming mothers."

Sofia adjusted her diamond necklace.

"You grew up in a family that could afford to send you on a trip to Italy to *find yourself*," Cal continued. "My family couldn't afford for my brother and me to eat every day when we moved to America. I was forced to join the military because my parents did not have the means to take care of us. Do you have any idea what that's like?"

"No."

"So how could you ever truly understand the problem?" he continued. "All you see when you look at the Valhner brothers is two rich businessmen. I see two men who've profited from this broken system to fuel their greed and desires."

Sofia exited the dressing room.

The fabric of her dark blue dress flowed like water. The deep cut of her neckline displayed a beautiful diamond necklace. Its shimmering reminded him of moonlight on ocean waves.

She was beautiful, but the kindness in her smile was gone.

She stood inches from him now, the look of pure venom in her eyes such a sharp contrast to the sweetness of her perfume.

"You have no idea what I see, Cal. You assume I'm like these people when you know nothing of my past."

Cal bit the inside of his cheek, wishing that he'd held his tongue.

"You get angry with people for assuming you're some hero who ended Max's life. How is that any different from what you are doing now?"

Gone were the soft brown eyes of a journalist attempting to charm him, now there was fire in her gaze. It was as though a veil had lifted, and he saw past the kind journalistic facade for the first time.

"You have no idea who I am or the things that I've gone through."

CHAPTER 20

———

The town car sped through the streets of downtown Washington, DC. The city's monuments and historic buildings were bathed in the golden hues of the setting sun. The two glasses of wine Sofia had on the plane were beginning to wear off. The cold clarity of sobriety returned as they passed the Federal Reserve Board building.

The tension from their argument at the boutique still hung in the air between her and Cal. He didn't apologize. She had no intention of bringing up the topic again.

I have a job to do regardless of what he thinks of me.

The soft glow of Cal's computer screen illuminated his face. She glanced at what he was doing. She expected to see more Bitcoin transactions, but instead, she saw social media feeds.

"We're not the only ones following the case," he stated as he caught her eye. "Many people around the world are receiving chunks of the Valhner and Castillo fortunes. Whoever we are following is gaining public support."

"Interesting," she said. "It's almost like giving people free money makes them like you more."

The corner of his mouth turned up into a smile.

Perhaps he'll still open up to me after all.

"Do you have any idea who is receiving the bitcoin?" she asked.

"Most of the users seem to be in Africa and Central America. I don't think that's a coincidence. Whoever we're following is giving back to the very people these men harmed."

The town car slowed to a stop as they arrived back at the plane to pick up Harold. He entered the car in a new outfit. Still completely grey, but a few shades darker. The jacket was precisely tailored with a charcoal tie.

"You have quite the diverse wardrobe, huh?" Cal asked.

Harold said nothing.

The three of them rode in silence for the first few minutes of their trip toward the Watergate Hotel. Harold rolled down the window and lit a cigar with a match. Sofia watched some of the stress melt off his face as he pulled smoke into his mouth.

"Unfortunately, I've heard nothing from Jonathan," he said between drags on the cigar. "But I was able to get in contact with the concierge who is organizing the party."

Harold looked out the window as they passed by the Washington Monument.

"A down payment is required in order to take part in the festivities of the penthouse," Harold began, looking intently at Cal. "A down payment *exclusively* accepted in bitcoin."

"Interesting," Sofia said.

"Do you even *have* any bitcoin to pay them with?" Cal asked.

"It's not the sort of thing I invest in," Harold said. "I'm skeptical it'll be around in another decade."

"You know it's the most successful computer network in human history, right?" Cal asked. "It's literally never been hacked since its genesis block on January 3, 2009. Is that not long-term enough for you?"

"I've worked for Federal Reserve Board members, Cal. They are intelligent and well-meaning people. I trust in them more than some made-up internet money," Harold said. "The US dollar has been the strongest currency in the world for hundreds of years."

"That's not true," Cal said. "The US dollar has only been the strongest and most widely used currency since the Bretton Woods Agreement in 1944. Despite the religious fervor most Americans assign toward their almighty green paper, historically, it's a new concept."

Sofia smirked at him as she watched Harold grow more annoyed.

"And the people you work for have rapidly debased it," Cal continued. "Destroying the entire middle class and the American dream alongside it."

"Some of the people I work for are Ivy League economists," Harold said. "I trust them more than you. I'll continue waiting for people to realize that Bitcoin is a digital scam."

"So would this be a good time to talk about how you're going to pay me?" Cal asked, reaching into his vest pocket and handing Harold a business card.

"What's this?"

"It's my Bitcoin address."

"Can I have one?" Sofia asked.

Cal handed her one. She looked it over, running her fingers over the embossed lettering. It was a straightforward card with only two pieces of information on it. It read *'Calvin Lamarck'* in large letters, accompanied by a QR code beneath.

"You can pretend this network has no value," Cal said. "But anyone in the world can send bitcoin to that address. No middleman. No asking for permission. My private keys are geographically distributed across multiple locations in the United States. Can't do something like that with a bank."

"Can the two of you stop for a moment? We are almost at the Watergate," Sofia said, as she tucked the card into her pocket. "Are we going to be able to get in the party or not?"

"One of our employers acquired some bitcoin and used it to pay for both of our spots," Harold said.

"Only two spots?" Cal asked.

"Sofia will not be joining us," Harold said. "Regardless of how much of my money you decided to waste on her attire."

Sofia immediately felt acutely aware of the heavy diamonds that hung over her collarbone.

"You told us we needed to look the part," Cal said. "If it were up to me, I'd still be wearing jeans."

"No," Harold said. "I told *you* to look the part."

"You have to be kidding?" Sofia asked as she readjusted her dress, being exceedingly careful not to wrinkle it. "It can't hurt to have more help."

"I hired Cal for a specific reason," Harold said. "He's been in violent situations in the past. If something goes awry, I know that he'll be able to handle himself. The same cannot be said of you."

"I'm not going to be a liability," Sofia said. "I interview people professionally. We have more information about the wait staff on the yacht because of me."

"And how well did that go?" Harold asked. "I can't help but think that if you and Cal hadn't been so involved, they wouldn't have run from the scene of the crime."

"We got tons of information about Rafael's business dealings. We—"

"I'm acutely aware of the things that Mr. Castillo has been accused of," Harold said. "The only thing your actions did was create problems."

"I made her a promise," Cal said.

"Vizcaya was already a crime scene when we got there. This is different. We could be walking into a dangerous situation. She's not coming."

"Then I'm not going."

Harold blew smoke out of his flared nostrils. He set the cigar down and leaned forward. "Do you really think it's wise to bargain with me, Cal?"

Sofia sensed something chilling behind Harold's words. She couldn't tell if Cal picked up on it or if he simply didn't care. It was the first time she truly understood how seriously Harold took his occupation.

The car stopped at the Watergate. Sofia wanted more than anything to get out of it.

"Do you really think it's wise to threaten me, Harold?"

"I do what I have to do to accomplish the things I have to accomplish. You still don't grasp the magnitude of this situation."

"Please enlighten me then."

"Do you know what city in the USA has the highest wealth per capita?"

"I'm not interested in billionaire trivia."

"This one," Harold replied. "DC is the epicenter of power in the modern world."

"It's also the epicenter of bureaucratic bullshit."

Harold ignored Cal and turned his attention to Sofia.

"If you don't show up to work, what happens? Maybe the story goes out late? Maybe your boss gets mad at you?"

She nodded.

"That's not what happens if these people go missing. They are the hidden powers that make our society function. Without them, systems collapse. People die."

She didn't respond. She didn't know how to respond. The more she connected with Harold's grey eyes, the smaller she felt.

At the same time, Sofia watched something shift inside Cal. His jaw clenched, and fire burned in his eyes. It felt like she saw a part of him for the first time. The kind, technologically savvy Cal was only a fraction of what existed within him. There was a soldier inside of him.

This was the man who took Max's life.

"You say these things in an attempt to exude power over us," Cal said, placing his hand on Harold's shoulder, his eyes only a few inches away from Harold's. "But your posturing means nothing to me."

Cal opened the door, and the sounds of the city began to pour in. The smoke from Harold's cigar seeped out through the open door into the evening air.

"I don't respect you," Cal said. "I don't respect the people you work for. This style of power signaling may work on the people of this city, but it means nothing to me. Sofia will be joining us this evening, or I will not be assisting the investigation any further."

"Is that all?" Harold asked through clenched teeth.

"You will also begin treating Sofia respectfully. She is offering us her help."

Harold's mouth twisted into a scowl, but he gave a begrudging nod.

Cal stepped out into the evening air and stood up beside her.

"Shall we?" He asked as he turned, offering her his hand. She took it, and he helped her out of the car.

The night air felt cool against her skin.

"I'm sorry," he said as she connected with his kind blue eyes.

"For what?"

"For assuming I know everything about you. For treating you like you were just another rich person who doesn't understand what it's like to experience hardships. It won't happen again."

"Promise?"

"I promise."

"Good," she said. "Can I tell you something?"

"Please."

"As your freshly appointed therapist, I think it's important for you to recognize that you might carry some baggage toward people wealthier than you."

"Is it that obvious?"

"You might want to dial it back a little," she said. "At least before we enter a party surrounded by the DC elite."

"This is going to be a long night, isn't it?" Cal said as he looked up at the Watergate Hotel.

"It's certainly going to be interesting."

CHAPTER 21

SIX YEARS EARLIER

As Nahla looked into Tariq's eyes, she saw how much the tyranny of Sudan had transformed him. His eyes held a deep sorrow that hadn't been there before Hashim died.

That's exactly why you need him. He knows this country better than you do now.

"Are you ready for this?" Tariq asked. His voice was deeper and his beard thicker than the boy she'd left behind. The two years since Hashim's death had made him a different man.

She nodded, placing a microphone discreetly between the folds of her thobe, inserting a tiny receiver into her ear. The subtle scent of spices from the bustling streets of Khartoum wafted through the window. It mixed with the heavy, oppressive heat that always seemed to hang in the air.

It's incredible how quickly I've forgotten the small details of my former homeland.

"You need to be careful," Tariq said.

"You think I don't know that?" Nahla replied. "I don't take bringing down a genocidal dictator lightly."

"If you misstep, it means death for both of us."

"And if I *don't* do this, Sudan will fall deeper and deeper into despair."

Nahla watched Tariq's eyes drift off into a distant place. He knew better than she what was at stake. He was the one still living in it. He remembered watching Hashim die with the same clarity that she did.

It appears to have tortured him even more than it has me.

"I owe you an apology."

"For what?" he said. As he spoke, she remembered the mannerisms of the Tariq she once knew. The Tariq she'd held resentment toward since the day she left.

"I should never have left you behind."

"I can't accept your apology."

The door behind them slammed open. Two servants walked in, carrying tablecloths and silverware, moving past them and into one of the other floors of the mansion. Voices echoed in the distance. One of them was al-Bashir's.

"No matter how much you hate me, I assure you that it is nothing compared to how much I hate myself," Tariq said. "Hashim's death falls squarely on my shoulders. When you arrived at my doorstep…"

A tear formed in his eye. He wiped it as he looked out over the skyline. Their old home was somewhere in the distance.

"...I was certain you were going to come back and kill me," he began. "I *wanted* you to kill me. I've been waiting for it, hoping for the regret to finally be over. But when you asked me for help..."

Fuck. He's more lost than I am.

"Why would you ever think that?" she asked.

"I've never stopped thinking about the way you looked at me that day. You may have changed. You may have moved on and left this country, but I know the girl you once were."

"And what do you know of that girl?"

"I know how much she desires vengeance. I know she'll stop at nothing until she finds it."

She reached out, touching him on the arm. The warmth of his skin felt like a lifeline, grounding her in the moment.

"A part of me will always hate you," she said. "But I also owe you a debt. You could have told them about our bitcoin, and you didn't. You allowed me to escape."

He was silent, staring down at her feet.

"Remember what Hashim taught you," she continued. "The toxic snakes that run this country have caused us to blame each other for the evil that they created. One of those snakes lurks in the next room. Let us be rid of it."

He smiled at her, cautiously, but with a look in his eyes like he believed her.

Do I believe in myself?

She couldn't help but feel repulsed by his desperation, but she couldn't dwell on it. It was time to act. It was time to find proof.

He wiped a tear from his eye, then placed both

earpieces into his ears. Nahla straightened her uniform and entered the servants' quarters.

The simple, coarse fabric felt heavy against her skin, a far cry from the elegant Sudanese dresses she once wore as a girl. Al-Bashir forced all of his female servants to wear traditional hijab with muted colors. She hated it, but it would allow her to play her part. They left the room, Tariq headed to a makeshift control room in the back of a van, and Nahla went into the kitchens.

"Why are you standing around?" the kitchen boss barked at her. "The kisra should have been out there five minutes ago."

Nahla smiled and nodded, grabbed the plate, and entered the dining room. She lingered for a moment on the slight sour aroma. She hadn't tasted fermented sorghum flatbread in years. The smell tugged at her heart. A part of her would always call this country home.

She was dressed in the same garb as the rest of the servants, moving through the mansion without attracting attention. She was only a servant, as forgettable as one of the beige couches lining the sitting area of al-Bashir's mansion. She kept her head down as she approached the table.

The grand dining hall was filled with a lingering haze of shisha smoke.

The moment she entered the dining room, her heart lurched.

There he is.

Cautiously, she moved to the table and placed the plate of kisra down in front of him. Omar laughed at a joke with some of the other men in the room.

He was dressed in his full military garb, the gold and red of his medals glimmering in the low light of the room. All she could think about was how much she wanted to rip them off his chest. This man enjoyed luxuries while millions of people in his country suffered from his cruelty.

Where are they?

The two defense contractors she was hoping to record al-Bashir talking to were nowhere to be seen. They must be somewhere else in the mansion, but she was too far in to wait.

All I can do now is get the microphone as close to him as possible.

She moved to the other side of the table, cautiously clearing plates and bowls from the table.

Her heart raced.

She was close enough to touch him now. Close enough to kill him. It would only take a second. She would grab his head and jam a table knife up through the bottom of his jaw. The image of him bleeding out across the expensive rugs that lined the floor flashed in her mind. She would die, but would it not be worth it? Her life was such a small price to pay for the genocide he'd caused.

'I only regret that I have but one life to lose for my country.'

She shook the thought from her mind and reached into her pocket, grabbing the microphone and placing it into her palm. Slowly, as she pretended to gather plates, she prepared to hide it beneath the table.

She slipped. Bumping a carafe of wine.

It crashed to the floor.

Fuck.

Omar al-Bashir's laugh transformed into anger, along with the mood of the entire room. He grabbed onto her wrist. His fingers squeezed into the bones of her forearm, the microphone still in the palm of her hand.

"What have you done?" he shouted. The kind face he wore for the ambassadors transformed into a scowl.

The wine soaked across his green military jacket. Like blood from a wound seeping into his medals and ribbons. She clenched the microphone with everything that she had. Opening her palm might cost her life.

"I'm… I'm so sorry."

He stared back at her as though she were a small, worthless piece of filth. Why did she think she could do this? No one could stop the kind of power this man controlled.

"What are you waiting for?" he questioned.

She opened her mouth, but the aggressive glare he shot her pushed all the words from her mind. She was frozen. Motionless.

"Clean," he said, releasing her wrist. "Now."

She nodded. She no longer cared about the microphone or the mission. She just wanted to get out of the room. Tariq's voice rang in her ear, but she didn't even register the words. Everything seemed distant.

She dropped to her knees, removing her apron and attempting to blot it over the large spill of wine. The material didn't absorb anything, but she didn't care.

"Can you believe this dumb bitch?" he said to the table of men. "Just as I was telling you about the quality of the women in my mansion."

Finally, the silence broke. The other men at the table laughed with Omar.

"The rest of them understand the meaning of respect. If they get your lap wet, it won't be an accident."

He smacked the back of her head.

She did everything in her power not to let out a whimper.

She continued to rub her apron over the wine spill, but she mostly just moved it around. It didn't matter. Anything that kept her out of sight from all the men at the table, anything that kept him from paying closer attention to who she was and why she was there.

"The rest of my women are ready to serve you in whatever manner you deem… *necessary.*"

"Is that why those two brothers were in such a rush to get upstairs?" a man at the table asked.

Omar leaned forward, beginning to talk quietly to only those in his direct vicinity.

"You think I leave my best wares out to wander the house?" he said. "Don't let this clumsy one fool you. The finest women are kept in my private quarters. As long as you are under my roof, whatever is mine is yours, gentlemen."

"Get out of there," Tariq said in her earpiece. "Now."

She didn't dare move. Not yet. She was so close to the table, so close to finishing the task she'd come here for. They were so close to bringing this man to justice.

"I've grown quite tired of African women," al-Bashir said. "But I have all sorts of different flavors in my collection. It all depends on how refined your tastes are."

"I personally don't like mine too refined if you catch my drift," said one of the men.

Omar smiled widely, his teeth stark white against his dark skin. "The south end of the second floor will have everything that you could ever hope to choose from."

Now. Do it now.

She switched the microphone to the hand closer to the table. She stood up and faced al-Bashir.

"I'm so sorry, sir," she said, taking a deep bow. At the bottom, she slipped the microphone under the table directly in front of al-Bashir's seat.

She prayed the microphone would stick to the underside of the table. She could barely breathe. If the bottom of the table were too smooth and the microphone dropped to the floor, it would all be over.

He'll torture and kill me. The people of this country will continue to live beneath his tyranny.

She stood up, then began to step away, quickly moving back toward the kitchen. She could finally get the hell out of here.

"Stop," al-Bashir said. Nahla turned, her heart pounding as Omar stood up from the table and walked toward her.

She froze, clutching the apron in her hands.

He stopped and extended his wine-stained jacket toward her.

"Speak with the servant in my room. Tell him to clean the medals, then return with a new jacket as soon as possible."

"Yes, sir," she said. She bowed once more, her voice trembling despite her efforts to remain calm.

Then he stepped even closer to her, his breath hot against her ear as he whispered. "If it happens again, I will cut off your hand."

Then he stepped back, smiled at her with those small white teeth, and walked back to the table.

"Well?" Nahla asked under her breath, still trying to regain her composure. "Did you get it?"

"I hear him loud and clear," Tariq said. She could hear the slight smile on his face. "Now get the hell out of there."

"You heard the man," Nahla said, moving back to the kitchen. "I have to speak with his servant."

"No," Tariq stated, whatever patience that was once in his voice now gone. "We talked about this. You're done. Get out."

She didn't respond to him. Instead, she moved toward al-Bashir's room, toward the servants' quarters.

"Every step you take inside that building is a risk of losing everything you've been working for."

There it is. He's still weak. He may have been willing to help me, but he's still controlled by fear.

"These are our people, Tariq," she said. "Are you going to help me, or are you going to sit here and listen?"

He remained silent for a moment before responding. "You put both of us at risk. If you are captured, everything that we have worked for is lost."

She didn't respond. Instead, she moved back through the kitchen. She ignored the shouting cooks and slipped up the servants' stairs to the second floor.

"Where are you going?"

"Did you not hear the man?"

She checked behind the first door. Locked.

She checked the second.

The door swung open into a bathroom. She stepped inside, her reflection in the mirror looking back at her with determination.

"Can you see any of the second floor right now from your current position?"

"I see you on the west side," he said. "There are a couple of servants throughout and a room on the south end with many different body heat signatures."

"I'm going to need you to get the van ready," she said. "Clear out the back, we might need some extra space."

No reply. He may have been angry, but he would help her. She still had that much faith in him.

She threw the military jacket down into the sink, examining it closely until she found what she was looking for. She ripped one of the badges off the jacket and then tossed the rest of it into the garbage can in the corner.

Nahla reentered the hallway, now moving slowly through the second floor. The floorboards creaked beneath her feet. She paused, listening for any sound from the rooms beyond.

Then she heard a whimper.

Hurriedly, she burst through the door.

A soldier with a gun turned toward her.

Holding up the badge she had taken from al-Bashir's jacket, she held her breath as he examined her. His eyes reminded her so much of the brutish soldier who took Hashim's life all those years ago.

Could this actually work?

The room was filled with women prisoners, many of them bound and gagged, all of them trying not to look at the scene happening in the corner.

Two men were having their way with one of the women on the bed.

Two men she'd hoped to record talking with al-Bashir.

The Valhner brothers.

William held her down to the bed and had his way with her, while James held a kitchen knife up against the side of her head.

"You best get still if you want to come out of this in one piece," James said as he held a knife up to the woman's neck.

Tears streamed down the faces of the other women, forced to watch as one of their own was defiled. They prayed they wouldn't be next.

Nahla clenched her jaw and forced herself to look away from the woman on the bed. It took everything in her power to keep her voice steady.

"I… I come with a message," Nahla said. "The President has an important announcement. He wants all his guests to return to the dining room."

The woman beneath William squealed and tried to free herself.

"Stay still, bitch," James said. "You aren't going anywhere."

"Our guests are…. occupied," the soldier said.

She felt her stomach turn, but she had to keep her composure. She kept her face pursed, emotionless.

If I want to save these people, I have to remain level-headed.

"The President's message is military in nature. He has commanded that all his security details be present when he—"

The woman screamed.

Nahla watched as James's knife sliced through the back of her ear.

Blood splashed over the white sheets.

"Stop!" Nahla yelled, unable to hold back any longer.

Both of the brothers stared at her with fire in their eyes.

"The President commands your presence," Nahla said.

"Are you serious?" William asked, his chest covered in spattered blood.

"Do you want to have to tell the President why his two esteemed guests were not in attendance?" Nahla asked the soldier.

She watched the fear crest over the soldier's eyes.

"Get dressed now," the soldier said. "I'll be escorting you to al-Bashir myself."

"Thank you," Nahla said to the soldier. "You have my personal assurance that not a single person will leave this room."

She watched as the brothers hastily put their clothing back on, leaving the woman clasping onto the side of her face as blood poured over her hand.

The men left.

"Tariq," she said into the microphone. "Get ready to drive fast."

CHAPTER 22

———

The elevator doors opened.

Cal stepped into the penthouse.

The marble flooring that sprawled across the entryway caught his eye. It resembled the interior of a precious gemstone. Swirls of earthy tones mingled with veins of gold and bronze, it was as if the floor had been carved directly from the heart of an ancient stone.

Against the far wall, there were hundreds of masks. Each one was unique, organized by color. They ranged from simple designs to extravagant jeweled creations.

The concierge desk was in front of them. Behind it, staff members wore dark black suits and dresses, with matching black face masks. Each of them looked like a living shadow compared to the colorful masks designated for each of the guests.

Is that how the hyper-wealthy like to view their servants? As shadows that fade into the background. Forgettable and unimportant.

Cal analyzed the room.

He had no idea what they were walking into, but he was already calculating escape routes. The only visible exit was a stairwell beside the elevator. None of the masked guests appeared armed, but tailored suits made it easy to conceal a pistol.

"Do we need to have some kind of plan?" Sofia asked.

"What do you think, Cal?" Harold asked, his voice laced with sarcasm. "You seem to know *exactly* what we should do next. Why don't you tell us how we should proceed?"

Cal said nothing.

"Welcome to the Watergate," the concierge said. Her demeanor was welcoming, but something about the way she looked at them was unnerving. Cal couldn't help but wonder if she knew about any heinous events planned for the evening.

"It's best to do this part myself," Harold said under his breath.

"Harold is probably worried we'll try to tip the servants," Sofia whispered to Cal as they stepped away from the concierge desk. "We might ruin his reputation if we treat the help like actual humans."

The two of them walked over to the wall of party masks.

Despite Sofia's sarcasm, Cal sensed her growing nervousness around the situation.

"Do you have any advice for me?" he asked, hoping the conversation would distract her from the stress of what lay ahead.

"I was thinking about asking you the same thing."

"Really?"

"You dealt with dangerous and stressful situations

all the time when you served. How did you deal with it?"

"To be honest with you, I was good at it long before I joined the military."

The curious look on her face implored him to continue.

"Yugoslavia was a stressful place to be a kid in the early '90s," he said. "People hear the word hyperinflation and think it means things just got expensive. They don't realize how a country's money collapsing brings down every facet of society."

Cal grabbed a blood-red mask and rolled it over in his hands.

"As the money became worthless, we were forced to buy the most basic things on the black market. I'm not talking about luxury goods or drugs. We were forced to barter for flour, eggs, and medicine. If a government official caught you doing it, you could be killed."

He set the mask down and looked at her. There was no pen and paper. No journalist. Just Sofia's curious eyes looking at him in the same way that she did on the plane.

Like someone who genuinely wants to understand who I am.

"Each time my parents left home, my brother and I knew it could be the last time we'd ever see them."

"Shit," she said as she reached out and touched him on the shoulder. "I'm so sorry."

"We survived," he said. "And now I'm basically immune to the things that stress most people out."

"What stresses you out then?" she asked.

"Making small talk with a bunch of two-faced rich people."

She laughed.

"I don't even know what I'm supposed to say to them," he continued.

"I'd recommend you try to not mention Bitcoin for at least five minutes. Consider it an exercise in self-control."

"No promises," he said as he smiled at her. "I assume a beautiful woman like you has been to events like this. Got any advice?"

"Didn't you promise you were going to be done assuming things about my past?"

"Is that a yes or a no?"

"I have," she said begrudgingly. "But nothing quite like this."

She grabbed a dark wooden mask, putting it up to her face, and smiled at Cal.

"There are two kinds of rich people," she said. "Those who want to look rich and those who don't. Usually, the most successful ones are the quiet ones, spending more of their time observing than talking. I suspect those will be the ones you'll get along with better."

"And which kind is Harold?"

Sofia smiled back at him.

"Most of what makes a good journalist is simple," she continued. "Ask good questions and genuinely listen to people's answers. People love talking about themselves. That applies doubly so to successful people. Outside of that, stick to safe topics."

"So I *shouldn't* go around telling them they're about to get murdered by a Robin-Hood-esque cult?"

Sofia put the wooden mask back on the shelf and gave him a glare.

"Fair enough," Cal said. "I'll keep my mouth shut, but I can't help but think about how the Robin Hood legend has similarities with the people we're following."

"You're going to go into a whole thing about it, aren't you?"

"I was considering it."

"Well, let's hear it then," she said as she chuckled at him.

"Robin Hood was the first prominent story in human history where the hero fought for financial equality, but he did more than steal from the rich and give to the poor. He opposed taxation by the local aristocracy and fought against economic oppression."

"Sounds like someone I know."

"Like many old tales, the story's nuance was lost with time. Today, many poor people root for Robin Hood because they would love to see the rich elites of the world robbed."

"You don't?"

"No, I don't," Cal said as he grabbed a grey mask that looked as though it would match Harold's attire. He ran his fingers over its textured surface. "Stealing from or killing people does nothing to fix the underlying economic problems if the system remains unchanged."

"I'm starting to think your interest in economic inequality might be even nerdier than your obsession with Bitcoin."

"Both things are related," Cal continued. "Financial inequality has been plaguing humanity for tens of thousands of years, but it's never been worse."

"That seems impossible."

"It's even worse today than when Karl Marx criticized the bourgeoisie for exploiting the working class. But it shouldn't be. Technology allows us to make food and goods cheaper than at any other time in history. We should have more abundance than ever."

"Then why don't we?"

"Because our monetary system is broken," Cal said. "Economics is more than boring numbers. It's the underlying cause behind most human suffering. We may live in a highly technological age, but the gap between the lowest and highest in society has never been wider."

"Didn't they literally guillotine rich people during the French Revolution because of wealth inequality?"

"Thousands of them, including King Louis XVI and Marie Antoinette. Class-based struggles have fueled genocides. It's historically been one of the greatest hotbeds of conflict and violence."

"If the wealth gap is worse now, why aren't there more revolutions?"

"You and I walked past the place where the Occupy Wall Street movement took place when we met this morning. Crowds rallied against the one percent and criticized the banks that got bailouts during the 2008 Great Financial Crisis."

"But nothing really ever changes, does it? All the same problems persist."

"To the uninformed," Cal said, with a smile. "But something did change. Something unstoppable and technological."

"You never shut up about Bitcoin, do you?" she said, smiling and looking at the wall of masks for something that suited her better.

"You got me," he said. "The network was a technical revolution born from the resentment of the rich getting bailouts during the 2008 crisis. If it succeeds, it will radically reduce the inequality gap caused by our government printing infinite amounts of money. Bitcoin forces individuals and organizations to play by a set of rules they cannot change. It makes them honest. Paradoxically, big Wall Street money moving into the Bitcoin network makes every single sovereign user of the network better off."

"What do you think?" Sofia asked, changing the subject and holding a deep sapphire mask up to her face. "I want something that says 'mysterious' but also 'I'm old money and have no idea how much a gallon of milk costs.'"

He wanted to tell her that she looked stunning, that the mask she picked out matched the grace with which she carried herself. He wanted to tell her how much he regretted making assumptions about her. He wanted to tell her how much he appreciated not being alone with Harold for whatever lay in front of them.

What if the feelings she's trying to evoke in me are not real? She knows so much more about me than I do about her. This is her profession. She wants me to open up.

"That's the one."

Harold returned with the concierge at his side. He now wore a mask that looked as though it was shaped out of a bar of solid gold.

"Everyone wearing a colored mask is a party guest," the concierge said, gesturing toward the sapphire mask Sofia wore.

Beneath its sapphire surface, Cal could see that she looked nervous again. He could feel his heart racing as well.

"Staff members will be wearing plain black masks like mine," the concierge said, pointing toward her own. Then she handed Cal a golden mask. It was heavy in his hands. "This allows you to enter any room you wish and play at the high-stakes tables. The games begin when you step through these doors."

Then the concierge led the three of them into the heart of the penthouse.

CHAPTER 23

———

Sofia followed Cal and Harold through the long hallway.

They passed smaller rooms and a staff kitchen. She looked through the door window to see more black-masked people organizing food and drinks for the party.

The penthouse was dark. The entire space was illuminated by low, flickering candlelight. Electronic orchestral music echoed through the dimly lit space. No words. No lyrics. Just a driving rhythm that vibrated deep beneath her sternum.

Burning incense filled the air with the scent of lemon and gin.

The long hallway opened up as they entered the main room. In the center, hanging above the dance floor, was a multi-tiered crystal chandelier. Each finely-cut teardrop caught the flickering candlelight and transmuted it into soft rainbows that shimmered over the shoulders of the dancers below. Masked people twirled and spun to the music in the low light.

Immediately, Sofia noticed the response to her wardrobe. She felt the kind of physical confidence only a dress could bring. Every male eye in the room was upon her.

Attention is power, as long as you understand how to use it properly.

Sofia adjusted her diamond necklace, grateful to be hidden behind a mask. She watched a handful of other people, adorned with golden masks, go deeper into the penthouse.

"Now what?" she asked as they approached the middle of the room where people danced around them.

"I think we try to blend in," Cal said, then extended his hand to her. The corner of his mouth curled into a smile beneath the gold of his mask, the blue of his eyes flickering against the low light.

She gave him her hand.

"The clock is ticking," Harold said sternly. "We need to act immediately if we want to figure out what's happening here."

"I plan to do just that," Cal said, wrapping his calloused hand around hers.

He pulled her out onto the dance floor.

"But first," he whispered to her. "I figured we could have a little fun."

He spun her around, his hand on her back, the other holding hers. He moved with surprising fluidity. She barely had to think as she allowed his body to guide her. Sofia found herself surrendering to the rhythm as Cal dictated the flow of their movements.

The anxiety she felt only moments ago in the entryway quieted. There was only music. Each step, each turn, felt like a conversation without words. Her eyes flicked to the other dancers, but they were nothing more than blurred figures in the periphery.

He spun her out, and she twirled with a grace she hadn't known she possessed. Then he pulled her back in, his strength evident as he effortlessly controlled the momentum. As the song built to a crescendo, their movements synchronized.

Conversation flowed so naturally between them, but *this*, *this* was something else entirely.

Cal pulled her close as the music began to slow, so close she could feel the heat radiating from his body.

"What do you think?" he whispered into her ear. The warmth of his breath on her ear sent a shiver down her spine.

"Where did you learn to dance like that?"

The corner of his mouth turned up into a smile.

"No, I mean about the party?" he said. "I still think our best exit is back the way we came in. Based on where people are congregating, it appears many of the guests wearing gold masks are going into the back rooms."

That was not what I was paying attention to.

"Some of the staff members in all black don't move like hospitality. They're too alert. Jonathan must have hired ex-military operatives to be discreet security for the party."

He turned their bodies, sweeping her around in a circle as they began to dance slowly. Behind her, giant windows overlooked the city. Fireworks exploded in the distance as people celebrated the upcoming Independence Day.

She looked around, examining the masked people around her, wondering if any of them were famous politicians or senators. She understood why they wanted to wear masks. Public figures surely longed for anonymity, yearning to retreat from constant scrutiny.

"The gold masks seem like a good place to start," Cal said. "We should follow the money."

"We'll have to split up," she said, looking around the room, curious where she should start her investigation.

He guided her around the dance floor, spinning her once more before settling back into a comfortable pace with a better view of the surrounding party.

"Spain," Cal said, as they passed in front of another dancing couple. His freshly shaven jaw shifted into a smile beneath the golden mask.

"What?"

"You asked where I learned to dance," he said. "I was stationed in Base Naval de Rota on the southwest coast of Spain. The culture down there was big into dancing. I was a young man at the time and had little else to do on the base."

"Interesting," she said. "Did you learn a lot about yourself during that time there?"

"Of course."

"Well, that's ironic."

"How so?"

"One might say that you found yourself while traveling in Europe."

The serious demeanor dropped from his face for a split second as a bright smile spread across his mouth. After a few seconds, he went back to cautiously scanning the room with his eyes.

"It wasn't like that," he began. "My whole life was work there. We were only allowed to leave the base for short periods of time, and if you wanted to meet any Spanish women, you had to learn how to dance."

"You sound like a liar to me."

He smirked.

He spun her around again, their dancing now bringing them closer toward the bar and the crowd surrounding it.

"I'm sorry," Cal said.

"For what?"

"I've been on edge since we met today, but it isn't you. I hate being surrounded by people like this. It's a constant reminder of the poverty that I grew up in, and how oblivious these kinds of people are to it. I apologize for judging you too harshly. I appreciate having you here today."

She looked into his eyes, wishing the golden mask were removed, so she could better read his facial expressions.

"It's not your fault," she said. "I've been so busy asking more questions about you without sharing anything about myself in return. It's my fault, not yours."

"Maybe it's my turn to ask a few of the interview questions?"

She gave him a welcoming smile.

His eyes beckoned her to say more, but she held her tongue.

She looked at the people surrounding them, some of whom might be in grave danger. She thought of her boss, and a wave of anxiety swept over her again.

I can't let my guard down, but would it be so wrong to enjoy the ride?

Just as she was beginning to feel comfortable being herself in Cal's presence, a hand reached out and grabbed her shoulder.

CHAPTER 24

SIX YEARS EARLIER

N ahla stood on the steps of the New York Stock
Exchange, taking in the historic facade. The Co-
rinthian columns gleamed in the morning light.

"We should be preparing for our next deposition at the United Nations right now," Tariq said as they walked to the security entrance. He'd cleaned up his appearance since she'd first arrived at his doorstep in Khartoum. The more clean-cut he kept himself, the more he looked like her uncle.

"Rehearsing one more time isn't going to change anything," Nahla said. "The recordings we have of al-Bashir are indisputable. But if we are going to try to change this world, we must better understand it."

"The only thing I need to understand is who is responsible for keeping al-Bashir in power."

"It's Senator Rosewall," Nahla said. "But she isn't the only one profiting from the unrest in Sudan. Many defense contractors make money from the wars that the USA exports globally. Some of those companies' stocks trade on the NYSE."

A senior official from a large brokerage firm approached them with a smooth smile.

"Welcome," he greeted them with an overly formal tone.

They followed him to a side entrance, away from the swarm of tourists snapping photos of the iconic building. The security checkpoint was discreet, tucked behind unmarked doors.

"Your connection from the Sudanese embassy spoke highly of you, Tariq," the official said.

Nahla connected with her cousin's eyes. She had never understood his yearning for a quiet life in Khartoum, but he was giving it up for her. If they failed to overthrow al-Bashir, the home they once shared would be lost to them forever.

Two NYPD officers watched them as they passed, eyes scanning for any sign of threat. The senior official handed over pre-registered badges, each one bore a metallic NYSE seal. They passed through metal detectors, underwent biometric scans, and had their ID's verified before being allowed to enter.

The doors slid open to reveal the grandeur of the trading floor, where the early morning calm was punctuated by the quiet hum of computers and whispered conversations among brokers preparing for the day's action.

It was different from what Nahla had expected.

There were no shouting men and high-stress stockbrokers. The old marble building was filled with computers and screens everywhere.

Nahla walked between the rows of computers, looking at the various stock tickers that surrounded the floor. Spectators gathered in awe of the history that laced these walls.

That wasn't what she felt.

These people make me sick.

Rich men in suits speculated on valuations, obsessing over the stocks prices and numbers. All the while, the financial system ignored people like her. This place, the center of global finance, was an insiders' game.

There were no Sudanese companies represented here. This place was said to be the center of global financial power, yet it brought no benefit to most people in the world.

"They walk around like their price fixation is critical to the functioning of human society," Nahla said. "Meanwhile, the people who make *real* things grow poorer with each passing year."

"Do you think we can truly make a difference?" Tariq asked.

"If we can show the world the evils taking place inside Sudan's borders, we can create change," she said. "We have to remain optimistic. This country was built upon free speech and the fight against tyranny."

The weight of the task ahead settled heavily on Nahla's shoulders. More than a speech, it was a plea for action, an appeal to the collective conscience of the world's leaders. She envisioned what it would be like to confront Senator Rosewall again. To show them the truth of how the world was profiting off of a warlord in Sudan. To make her face the consequences of her actions. The thought gave her strength, a fire burning in her chest.

A commotion began in front of them.

A group of people stood ahead of them on a balcony, preparing for the opening bell to ring.

"It's ironic, isn't it?" Tariq said. "This country pretends to be the center of economic freedom, but its people are only allowed to trade their stocks when the government regulators allow. Nine-thirty to four. Monday through Friday."

Nahla smiled.

Meanwhile, the Bitcoin network let her send money anywhere in the world, regardless of time, without asking a single person for permission.

Many of the companies trading held bitcoin on their balance sheets. Nahla resented this. Wall Street money was trying to adopt the very network that could bring freedom to people like hers. They would manipulate it. Financialize it. Corrupt it.

The bell rang, and people around them cheered. The market was officially open, and traders would begin their day.

"Enjoying the festivities?" asked a gravelly voice from behind them.

Nahla turned on her heels to meet the eyes of a man dressed all in grey.

"Who are you?" Nahla asked, immediately put off by the way he was looking at her.

"My name isn't important, but *who* I work for is."

Nahla studied the lines in his face. Something about his gaze unsettled her. The scent of cigar smoke lingered on his tailored suit.

They'd planned for weeks to get a security clearance for the NYSE.

Whoever he is, he must have powerful connections.

"I'm here to help you," he said. "You are about to make a catastrophic mistake."

She looked at Tariq, who also stood still. She saw that same flash of fear in his eyes, that same flash of weakness that she knew still resided within him.

"You need to withdraw your case from the United Nations."

Her heart dropped out of her chest.

"Absolutely not."

"Nahla," the grey man continued, a large smile on his face that was far from being kind. "I'm simply here to give you information. I would be remiss if I allowed you to simply walk into the UN building tomorrow and present... knowing what it is that I know."

"What do you know?"

"Sudan recently entered into a complex economic relationship with China. Senator Rosewall has made it clear that she does not want to upset that relationship. We are on tumultuous ground with them to begin with. The information you are planning to present will jeopardize that relationship."

Nahla wanted to scream.

She imagined herself grabbing this man by the neck and clawing out his throat.

"I care not what kind of *relationship* China holds with the genocidal dictator of my country. I don't care if Senator Rosewall's investment portfolio tanks because of my actions. The world needs to see exactly what is happening and what will continue to happen if we do not expose the toxic infection of their economic interventionism."

"Ah, but you should," the man said with a casual tone, as if the threats he was issuing to them were just a normal day for him. "You and Tariq will have to face the consequences of your actions."

"A tiny sacrifice for the betterment of people who cannot defend themselves from people like you."

"You know nothing of myself or the people I serve."

A group of brokers walked past them, talking enthusiastically about a stock they thought would have a big run-up in the afternoon.

"I'm familiar with your type," Nahla stated. "Someday, men like you will have to pay for the atrocities that you've helped to fund."

"Maybe one day," he continued. "But today I have a message to convey. A simple one, but you would be wise to adhere to every word."

"And if I continue to show the world the evils that are taking place within it?"

"Then there will be consequences."

"And they will be worth it."

"Let me put this more plainly," the man said as his grey eyes narrowed. "Your deposition with the United Nations has been canceled. My employer has been kind and not yet taken further action. However, if any of those recordings see the light of day, the two of you will be sent directly back to al-Bashir and your lives will be forfeit."

"I will see you undone."

The grey man gave a spiteful smile in response. "You do not want to start this fight. The people you prod are far more dangerous than you."

"'I have not yet *begun* to fight.'"

"Goodbye, Nahla. If you are wise, you will never see me again."

The realization hit Nahla like a wrecking ball.

I've failed the people of Sudan. I've failed Hashim.

The bustling lobby of the New York Stock Exchange was too much for her. No matter how nice the clothes she wore, no matter how much she tried to play their game, she would always be an outcast in this world of fancy granite floors and wealthy men. The polished surfaces, the technological lingo, the well-dressed diplomats.

It all felt like an elaborate lie.

She couldn't breathe.

She was suffocated by the stagnant air of the old building. The walls seemed to close in on her, the bustling sounds of the trading floor amplifying her sense of failure. She ran to the exit, the heavy doors swinging open, revealing the bright sunlight of Wall Street.

She ran.

Past the crowds of people that craned their necks at the old architecture of the city, past Trinity Church, past the throngs of people on Broadway.

I'm still a foolish girl. How did I think I could change the world?

She was just like all the other young women who had tried before her. They came to this city with optimism and hope, only to be crushed by bureaucracy.

Tariq shouted her name, but she couldn't stop.

The crisp New York air filled her lungs.

Broadway split in front of her.

At its center, the giant bronze bull stared into her eyes, the symbol of a financial system that left her people unrepresented. Off in the distance, she could see Valhner Tower, the evil men she'd seen commit vile acts with her own eyes still had not met the consequences that they deserved.

This cannot be tolerated. Someone has to do something.

"Nahla," Tariq said as he finally caught up with her. "Stop."

Around them, the crowd was bustling. An endless sea of people in suits.

"Years of work," she said. "Years of sacrifices. The risks I took to get close to al-Bashir were all for nothing."

"That's not true. Those women are free now because of you. Perhaps that's good enough?"

"Good enough?" she yelled at him. "The world falls deeper into ruin because of the toxic system that these people continue to perpetuate. Have you not changed at all?"

He looked back at her, and she felt sorry for him. The agency she wanted to see in him wasn't there. He was still the scared boy who turned on his own father.

No. That's not fair. He's trying to change. He believes in me, regardless of how I feel about him.

"All is not lost," Tariq said. "We can return here in a year and find a different strategy, this time gaining more support from—"

"I'm done with bureaucracy," Nahla said. "Never again will I ask the elites for help with a problem that they created."

She collected herself. There was a fire burning inside her that she hadn't felt since the day she watched Hashim die.

"The people complicit in funding the warlords and dictators are sitting inside federal buildings, smiling and shaking hands. I've tried to play their games, and I've failed time and time again. All the while, they get rich and profit off the suffering of our people."

She thought back to how much she idolized the United States when she was younger. The freedom and opportunity she had dreamed of were a lie.

"Nahla, what are you saying?"

"It's time to take a different approach. It's time to play a new game. It's time to make these people experience the hopelessness they've subjected the rest of the world to."

She looked at the bull, disgusted by the financial system that systematically stole from the poorest in society. She looked at the crowds of US citizens, the people of the country she'd once held in such high regard. The country that had given her so much hope. The country that was all a lie.

"I'm going to burn them to the fucking ground."

CHAPTER 25

———

C al watched Sofia jump in shock as Harold placed his hand on her shoulder.

"Did I interrupt something?" he asked with a judgmental tone.

"What have you found so far?" Cal asked as Sofia regained her composure.

"A few of our employers are here," he said, his voice quiet. "I just spoke with one of them."

"Who are they?" Cal asked.

"You understand the point of a masquerade is anonymity, right?" Harold asked. "I cannot divulge that."

"It's hard for me to help you without all the facts."

"You have as much as you need," Harold said. "How do you think we should proceed?"

"I think we need to follow the money," Cal stated, looking to one of the adjacent rooms beyond where he saw people seated at poker and blackjack tables. "If wealthy individuals are the targets, we should be near them."

"I have some ideas too," Sofia said, looking at a man wearing a golden mask seated at the bar. "But I'm going to need the two of you to leave me alone to do it."

"I suppose you might as well put that beautiful dress to work," Harold said. "I did pay an exorbitant sum for it."

"Of course, Sir Harold, your charity humbles me," Sofia said, followed by an exaggerated curtsy. "I'm forever indebted to you and your patronage."

Cal didn't even attempt to hide his laughter as she walked off toward the bar.

"How's your poker game?" Harold asked Cal.

"I played a time or two in the military."

"Did you ever win?"

"Occasionally."

"What's the most you ever lost in a hand?"

"My lunch money."

Harold looked appalled.

"How would you play pocket jacks?"

"Is there a point to this?"

"I'm trying to figure out what I'm working with."

"They're a strong hand, but you can't fall in love with them. You have to be willing to let them go."

Harold seemed to be satisfied with his answer.

The pair of them walked into the next room.

It felt like they walked onto a Las Vegas casino floor. The scent of tobacco floated throughout the space. The table in front of them was surrounded by men wearing golden masks.

It appears we've found the money.

Cal led them to a spot with a good vantage point over the entire room. They stood next to the giant glass windows that overlooked the DC skyline as they waited for a spot at the poker table to open. He looked down over the waters of the Potomac River, watching as a yacht passed beneath one of the arches of the Francis Scott Key Bridge. Across the penthouse, Cal watched as Sofia sat next to a woman in a green suit at the bar.

"I have to be honest with you about something," Harold said. "I'm beginning to get frustrated that you aren't taking this seriously enough."

"I assure you that's not true."

"The way you were dancing with Sofia says otherwise," Harold said. "When I hired you, I assumed someone who would be slightly more... *professional*."

"What's that supposed to mean?"

"It means I messed up," Harold said. "I should have hired somebody who would take their job more seriously."

"That's a lie."

"Case in point," Harold said. "This is no way to communicate with your employer."

"What you want has nothing to do with professionalism," Cal said. "You want somebody you can control. Somebody who looks at this luxury and excess and is willing to do anything you ask of them."

"That's not true—"

"You know it. I know it. There is no point in debating it. You need to move past it."

"How can I move past it if I'm not able to trust you to have my back?" Harold said. "My friend is still missing. For all I know, one of these masked people could be plotting to end my life right now, and I'm stuck here with someone I don't trust."

"Look at me," Cal said, grabbing Harold by the shoulder. "We don't have to agree on everything to work together. I don't know these people personally, but I assure you that I will do everything in my power to help you stop these people."

"Everything?" Harold asked. "Says the man that refuses to carry a weapon."

Cal didn't respond.

"Every step of the way, you treat me like I'm some pretentious asshole," Harold continued. "If we are going to work together, you need to treat me with respect."

"Because you *are* a pretentious asshole," Cal said. "You need to accept that flashing your money or using intimidation tactics is not going to work on me. I'm here because I want to be. We're on the same team."

"In what way?"

"Bitcoin is a *peaceful revolution*," Cal continued. "But what we are witnessing today isn't peaceful. If whoever we're chasing is successful, the Bitcoin network could become further associated with violence. This tool can bring so much hope to humanity. I don't want to see its reputation tarnished."

"You're willing to put your life on the line for some ethical beliefs about a computer network?"

"Absolutely."

"Didn't you tell me Bitcoin couldn't fail?"

"Bitcoin will produce block after block roughly every ten minutes for the rest of time. It doesn't matter what either of us thinks about it. It will continue to adhere to the most predictable monetary policy humankind has ever known. Millions of people around the world will continue using it as a savings technology regardless of what happens tonight."

A small cheer erupted from the poker table behind them as a man won a large pot, adding a large stack of chips to his own.

"But *we* can fail to convey that message to humanity," Cal said. "I don't want to see the very people that could benefit most from this technology refuse to use it because they associate it with violence."

One of the losers of the hand stood up and left the poker table. A couple of new men in gold masks sat down in their place.

"You and I both want to stop whoever is doing this, but I'm not your employee to be commanded. I will continue helping you, but only if we work together as peers."

Harold gazed at Cal with deep skepticism. It was the same look Colonel Blackwell used to give him.

The look of someone who doesn't understand me but desperately needs my help.

"Deal," Harold said. "But will you follow my lead, so we can get Jonathan out of this alive?"

"If you'll be honest with me about why you care so much about him."

Harold paused for a long moment, choosing his words carefully.

"We're still friends, but we used to have a much more intimate relationship."

Interesting.

"I appreciate the transparency," Cal said.

"I can see the way you resent everyone at this party," Harold continued as he looked across the penthouse.

"But some of the guests here are the most generous people I know. Jonathan is a great man. He uses his wealth to erase medical debts for low-income families."

"I understand that, but—"

"Do you? You act as if rich people are evil. It worries me that you may be more aligned with whoever it is we are chasing than those you need to protect."

"Just because I hate the monetary systems that create wealth inequality doesn't mean that I hate individuals who've had financial success. Our world cannot operate without people who leverage technology to create a better life for the rest of us. The thing I *detest* is bureaucratic elites who got rich by siphoning the financial life force away from the unknowing masses."

"Is that a very Cal way of saying that you're willing to help me?"

"Something like that," Cal said as he extended his hand. "For now, we are aligned. Let's stop anyone else from getting killed."

Harold met his eyes and shook his hand.

"Where do you propose that we begin?" Cal asked.

Harold pulled out a small leather case from his suit pocket, grabbing one of his cigars and cutting it.

"You wanted to follow the money," Harold said as he used his pocket lighter to carefully toast the bottom of the cigar. "Well, some big money just sat down at the poker table."

CHAPTER 26

———

Their faces may have been hidden, but Sofia felt their eyes.

Judging.

Longing.

She was no stranger to beauty. It was a tool she'd often wielded against men to get the story that she needed. This was different. The expensive dress and diamond necklace caught everyone's eyes. The surrounding women were well-dressed, but most of them were attempting to be discreet. The goal was anonymity. She'd failed at that.

If I can't fit in, I might as well embrace it.

She approached the bar.

At first glance, the bar seemed completely normal. The entire back shelf was covered in various colors of alcohol. Low lights highlighted the bottles with their distinct vintages. But beneath the dark glass counter lay a variety of different substances.

Cocaine, ecstasy, and psilocybin were labeled beneath the glass.

Shit.

A bartender handed a needle to a man wearing a red mask at the end of the bar. He immediately shot it into his arm, bliss slowly melting the rigidity out of his body. Behind all of them was the skyline of DC. The penthouse looked down on it from above, like a castle looking over the fields of the servant class.

Sofia settled onto a stool beside a woman in a green suit whose massive emerald necklace made Sofia's diamond one look like play jewelry. The woman snapped her fingers in the bartender's face to get his attention, pointing at her glass to demand a refill.

I understand where Cal is coming from. I can't stand these people.

A few minutes later, the bartender returned. He tried his best to hide the annoyed look on his face while he refilled the woman's glass.

"What's your vice?" he asked, turning to Sofia. Wearing the same black mask and black attire as all the other staff members in the establishment.

"Do you have a Bisol Cartizze Dry?"

"I think we do," the bartender said, turning around to fetch it.

As soon as he stepped away, Sofia began snapping at him just like the lady in green had.

The bartender spun on his heels, with a confused look on his face.

"Oh, my mistake," Sofia said, with a coy smile on her face. "I thought being an insufferable bitch was the only way to get noticed here."

The bartender tried his best to hide his laughter before he left to fetch her wine.

"You can't be serious?" the woman in green said as she clutched the gigantic emeralds of her necklace. For a moment, Sofia thought she was going to get slapped.

A man sitting at the corner of the bar began to chuckle as the woman in green left the bar. His well-defined jawline protruded from the bottom of his golden mask.

"That was bold," he said.

Sofia looked him over. Despite the mask, she could tell that he was tall and confident, with long, thick hair hanging over the edges of his mask.

"Do you have any idea who that was?"

"No."

"It's probably better if you don't know," he said as the corner of his mouth turned up into a smile. "What brings you here?"

"Do you recognize the irony of asking that question to someone wearing a mask?"

"Do you recognize that looking *that* beautiful in *that* dress makes you quite memorable? Even if you turn me down and walk away, I certainly won't be forgetting you."

"Shall we test that?" she asked, standing up from her seat like she might leave.

"Wait," he said, gently touching her arm. "Is it so bad that I have an interest in a beautiful woman who chose to sit next to me at the bar?"

"And if I'm not interested in small talk?"

The bartender came back, placing the glass of Prosecco in front of her. She took a sip, its flavor transporting her back to one of the wineries she visited during her time in Italy.

"Then let's skip it entirely," the man said. "No small talk, no names, no pleasantries."

"Go on."

"Everyone in this place has things they'd rather keep secret," he said. "Let's trade. I'll tell you one of mine if you tell me one of yours."

"A secret?"

"Let's embrace the anonymity and have a little fun."

"Deal," Sofia said, turning her chair to face him, wondering if she'd chosen the right rich man to approach. "Go ahead."

"I enjoy my job."

"Oh wow," Sofia said. "That's riveting."

He smirked before continuing.

"I'm not supposed to," he continued. "No child dreams of being the person they bring in to fire people. No one goes to business school wishing that one day they will specialize in mass layoffs. I've always thought there must be something wrong with me. What kind of sick person enjoys watching people's professional lives get ripped out from beneath them?"

The man laughed before continuing.

"I've never been able to admit that to someone in my personal life. I have to pretend like my job rips me apart. They even pay for us to have a psychiatrist after particularly large layoffs. If I ever told them the truth…"

Sofia had to gather herself.

Your job is to charm, regardless of what you think about him.

She reached out and touched him on the arm. Regardless of how sick and depraved she found him, their time was limited. She needed to gain allies.

"The truth is the truth," she said. "Regardless of how uncomfortable it is."

"I enjoy playing executioner," the man said. "Plus, it pays the bills for places like this. I can't stand hanging out in bars with the general public. Their addiction to failure rubs off on you."

The bartender handed a few joints to an older couple at the end of the bar who couldn't seem to keep their hands off one another.

"Felt good saying that out loud," he said. "Your turn."

"I'm way out of my depth here," Sofia said.

"Aren't we all?"

His eyes bore into her. She couldn't risk creating a fictional story. She'd have to give him something real.

"This is all a lie," she said. "I'm a liar."

The man toyed with the ice cubes in his drink.

"This person you are talking to right now," she said. "I'm playing a role. I'm actively doubting every decision I've made over the last couple of days, and now I'm far too deep into a world that I barely understand."

"Well, you look like you know what you're doing," he said as his eyes drifted down past the diamonds of her necklace.

"I shouldn't be telling you any of this," she said, gently placing her hand on his shoulder. Letting it linger for only a moment, she watched the corner of his mouth curl up into a smile.

"There are plenty of substances behind this counter that can help with indecision and anxiety," the man said, as he gestured for the bartender. "Whatever you want is on me."

"I appreciate the offer," she said. "But this wine is doing its job just fine."

Out of the corner of her eye, she spotted a group of staff members moving through the penthouse with urgency. The concierge walked in front of them, commanding orders.

Is something wrong?

"Actually," Sofia said, beckoning the bartender back over again. She looked down at the case, full of all sorts of different illicit substances. "There *is* something that I would like, but it might sound like a strange request."

CHAPTER 27

ONE DAY EARLIER

"No more," James Valhner begged from the next room. "I'll do anything."

Nahla's heart raced as she listened to his screams.

She wasn't sure how it would feel to hear them. To know their deaths were her choice. She thought she might feel remorse. She thought she might feel guilt.

She didn't.

Instead, she felt envious.

A part of her wished she were in the room herself, watching it happen, listening to their screams, and seeing the two powerful men beg on their knees for her forgiveness.

No suits or bureaucrats this time around.

She'd spent the last five years planning for this moment. Meticulously identifying politicians and businessmen who profited the most from abusing the poor.

The time was finally here, and this time she was going to force the change she wanted to see in the world.

It begins with blood.

"You fucking bitch!" William Valhner shouted at the top of his lungs between the gasps of pain coming from the next room.

Nahla smiled.

Tariq squirmed as he stepped into the room. His face was pale.

"The temporary walls are set up around the Bull of Bowling Green," he said. "The city is under the impression it's a restoration project. I've programmed them to drop at exactly seven tomorrow morning."

"You don't have to be here for this part," Nahla said to him, her voice calm despite the violence.

The years of living in America had been good to him. Nahla watched the life come back into his eyes. It was incredible how much more vitality a person was capable of when not under the rule of a genocidal dictator. She wondered how much distance from the city where he killed his father played a role in that.

The passage of time has a way of dampening all traumas.

"I may be on the technical side of this plan," Tariq said. "But that doesn't make me any less complicit. I need to hear this."

His clenched jaw betrayed his composure. Nahla respected him for it. Perhaps he would be able to harden his heart and do what was required after all.

"Just think about how many people they've subjected to pain," Nahla said.

Another desperate scream echoed from the room.

"They supplied al-Bashir with more weapons than anyone else. I saw in person the brutality they'd subjected others to in his mansion."

A saw turned on in the next room.

Tariq's face went pale.

"How are we positioned financially?" she asked Tariq, hoping the technical talk would distract him from the sounds of the brothers being tortured.

He reached into his back pocket and placed two small metal tablets on the table, each with a list of twelve words.

"The funds on these two wallets have been confirmed on the timechain," he stated. "Within a few hours, on-chain investigators like Captain Lamarck will see exactly what we've done. The savvy ones may even be able to conclude *who* we've done it to."

"And the distribution?"

"I was able to find millions of Bitcoin addresses that originated from exchanges in Africa. From there, I filtered it down probabilistically based on their on-chain actions, targeting smaller UTXOs."

"In English, please."

"This shit is complex," Tariq said. "If we are a team, then you need to understand it all, too. I'm not dumbing it down for you."

"We each have our roles," she said. "You have your strengths, I have mine."

"The Valhner brothers' funds have been divided equally. They're being sent to ten thousand random Bitcoin addresses across Africa."

"Has it completed?"

"Fortunately, the mempool was clear enough that I was able to get them all through over a couple of hours."

"Thank you," Nahla said as another scream echoed through the room.

Tariq clenched his teeth.

Nahla understood the incentives and cryptography that made Bitcoin function at a high level, but searching through the timechain and sending thousands of Bitcoin transactions was beyond her capabilities.

As long as most of the bitcoin found its way to active addresses, it would be enough. Even if they accidentally sent some bitcoin to an address no one controlled, it didn't matter. If no one had the keys, it would be forever inaccessible.

Like a small donation to every other person using the Bitcoin network. Making everyone else's bitcoin just a little more scarce.

"Please," William Valhner began begging from the next room. His voice was laced with the same kind of despair that he'd once subjected those women to in Khartoum.

The sound of ripping flesh came from the next room. Followed by deep guttural sobbing.

Tariq almost vomited on the spot.

"I assure you that I can take it from here," Nahla said. "Go."

He nodded and left the room.

Nahla reached down and grabbed the two metal seed phrases from the table. Each was engraved with twelve words.

They were many years and thousands of miles away from what happened in Khartoum. Even so, there was a part of her that resented him. He was the closest family she had left. He was the only person who would ever understand those parts of her past. Unfortunately, it didn't change the feeling of distrust in her stomach every time she looked into his eyes.

I need to get these thoughts out of my head. Tariq is no longer that feeble boy, and I am no longer that afraid little girl.

She thought back to the men who had come to her door that day. She remembered the hole in her heart that was left when Hashim bled out in front of her. For years, she fantasized about what it might be like to go back to Sudan and kill the soldier who stabbed her uncle. It always left a hollow pool of rage in her chest.

A rage she looked forward to tapping into today.

She grabbed the knife and the seed phrases and stepped into the room.

CHAPTER 28

———

" I fold," Cal said, tossing his cards toward the dealer. "And here I was thinking you had balls," said the man across the table.

His gold mask looked just like Cal's, but it felt like an extension of his personality. He wore a brown suit, but every piece of his jewelry was gold. An extravagant necklace hung around his neck, and nearly every finger had a ring on it. His beard was trimmed a little too meticulously. The sharp lines made him look more like a comic book character than a real person.

"What gave you that impression?" Cal asked as Harold slowly breathed out two small smoke rings that drifted lazily across the table.

"I saw the woman you walked in with. I assumed the man she came with would be a little more *assertive*."

"My disposition has nothing to do with the quality of the cards I'm getting."

The man gave him a judgmental grin.

No poor man has ever looked at me like that. This asshole seemed like the type that might wind up with twelve words carved into his chest.

Two more players at the table folded. The man smiled as he was the only one remaining. He flipped his cards face up as he tossed them to the dealer. Seven and eight, off suit.

"I'll gladly keep taking your money if you're gonna let me win with this garbage."

The dealer grabbed the cards off the felt and shuffled them together with the kind of dexterity that can only be gained through thousands of hours of experience.

Harold continued to puff on his cigar as the smoke gently flowed throughout the room. He cast Cal a glance through the eye-holes of the mask, looking at the man, then back to Cal again.

Perhaps this man is worth getting information on.

Before he had time to dwell, more cards were dealt. The dealer tossed out the cards across the table, and it was back to the action again.

A seven and an eight of spades.

Fitting. Same two cards that asshole threw away, but the same suit.

After the small and big blinds, the focus was once again on the man in brown.

"Raise five grand."

Cal looked at his pile of chips. The smallest one was $1,000. Betting more than most people made in a week made him want to throw up.

"Raise ten grand," Cal said, attempting to be as cool and confident as possible.

"Call," Harold said between puffs of his cigar.

The rest of the players around the table folded, and the play went back to the man in the brown suit. He played with his chips, dividing them into stacks and shuffling them together with precision.

"Big dog finally decides to play," the man said slowly. "I'd re-raise you, but I'm afraid you'd bitch out and fold again. I'll call."

The man tossed the rest of his chips into the pot. Cal's heart pounded in his chest. It wasn't even his money, but he couldn't help but grow anxious thinking about how much he stood to lose.

The dealer discarded a single card before revealing three face up on the table.

Queen of diamonds.

Nine of spades.

Ten of spades.

Cal did his best to hide the emotion that lurched through his entire body as he looked at the cards. He now had a chance at both a straight and a flush draw. A six or a jack of spades guaranteed him the win. He started calculating the odds of hitting one of those cards before he noticed the man in brown staring holes into him.

He's not even watching the cards or the other players. He's just staring me down.

"Fifty thousand," the man said, confidently throwing an even larger stack into the pot. "Let's see if this pup's got any bite."

The amount made him weary, but not because he might lose it. He didn't care if Harold had to spend more money on their investigation. It wasn't about him losing so much as he didn't want the man in brown to win.

That's what he wants. No more thinking. Trust your gut.

"One hundred thousand," Cal said, re-raising.

"Call," Harold said.

Cal glanced at Harold, but the golden mask made his expression hard to read.

Was that some sort of approval?

"We've got a nibble," the man said. "Now let's see if they'll come and play for real. All in."

The man pushed the rest of his stack out onto the table.

Cal had a solid hand. Although far from a sure thing, his odds of a flush or a straight draw were decent. But winning wasn't the goal. He was here to get information about these people. If he lost the hand, it would be over.

"You look a bit scared," the man said.

"And you look like a rich prick."

"A rich and reasonable prick," the man said. "I'd be willing to make an offer."

"Not interested."

"I don't need your money."

"You sure about that?" Cal asked. "Seems like you could stand to hire a better barber to fix what's going on with that beard of yours."

"You can keep your chips, but if I win, I get to spend the rest of the evening with that beautiful lady you came in with."

"Something tells me you wouldn't be her type."

"She's certainly mine."

Cal said nothing.

Stay level-headed. He's trying to trigger your emotions.

"I'll tell you what, big dog," the man continued. "For an evening with your woman, I'll throw in a kicker. Information."

"What kind of information?"

"The kind that can make you rich, if you're better at placing bets in the financial markets than you are at cards."

Harold looked at him. His eyes imploring him to accept.

"Political information," the man continued. "The type of thing that could be advantageous if properly applied to the stock markets at the right time."

"No," Cal said, connecting with the man's eyes. "I fold."

Cal tossed his cards toward the dealer. Face up.

Harold's jaw dropped.

"I can't decide if you are terrible at poker or a loser," the man said.

"Sofia is not *mine* to bet."

"That's such a shame. I would have shown her the best night of her life."

"She would have seen through a manipulative asshole like you in seconds."

"I'll take the deal," Harold cut in.

What?

"Well, well," the man said with a grin growing on his face. "What is this?"

"Sofia works for me," Harold said to the man. "And I'm willing to take that bet. I call."

Harold refused to meet Cal's eyes.

"I'm in," said the man, reaching out and shaking Harold's hand. "Let's see what you've got. I'd love to have her sitting on my lap the rest of the night."

Harold flipped over his cards. Pocket nines. Including the flop, that gave him triple nines.

"Respectable," the man in brown said. "Unfortunately, that ain't going to get it done."

The man flipped over his cards. Pocket queens. Giving him triple queens and the best hand on the table.

"What does your girl like to drink?" brown suit asked Cal.

Neither Harold nor Cal responded to him. The dealer looked across all of their faces before unveiling the next card.

Jack of spades.

I would have had a straight flush.

The feeling of regret quickly subsided. No matter how much he wanted to beat this man, nothing was worth gambling with Sofia.

"It's poetic, I'm going to beat you with queens," the man sneered. "These three beautiful ladies are going to get me in one of those back rooms with your beautiful lady."

Slowly, the dealer unveiled the next card.

Nine of diamonds.

Harold hit on four of a kind, beating brown suit's full house.

Cal exhaled. He hadn't realized he was holding his breath.

"Fuck," the man in brown said.

"So what kind of industry are we talking about here?" Harold asked. "Insider trading is one of my favorite pastimes."

Cal blinked.

Then he blinked again.

It wasn't just his eyes playing tricks, and it wasn't Harold's cigar smoke. The room was growing hazy. He looked up and saw it.

A dense white fog began to descend from the ceiling.

CHAPTER 29

———

Sofia watched the white gas swirl overhead, creating a ghostly haze over the room. It was time. The reason they were here.

I know what comes next.

Cal grabbed her wrist.

"We have to move. Now."

There was a shift within him. The joy she'd seen in his eyes on the dance floor was now gone. The military man was fully activated. As the rest of the people in the penthouse were beginning to panic, he switched on.

He pulled her through the room.

Harold followed close behind.

They ran past a group of people. Some of the more astute guests crouched low to avoid the falling fog. Others covered their faces with their shirts, hoping to protect themselves from breathing in the gas. Sofia did her best to calm her mind, simply putting one foot in front of the other.

There was a scream from the other side of the room. A dancing woman collapsed to the ground. The sight of her limp body spurred Cal to move even faster.

Time is running out.

The gazes of the party guests were beginning to grow distant. The music was still playing, but panic overtook the room. People were pushing and shoving, desperate to find an escape from the descending fog.

"Where are you taking us?" Sofia asked.

He didn't answer. He just kept moving toward the entryway of the penthouse. They entered the hallway, farther away from the rest of the panicking crowds in the penthouse. The gas filled the room. She could feel it in her lungs. Her vision was starting to blur, the edges of her sight growing fuzzy.

The entryway came into view.

"Stop," she shouted, planting her heels and pulling Cal toward her.

To her right, she looked through the window pane of the door to the staff kitchen. Gas fell from the ceiling there as well.

"We have to go," Cal yelled.

She ripped her arm away from his.

"I need you to trust me."

She looked into his eyes, trying to leverage all the trust they'd built. She opened the door to the kitchen.

"Where are you taking us?" Harold asked.

She didn't answer. She *couldn't* answer. If she did, they wouldn't follow her.

"Please," she begged, beckoning them to enter the kitchen.

They listened.

Sofia didn't follow.

Instead, she stepped back into the hallway and closed the door, placing a padlock over the handle. Cal lurched toward the door, his eyes desperately searching hers through the kitchen window.

"I'm so sorry, Cal."

Sofia reached into her purse and pulled out a gas mask. She pulled it over her face and immediately took in a deep breath of filtered air. Her mind cleared. Cal and Harold's eyes grew more distant. A look of rage came over Harold's face before he stumbled and fell to the ground.

The gas aggressively filled the smaller space now. She watched as Cal's angry gaze became more distant, his movements slow and lethargic.

"Why?" he asked as he lost consciousness and passed out onto the floor.

Her job was complete.

Now to find Nahla.

CHAPTER 30

———

FOUR HOURS EARLIER

Nahla stood atop the Watergate's Penthouse Suite and looked out over DC. One of her team members cleaned up the bloodstain where she had killed Jonathan earlier in the evening.

Party goers would be arriving soon.

She looked out over the Potomac River as the final rays of the sun set on its gentle waves, painting the sky with hues of orange and pink.

The Valhner brothers were dead.

Rafael Castillo was dead.

Each of their immense fortunes was now distributed to thousands of Africans and Central Americans. The first two steps in marketing her plan to the world had gone perfectly. The same fate was coming soon to the Land of the Free and the Home of the Brave.

From the top of the penthouse, Nahla could see all of them moving. The manipulative cockroaches that called themselves public servants. The very people this building had come to symbolize.

In the early 1970s, the Watergate Scandal opened many Americans' eyes to the rampant abuse of government power. It eventually led to the resignation of Richard Nixon. Corruption had once again overrun this city like a plague. The democratic system continued to vote for individuals based not on what was righteous, but on fear.

'A nation which can prefer disgrace to danger is prepared for a master and deserves one.'

Nahla picked up her phone and made the call.

"Hello, darling. How's Miami?"

"We are currently flying to DC," Sofia said. "I've just finished speaking with Cal."

"Right on time."

"Harold found the fake burner phone I planted. With some light encouragement, we left straight away."

"He's an evil man, but he's decisive. I'll give him that."

Nahla heard gentle piano music playing in the background of the plane.

"What will you have me do next?" Sofia asked.

"Whatever it takes."

Tariq stepped onto the balcony, visibly exhausted. Dark rings circled his eyes. She wondered if she looked just as drained.

There was silence on the other end of the line.

"Do you think you'll be able to manage that?" Nahla asked.

"Whatever it takes," Sofia repeated.

Nahla hung up and turned to Tariq.

"What was that about?" he asked, concern deepening the lines on his face.

"Just things finally coming together for us, cousin. We're going to have another special guest in attendance."

"Do you not see this as a risk? Bringing the man who is actively investigating us *closer* to our plan?"

There it was. The weakness inside him rising up again.

"Don't you think Harold deserves retribution?"

"I thought this was about more than revenge," Tariq said. "What happened to fixing the inequality that's plagued society for centuries?"

"It is," Nahla began. "The American Dream this nation was built upon is encapsulated in a singular emotion. *Hope.* The people in this swamp have been slowly siphoning that hope from their populace."

She looked over to the slow-moving waters of the Potomac River, the same body of water that once separated the Union from the Confederacy during the Civil War. It seemed fitting that she looked upon it now, as she prepared to wage her own war against the corrupt and broken system of this once-beautiful country.

"It's not enough to take their power, Tariq. We must destroy their hope. Let them think they're a step ahead. Let them cling to their optimism until the moment their throats are slit. Harold is their puppet. If we control him, we can destroy them."

CHAPTER 31

———

C al awoke to the pinch of a syringe in his neck. He sat bolt upright, eyes wide as liquid fire shot through his veins. Memories crashed into his mind as the blood flowed back to his brain.

Sofia. Penthouse. Lies.

The room was dark. The only light came from the window of the kitchen door. The same one he watched Sofia betray him through. A light haze still hung in the air from the gas. He suspected they'd only been unconscious for a few minutes.

How could I be so stupid?

All his instincts in New York screamed for him to ignore her. Her tantalizing smile was just a lie to manipulate him.

Manipulate me for what exactly?

A soldier stood in front of them. He wore a black uniform, his entire face obscured by a gas mask.

Cal felt like he'd just been dragged out of a frozen river. He opened up his mouth, but the words wouldn't come. His vocal cords were still waking up, his throat dry and raw.

The soldier crouched over Harold, injecting him with the same substance. Cal watched a surge of energy rip through the grey man. His eyes snapped open, wild and alert. He slowly came into consciousness in the same way Cal had, slowly taking stock of his surroundings until his eyes fell on the corner of the room.

"Jonathan—" he began to yell, but the soldier snapped and gestured for him to be silent.

That's when Cal saw him. The bloody corpse of a man was tucked out of sight. It looked like he'd been there for a while.

Cal watched as a wave of emotions washed over Harold's face.

The soldier pointed silently toward the wall. Two sets of black uniforms and two gas masks hung at the ready. In silence, they dressed. Cal met Harold's eyes. There was confusion in them, but beneath it a pain unlike any he'd seen from him before.

I trusted her. This is my fault.

The soldier opened the kitchen door and led them back into the penthouse. The soldier was much smaller than Cal. He imagined himself overpowering the man, wrapping his arm around his neck, and choking him unconscious.

Would that even be wise?

Cal had no idea what was going on, let alone where they were being taken. The analytical part of his brain was very slowly coming back online.

For now, it seemed best to follow.

They entered the main room.

Sprawled out on the floor were the bodies of the party-goers. All unconscious. Many stripped naked.

The once-lively dance floor was now a scene of quiet horror. The grand chandelier illuminated a mess of lifeless human bodies. Soldiers in black military uniforms and gas masks walked amidst the bodies.

How big was this operation?

The three of them silently walked through the crowd of unconscious bodies across the floor. Some soldiers walked around with notebooks and cameras, taking pictures of the unconscious people.

Cal watched it happen this time.

A soldier slit through the carotid artery of an incapacitated party-goer with a golden mask, the blood pooling on the floor beneath them. Another soldier carved words into a party-goer's chest with a scalpel.

Blood pooled onto the floor. The smell of antiseptic mingled with the lingering scent of expensive cologne.

Don't linger. Head down.

"You three," one of the masked soldiers said, then he snapped his fingers in their direction. "Come here."

Cal saw another body on the ground as he approached the soldier. One he recognized. The man in brown, his golden jewelry now hanging off his lifeless, pale skin. Twelve words were carved into his chest.

Cal felt a pang of guilt.

Could I have done something to stop this?

"Which one of you is the tech?" the man asked them.

Cal cautiously raised his hand.

"Check and double-check each name on the list before you harm anyone," the man said. "A few of the people wearing gold masks are coming with us to the beach."

The beach?

Cal had so many questions, but asking anything might blow his cover. Their case didn't matter if he didn't get out of here alive.

The man handed one of the scalpels to Cal, still some blood on its razor-fine blade.

"Remember what we are doing this for," the masked man said to him. "Remember your *why*."

Cal froze for a moment as the man's eyes bore into him, looking for a response. Wondering what he should say back to him. The man searched for any sign of weakness or hesitation in Cal's eyes.

He'd spent so long studying their on-chain transactions, but standing here with them was different.

Do I truly understand their motivations? I have to act as though I do.

"They've stolen from all of us," Cal said. "It's time for them to repay their debts."

"Remember what she said to us," the man said as he placed a hand on Cal's shoulder. "'The tree of liberty must be refreshed from time to time with the blood of patriots and tyrants.'"

Cal nodded, and the man stepped away.

He let out a breath of relief.

Cal knew whoever they'd been following was well-funded. He knew that they had teams of people. But he hadn't expected *this*. The sheer scale of all the staff members and soldiers, each of them clearly aligned with some larger goal. This was so much worse than Harold's employers imagined.

The three of them continued on through the penthouse until they reached the entryway. The wall full of colorful masks watched them from across the room.

The concierge stood in front of them, but she no longer wore a black mask.

She was younger than Cal expected, with beautiful, rich brown skin and high cheekbones. Everything about her looked regal. Everything but her eyes. Her gaze bore into them with the kind of intensity that could only be earned through an intimate relationship with pain.

"Where are you going?" she asked. Her voice had a cold violence behind it.

They were only steps away from the exit to the stairwell. *So close.*

The soldier who had been leading them paused. The confident stride he'd been leading them with faltered.

The soldier removed his gloves, and Cal realized that it wasn't a *he* at all.

The soldier's hands were small.

Feminine.

Her fingernails ended in white French tips. Her skin was a deep olive tone.

Sofia slowly pulled off her gas mask.

Then Cal noticed it.

It was the first time he'd seen her hair up in a bun.

The backside of Sofia's left ear was covered in a network of scar tissue. Faint white stitch marks still lingered around its edges. It was subtle, but it looked like it had been cut off and stitched back on surgically.

"How?" he asked, connecting with the same brown eyes he had stared into as she locked the kitchen door behind them.

The passion that lingered between them as they danced was now gone.

It was replaced by fear.

"I'm sorry, Nahla," Sofia said to the concierge.

"What have you done?" Nahla asked.

Sofia didn't respond. Instead, she looked toward Cal and Harold as she threw open the door to the stairwell.

"Run."

CHAPTER 32

Instinct took over as Sofia rushed through the door behind Cal and Harold. The muffled yells from behind them bounced off the concrete walls.

"Stop them before they get to ground level," Nahla shouted from above. "Kill them if you have to."

They rounded the first corner of the stairwell. For a split second, her eyes met Cal's. His piercing blue gaze cut through the darkness, filled with a multitude of questions.

Will he forgive me? Could he ever understand?

They flew down two more flights of stairs. The door above slammed open, followed by the sound of boots running towards them.

Cal stopped, looking up the stairwell toward the incoming men.

"What are you doing?" she asked, her lungs burning.

"Keep moving," Cal said. There was no more kindness in the way that he looked at her. His gaze was cold and commanding.

Harold limped past them, still reeling from the lingering effects of the drug. His face contorted in pain. Sofia couldn't tell if it was physical or emotional.

I can't just leave them.

Cal rolled up his sleeves, revealing his muscular forearms. His hands flexed into fists.

"Go," Cal commanded.

There was no kindness in his voice. No warmth.

"I got you into this mess. I'm not leaving you."

He clenched his jaw in frustration. Two large men rounded the corner.

She froze.

Cal didn't.

He lunged forward, grabbing the barrel of the first man's handgun before he could raise it. He twisted the gun, disarming him and sending the weapon clattering down the steps below, then pushed the man in the chest and sent him crashing into the concrete floor.

The slam of his body reverberated through the stairwell.

Cal tackled the second man.

As soon as they hit the ground, he slammed an elbow into the man's jaw. He did it again. The man spasmed, desperately trying to grab at Cal.

Sofia regained her composure and raced to the gun, but the first man got back on his feet and came after her. He slammed her into the wall, jamming his forearm underneath her neck. The back of her head cracked against the concrete. Her world shook, and the edges of her vision went dark for a split second.

He pressed harder.

Sofia felt her voice box shift inside her throat, the taste of blood filling her mouth. The man's breath was hot against her face. She pushed back against it with everything she had, but she still couldn't breathe.

Out of nowhere, Cal's arm wrapped around the man's neck. He ripped the man off her. She nearly collapsed in exhaustion. She grabbed the gun from the floor and pointed it at the soldier's head. His face turned red, and the veins on his temple bulged.

"Put the gun down," Cal said to her as he tightened the grip on the man's neck. The man tried to yell something, but it was muffled by the pressure of Cal's muscular arm squeezing around his throat.

Seconds later, the man lost consciousness and went limp.

"He was going to kill me," she said.

"So you would kill him? Without a second thought?"

"Yes."

"Who the hell are you?" Cal asked.

She said nothing.

There was nothing she could say that would satisfy him.

He won't understand.

"I will *not* stoop to their level," Cal said, looking down at both of the unconscious men. "They are misguided."

One of the men began to stir.

"We need to move."

He didn't wait for an answer as he grabbed her wrist and pulled her down the stairwell. She'd spent so much time close to the man, but he'd only treated her gently so far. No more. There was something animalistic about the way that he forced her to follow him.

Sofia's lungs were on fire when they reached the bottom.

Harold was waiting alongside the town car.

"He would have killed you, Cal," she said, gasping for breath.

He didn't respond to her. Something had shifted in the way that he looked at her now. The warmth that had been growing between them was gone. The brightness in his blue eyes grew cold and distant.

"Who the hell are you?" Cal asked again.

Where do I even begin?

"I'm going to find that out momentarily," Harold said as he jammed her hands behind her back and forced her into handcuffs. He taped her mouth shut and threw her into the trunk of the town car.

CHAPTER 33

—

TWO HOURS EARLIER

N ahla's heart skipped a beat as she watched Harold get off the elevator.

You did well, Sofia.

Everything was falling into place.

A few of Harold's high-profile employers were already scattered about the party, and soon they would all die by her hand. She gathered herself, settling back into her role as the concierge, putting on a welcoming voice as she spun Harold deeper into her web.

It is nearly time.

The three of them approached.

Harold's cold, grey eyes looked just as she remembered. For a moment, Nahla felt as small and helpless as she did on the New York Stock Exchange floor. She took a deep breath and forced her mind to calm down.

"Welcome to the Watergate," she said, shifting the tone of her voice slightly deeper than normal to disguise herself.

Harold whispered something to Cal and Sofia, who proceeded to peruse the expensive masks covering the wall.

"I believe we spoke on the phone," Harold said.

"We did," Nahla replied "We have the two golden masks you requested set aside for the party."

"I'm afraid there has been a change of plans," Harold said. "Would it be possible to have another person join our party?"

Nahla watched as Sofia spoke with Cal. She played her role better than Nahla could have hoped.

"I'll have to check with my assistant," Nahla said. "But I'm sure we can make an exception."

She beckoned for Tariq.

"Yes?" he asked. There was a quiver in his voice. He'd always been so much worse at concealing his emotions than she had.

"There is a change of plans. We need two gold masks for Cal and Harold, and clearance for another guest."

"Two gold masks for Cal and Harold," Tariq repeated. "And clearance for Sofia."

Fuck.

Tariq left, oblivious to the misstep he'd just made.

"How did he know her name?" Harold asked, his eyes flickering between Tariq and her. The calm demeanor he initially put forward was gone. "I didn't even know that she was coming until a few minutes ago."

"We do extensive research on our guests," Nahla lied. "We approach our security with the utmost seriousness, scanning faces and recording every person as they get into the elevator."

The look on his face made Nahla question her decision to bring him here.

A silence hung between the two of them for a moment.

"You seem familiar," Harold said slowly, no longer looking around the room. His entire focus was directly on her, like a predator focused on its next meal.

"I get that a lot," Nahla said, continuing to mask her voice.

"I bet you do," Harold said with a darkness behind his voice, the same intimidating tone he'd used with her on the trading floor.

I can't let him play games. I just need to get him through that door.

"How long have you been working for Jonathan?"

"A few years," Nahla said, racking her brain for the information her team had given her about the senator. "But this is the first time I've organized one of his parties."

"I'm certain we've met before," Harold said. "Have you worked in DC for long? What about New York?"

Nahla could feel the anxious Sudanese girl within her flaring up. For a moment, she debated making up a false reason or story on the spot.

Everything she'd worked for could collapse with a misplaced lie. She took a deep breath and tried to calm her nerves. She forced herself not to think about the threats Harold had once issued her and the incalculable damage that he had done to the people of Sudan.

'It is better to offer no excuse than a bad one.'

"Would you like me to communicate a message to Jonathan?"

"I thought you said you couldn't find him?"

"We couldn't locate him earlier," she replied. "But he arrived just before you did. If you would like, I can tell him to speak with you."

"Please," Harold said, immediately shifting away from the intense engagement and into a kinder tone. "I fear he is in danger."

Too little, too late, Harold.

"Is this something my staff should be worried about?" Nahla asked.

"No, no, nothing like that," Harold said. "Just make sure he finds me."

The image of Jonathan's corpse tucked out of sight in the kitchen flashed through Nahla's mind.

"I guarantee you'll be seeing him shortly."

Tariq returned with the two golden masks for Cal and Harold. Completely oblivious to what he had almost cost them. Nahla took them, then led Harold over to the wall of masks.

"Everyone wearing a colored mask is a party guest," Nahla stated, gesturing toward Sofia's sapphire mask.

"Staff members will be wearing plain black masks like mine," she said as she handed Cal a golden mask. "This allows you to enter any room you wish and play at the high-stakes tables. The games begin when you step through these doors."

Then she led them into the penthouse.

CHAPTER 34

———

The rumble of the plane's engines was beginning to feel familiar to Cal, but the view in front of him was anything but routine.

Harold handcuffed Sofia's hands in front of her, securing her to a chair in the middle of the cabin. Duct tape covered her mouth.

No matter how much I've enjoyed looking into those kind brown eyes, she cannot be trusted.

Cal blinked hard, forcing himself to stay alert. The adrenaline of their escape from the penthouse had worn off, and exhaustion was beginning to sink in.

Harold ripped the duct tape off her lips.

"Shit," she said. "Was that necessary?"

"Yes," Harold replied.

"I saved both of your lives," she said, her voice strained. "Why do I need to be in handcuffs?"

"Because I can't trust you," Harold said, his tone cold. "I have another set for Cal if we don't get some immediate answers out of you."

"She lied to me more than she lied to you," Cal stated.

"But you're the reason she's here," Harold said as he clipped the handcuff keys to the table next to them.

Cal looked into Sofia's eyes. There was regret, or what looked like it, but he couldn't trust her anymore.

How badly have I misjudged you?

"I'm so sorry, Cal," she said.

"How long have you been working with them?"

"It's complicated."

"They always say that," Harold said. "Everything is always so *complicated* after you get caught in a lie. You've been wasting our time and sabotaging our investigation. You're the reason Jonathan is dead."

"I just risked my life to get you out of there."

"And you nearly cost us our lives by bringing us there in the first place," Harold said.

"Who was that woman?" Cal asked. "The concierge?"

"Her name is Nahla," Harold said, cutting the tip off a fresh cigar. He lit it, then took a long draw. The tremble in his hands faded.

"You knew her, too?" Cal asked.

"We have some *history*," Harold said, slowly letting the smoke seep out of his mouth and into the plane's cabin. "But it's not relevant, Sofia needs to start talking."

The plane hit a small patch of turbulence, and the glasses on the bar rattled against one another.

"Seems pretty relevant. The person systematically killing your employers just *happens* to be an acquaintance of yours?"

"I wouldn't call her an acquaintance."

"I don't give a damn what you'd call her. How do you know her?"

"Years ago, I was hired to communicate a message to Nahla," Harold said. "She and her cousin Tariq acquired incriminating recordings. They could have created political turmoil and cost my clients billions of dollars."

Sofia laughed at him.

"Do you have something to say?" Harold asked.

"By *communicating a message*, what Harold means is that he threatened to kill them if they didn't keep their mouths shut."

"Oh, that's just great," Cal said.

"Are you going to listen to her?" Harold asked Cal. "She led us to be slaughtered."

"She put her own life in danger to get us out of there. Why would she do that?"

"I know this might come as a shock," Sofia said. "But perhaps I'm not totally evil?"

"Then talk," Harold said.

"People like you are accustomed to getting everything that they want in life," Sofia said. "Nahla wants to rip these resources out from beneath your feet. This is about more than the bodies and crime scenes. It's about sending a message."

"What's the message?" Cal asked.

"There is a wealth disparity problem between Harold's friends and the rest of us," Sofia said. "Nahla believes she has a way to solve it."

"Lofty goal," Cal said.

"She cares about many of the same problems as you."

"I find that hard to believe."

"Why?"

"Because there is no world where going around and extracting wealth through violence has a positive outcome. We need to find peaceful ways to create change in the world."

"Nahla disagrees," Sofia said. "What is happening right now is the culmination of years of preparation and a large team."

Cal remembered what one of the soldiers said to him as they were escaping from the penthouse.

A few of the people wearing gold masks are coming with us to the beach.

He wondered what exactly they were planning to do next.

"You've only seen the tip of the iceberg so far." Sofia continued. "The Valhner brothers, Miami, and the Watergate... there is more to come. I don't know what it is, but they're planning something big."

"You don't know?" Cal asked.

"I was a small piece of her plan," Sofia said. "She only told me what I needed to know."

Another wave of turbulence. Harold grabbed onto the back of a chair to steady himself. Cal felt disoriented every time he looked into Sofia's eyes. The person he thought he'd come to know, the one he'd grown so comfortable with, was just a lie.

"Are you even a journalist?" Cal asked.

"Yes."

"Why tell the truth about that?"

"I've been a reporter for years. Traveling internationally, writing about dangerous people in dangerous places. Nahla wanted me to reprise that role to follow you."

A role. A part. That's all this had ever been to her.

"Nahla is no longer the same woman I first met.

There is a darkness that's grown inside her. A rage that's twisted her."

She looked at them, meeting each of their eyes in turn, her expression full of regret.

"Your hands are covered in the blood of the people who died at the penthouse," Harold said. "If you had come forward with this information, we would have been able to stop her."

"I can't deny that," Sofia said, looking at her feet. "I made a deal with Nahla to lure Harold to the penthouse."

"You *lured* us?" Cal asked.

"I planted the burner phone Harold found in Vizcaya, laying the breadcrumbs, so you'd find your way to the Watergate. I relayed every detail of your investigation to Nahla along the way."

"Was it worth it?" Harold asked. "If I don't decide to kill you, I promise that you'll spend the remainder of your life in prison for the crimes you've committed against your country."

"I could ask you the same, Harold," Sofia said, with a look of pure malice on her face. "How long do you think you'll spend in prison for the crimes you've committed? You are just an errand boy for sleazy politicians like Jonathan."

"Well, that makes my decision easier," Harold said. "I am *definitely* going to kill you."

"No, you're not," Cal said. "She has invaluable information."

"I'm not worried, Cal," Sofia said. "Harold enjoys talking down to me way too much to have me killed."

Harold glared at her.

"Nahla planned to execute you publicly alongside

your employers," Sofia continued. "I saved you. I'd
like a thank you."

"You killed my friend," Harold said. "Fuck you."

Cal felt the body of the plane jiggle around as another wave of turbulence rumbled around them. He
looked out one of the windows to reset his bearings
on their surroundings, but there was nothing but the
dark blue of night beyond.

"Why do any of this?" Cal asked. "Why work for
Nahla at all, just to betray her?"

"Closure."

"Closure from what exactly?"

"She gave me an opportunity I'd only imagined in
the darkest recesses of my mind. She gave me a chance
to *end* what started in Sudan. She gave me two beautiful gifts, served up on a bronze platter."

Cal could see the last reaches of Sofia's guard fall
away. The woman he'd mistaken as being fragile transformed in front of him with each syllable that came
out of her mouth.

"She let me kill the Valhner brothers."

CHAPTER 35

———

Sofia watched her words fall over Cal's face. The warmth that once grew in his blue eyes was now icy cold.

Is there any explanation I could give where he doesn't think of me as a monster?

Harold's hands clenched into fists. He now considered her complicit in Jonathan's death. He would never trust her again, even though she did save his life. He looked at her as if she were an object holding information he wanted to extract.

"How is that possible?" Cal asked.

"I told you as much of the truth as I could, Cal," she began. "I spent years of my life working as a journalist—"

"Just because some of what you said is true doesn't make you any less of a liar," Harold interrupted.

"She saved both of our lives," Cal said to Harold. "Shut the hell up for a minute and listen to what she has to say."

"I don't trust her."

"Nor do I," Cal said. "But that's all we have to go on right now. The only reason we are still on Nahla's trail is because Sofia told us where they were headed."

"And what if she's sending us in the wrong direction?"

"That's a risk we have to take."

"I'm telling the truth," Sofia stated. "While I was stealing uniforms and masks for you to wear, one of Nahla's men mentioned flying back to Jacksonville."

Harold glared at her.

There is no way back with him. Our relationship is permanently severed.

She didn't care.

"Why follow Cal at all?" Harold asked.

"I wasn't following Cal," Sofia said. "I was following *you*. Nahla's team has been watching your communications for years. As soon as you reached out to Cal, she saw an opportunity."

"It's literally all been lies then," Cal said. "From the first moment we met."

The way that Cal looked at her was more painful than the handcuffs that dug into her wrists. She wanted more than anything for him to understand.

"My interest in you was genuine," she said. "I'll always be a journalist at heart. From the first words I read about the takedown of Max Aldrich, I knew I wanted to learn more about you."

"No," Cal said. "You *used* me to get closer to Harold."

"You don't understand the position I was in."

"You're a liar."

"And a murderer," Harold interjected.

Another wave of turbulence rattled the plane, causing the glasses on the bar to clink together.

"Do you really think *you*, of all people, should be giving me ethical judgments, Harold?"

Harold said nothing. The tip of his cigar turned orange as he inhaled.

"How did you meet Nahla?" Cal asked.

"My specialty as a journalist was interviewing political leaders. I was quite good at it. I knew how to blend in and how to get close to people. *Dangerous* people."

Cal's eyes gave her that same skeptical look he had given her when they first met in New York. All the work that she'd put in to get closer to him was now gone. A part of her truly looked forward to spending more time with him and getting to know him better.

Is that how sick I am? Do I delude myself into thinking that I have feelings for a person just to get information?

She wondered if she'd lost herself in the lies.

"I was assigned to do an in-depth story on Omar al-Bashir," she continued. "The president of Sudan."

"The one charged with war crimes from the Darfurian genocide?"

"The things he *wasn't* charged with were equally terrible."

Cal leaned in closer, his expression intense. It was such a shame she wasn't able to interview him honestly. There was a story behind those eyes. It broke her heart that she'd never be able to write it.

"It took months to get into al-Bashir's sphere of trust for an interview. Things seemed so conservative around the president, but that's not the way things were behind closed doors."

Harold breathed out cigar smoke through his nose. He refused to meet her eyes.

"In a blink, my fortune changed. Omar's team grew paranoid and believed I was going to write a hit piece about him. I tried to show them my notes. I tried to be transparent. None of it worked. Instead of being treated like a guest, I was locked up in a room with many other women. I was beaten. Raped."

She looked down at her handcuffs. They reminded her of the weeks she'd spent locked up. She'd tried desperately to compartmentalize that part of herself, but the feeling of the cold metal digging into her wrists brought all those thoughts clawing back.

"I was immersed in luxury but completely helpless. I felt as though I was stranded on a life raft in the middle of the ocean, surrounded by water while dying of thirst."

She held back emotion.

No tears. Not now.

She didn't want Cal's sympathy. She was proud of her actions regardless of how they judged her.

"That's where I met the Valhner brothers. They traveled to Sudan to sell weapons to al-Bashir and his cartel."

She repressed another wave of feelings. It was more than a light bubbling of anxiety beneath her sternum. It was a lurching deep inside that made her want to vomit.

"The innocent journalist died that day."

She looked out of the plane window, thinking she sensed some movement outside. There was nothing there. Only the endless darkness of night as they flew through the sky.

"Then came Nahla. She didn't know who I was. She didn't ask for anything in return. She set us free and took me to a hospital."

"Why would she do that?" Cal asked.

"Whatever you think of her now, in that moment, all I saw was an angel. A savior. Nahla became who she is because she was forced to watch her country burn. No matter what she's done since, she acts out of conviction. I still believe there's good in her."

"What right do you have to judge if someone is good?" Harold asked. "You uprooted your entire life to murder two men."

"More of a right than you do," she said to Harold. "How many millions of lives have you impacted because of your actions as a political puppet? How many of your friends will die today because you silenced Nahla before she could expose al-Bashir?"

"Fuck you."

"What do you say, Cal? Does killing someone always make them a bad person?"

"Did you torture them?" Cal asked, his expression unreadable.

"Yes."

"Damn."

"I told them the same thing they told me," Sofia continued. "You're about to develop an intimate understanding of what it means to feel pain."

She saw it out of the corner of her eye.

Something was growing larger in the window behind Harold. Hard, angular wings that stood out against the midnight blue of the night sky.

A metallic glimmer.

A plane?

She watched it grow larger.

No cockpit. No doors. No lights.

"What is that?" she asked.

Before she got an answer, a flare burst from beneath its wing.

A missile was headed directly for the plane.

CHAPTER 36

———

ONE HOUR EARLIER

Nahla looked out the windows of the Watergate Hotel as her team attended to all the incapacitated bodies around the penthouse.

The plan was in motion.

The day was here.

She looked across the skyline of Washington, DC. Its monuments to power and corruption stood tall against the night sky.

I can't believe I once viewed this city as a beacon of hope.

She used to think the United States of America exported freedom, but the only thing it truly exported was its fetish for war. The Founding Fathers' ideals of sovereignty were now more present in freedom-enhancing technologies like Bitcoin than in this decaying country.

No government can stop it. No bank can block it.

It was a network incorruptible by populist politicians. Immune to the ever-turning tides of irrational democratic crowds. A network she would use to take from the rich and give to the poor.

Nahla couldn't believe she once stood before political leaders and pleaded for change. Those days felt like a lifetime ago.

How naive I was. This system could never be fixed from the inside.

Soft men now ruled this country. They'd never lived through a war. They'd never seen young men with rifles storm their village in the night.

Their weakness was her advantage.

Violence is a tool. It's ingrained into the human psyche. The frail elites of this city liked to pretend their abstract political positions gave them control, but all it took was a precisely placed blade to bring down their delusions of power.

"They've escaped," Tariq said, standing alongside the floor-to-ceiling glass window.

"How?"

"Cal incapacitated two of our men in the stairwell."

"Where are they headed?"

"The airport."

"This could spiral out of control if we can't get ahead of it," Nahla said as she watched the lights of a boat move across the waters of the Potomac.

"Was risking everything worth it?"

"You want to have this conversation again?"

"I've put my life on hold to do this with you," Tariq said. "I don't want to see us fail because of your need for revenge."

"The way you were living in Khartoum wasn't a life. That place was a dusty, garbage-filled prison."

"I *liked* my life there," he said. "I was surrounded by computers and things to fix. Not everyone has dreams of changing the world, Nahla. Some of us are capable of being happy with the small pleasures in front of us."

"Then why are you here?"

"I think you know why."

"Our men are willing to sacrifice their lives for this cause," Nahla said. "Will the guilt you feel toward me and Hashim provide enough motivation?"

"I'm here, aren't I?"

"Harold threatened you, too, Tariq."

"Which is exactly why you should listen to me when I tell you to stop. He's not worth it. We're so close to the finish line, and now we have another thread to untangle. How much does Sofia know?"

"Not much."

"Why did you trust her?"

"I saw a part of myself inside of her," Nahla said. "I saw firsthand what they did to her in Khartoum. I know better than most how it feels to carry around the desire for revenge."

"Just because you saved her life doesn't mean she is aligned with our cause."

"'The harder the conflict, the more glorious the triumph. What we obtain too cheaply, we esteem too lightly. It is dearness only that gives everything its value.'"

"Is that Thomas Paine?"

"He'll always be my favorite."

"Relating to Sofia's struggles doesn't mean you understand her."

"She's not blind," Nahla said. "She has to see that what we are doing is good for the world."

"Not everyone sees the world like you. Some of us recognize the problems, but few are willing to take action."

"And how far are you willing to go?"

He paused. It was brief, but Nahla sensed his hesitation. She wanted more than anything not to see it, but it was right there in front of her.

An image flashed into her mind. The image of a scared boy who stood in the hallway as he watched a knife plunge into his father's heart.

"I've been with you from the beginning," Tariq said. "I'll be here until the end."

"Thank you, Tariq," Nahla said. "I will not let revenge cloud my judgment again."

"What will you have me do?"

"Prepare one of the drones," Nahla said. "Locate their plane and strike them down before they reach their destination."

He nodded and made the call.

Nahla proceeded back into the main room of the penthouse.

No longer was it dark and filled with music. It was bright and silent. Bodies lay scattered. Some hung over lavish furniture, others crumpled on the floor. She wove through bodies and pools of blood until she reached her destination.

A woman.

Incapacitated.

Her body had been completely untouched as per Nahla's precise instructions. Her green suit was covered in spilled wine. The emerald necklace she was flaunting around the party lay haphazardly around her neck.

"Pleasure to see you again, Senator Rosewall."

CHAPTER 37

———

Cal saw the drone too.

He lunged toward Sofia, grabbing both her and the chair. At the same moment, the pilot of the plane attempted an evasive maneuver.

Their world tilted sideways.

It didn't matter.

The missile collided with the wing of the plane. The explosion was quieter than Cal expected. For a moment, everything was still. Cal grasped Sofia's still-handcuffed arms.

The wing ripped free.

The temperature plummeted as a frigid gust blasted through the cabin, carrying with it shards of glass and debris. Wine glasses and bottles shattered, their contents sucked out into the sky.

A surge of adrenaline coursed through Cal's body as he watched Harold get pulled toward the hole. The man desperately grasped the bar railing. It bent as it held his weight. The cigar was ripped out of Harold's mouth. He strained with everything he had against the vacuum.

"I'll come to you!" Cal shouted over the sound of rushing wind.

Harold shifted, adjusting his hands for a better grip, trying desperately to grab anything on the bar that would keep him secure.

But Harold's grip slipped.

He was sucked out into the night sky, the roar of the wind muffled the sound of his screams. Cal watched the realization of death cross Harold's face. The same shift he'd seen when he watched the life leave Max's eyes. Detached and distant. There was no one else he could command to save him. No amount of money could stop him from plunging to his death.

The grey man had finally faced a problem he couldn't solve.

The large rubber mat from beneath the bar was sucked into the hole after him. For a moment, the depressurization stopped. Cal braced against the window, fearing it might shatter and pull them into the abyss of the night.

The plane began to rotate.

Cal's head felt like it was going to explode. He pushed through the pain, grabbing onto the chair and pulling himself upward to grab one of the oxygen masks hanging from the ceiling. He wrapped one around his own face and then handed it to Sofia. She took in a few deep breaths, slowly steadying herself.

"We have… to get… to the cockpit," Cal said between breaths. "…Parachutes."

He looked back at the rubber mat covering the hole. It could give way without any warning.

We only have seconds.

He tried to find his bearings as his entire world began spinning faster and faster. There was no way to tell which way was up or down as the cabin rotated. He didn't let himself dwell on the image of the plane being ripped apart and crashing into the ground.

Cal stretched to grab the handcuff keys that hung from the table, but they moved out of reach at the last second.

Another wave of turbulence shook the body of the plane.

The keys rattled overhead.

He gave it everything he had and jumped. His fingers wrapped around the key, but he overshot as the plane's center of gravity shifted and flew into one of the overhead storage compartments. His rib cracked.

All the air left his body. A rush of panic came over him.

He met Sofia's eyes, wide and terrified.

Breathe. If I lose control of myself, we'll both die.

He forced himself toward her. Pain surged through the entire right side of his body, but he was able to grab hold of her handcuffs. Using the chairs as handholds, they climbed closer to the cabin.

Cal saw the parachutes.

The crash dislodged them, but their bodies caught against the grand piano. The heavy-duty bolts anchoring its legs to the cabin still held. Fighting the spin of the plane, Cal pulled himself toward them. They were civilian rigs, backpack style with no reserve chutes or automatic deployment systems. Cal's training kicked in. He tightened the straps and checked the ripcord.

Sofia struggled.

Her handcuffs prevented her from getting her arms through the parachute. As she tried to put a leg through, she tripped, bracing herself against the piano.

Its legs snapped.

It broke free.

The piano tumbled past her. As it crashed into the hole, the tension of the strings released, metallic snaps and wooden groans echoed up the cabin as the deafening sound of wind left the space.

The suction returned, ripping Sofia toward the hole. He watched as her parachute was ripped out of her hands, tumbling into the night behind her.

She looked back at him, sheer terror in her eyes. The same deceptive face that locked him in the kitchen only hours ago. The same brown eyes that had been manipulating him from the start. He had every right to hate them, but that wasn't what he felt. Something about the way she looked at him sent a vibration through his body.

The plane groaned around them as the pull of the wind grew stronger.

He stopped resisting it.

Instead, he lunged toward it.

He connected with Sofia's hands, then the two of them were sucked out of the plane into the inky darkness beyond.

CHAPTER 38

———

They plunged headfirst toward the ground.

The only thing tethering Sofia to reality was Cal's arms wrapped around her. She felt his heart racing. Wind howled in her ears as a piece of debris shot past their heads. The darkness pressed in from all sides, the only light coming from the distant glow of the moon.

"Hold onto me with everything you have," he said, his voice barely audible over the wind.

She wrapped her handcuffed hands around his shoulders. He adjusted his body slightly, and she could feel the muscles in his back tense as he changed their trajectory. Sofia smelled the light scent of aftershave on his skin, for a brief moment flashing her mind back to the image of him shaving. Before the penthouse. Before turning on Nahla. Before things got so much more complex.

With each breath, she wondered if it might be her last.

At least I won't die alone.

She knew right then she'd made the right choice in helping Cal escape from the penthouse. It didn't matter if he never forgave her. It didn't matter if he never understood what she'd done. He was a good man. At least she would know she did one thing right.

The parachute deployed with massive force.

Her legs slipped loose from Cal, her body weight ripped downward. For a moment, she thought she was going to fall to her death, but her handcuffs caught around Cal's back, yanking her left shoulder out of its socket. She screamed involuntarily as the canopy deployed. She tried using her breath to manage the pain, but it didn't work.

Shaking.

Heart racing.

Pain.

Cal wrapped his arms around her. It was so dark that she could barely see his eyes. Even still, she felt comfort in them.

The image of plunging into the sea passed through her mind. She envisioned the parachute smothering them. She envisioned thrashing and twisting in strings as they sank deeper and deeper beneath the surface.

The lights of a small town came into view somewhere beneath them. She let out a short-lived sigh of relief before wondering if they would now crash into a tree instead.

"Are you alright?" Cal asked.

"My life has been spiraling out of control," she said, looking up at his silhouette against the night sky. "And then we were ripped out of a plane."

He chuckled. She felt the vibration of his chest against her.

"I meant physically."

"I'll be fine."

He nodded, but he didn't look like he believed her. She wasn't sure she believed herself.

"Where are we?" she asked.

"I think we were flying over southern South Carolina when we were hit by whatever that thing was."

"It looked like a military drone."

"How did Nahla get a military drone?"

"She's extremely well-funded, and they've been planning for years."

"That only leaves me with more questions," Cal said. "But at least we got one answered."

"Which one?"

"If you are still working with Nahla."

"I already told you that I'm not."

"Forgive me, but I couldn't exactly trust anything you've said to me in the last day."

"Did the fact that she's attempted to kill me twice now finally make things clear for you?"

"It did actually."

"I've been as truthful with you as possible."

Cal didn't say anything. For a few minutes, silence hung in the air between them.

Sofia felt a wave of relief when the ground came into view. Cal adjusted the strings of the parachute, and they descended toward a clearing. Gently, he brought them to the ground, flaring the canopy at the last moment to slow their descent. Despite Cal's gracefulness, Sofia's bare legs were still bloodied as they crashed through grass and shrubs. She gritted her teeth again, determined not to let Cal sense any weakness.

"You've done this before, then?" she asked, brushing herself off.

"I went through Jump School before transitioning to the Cybersecurity unit... I figured that a journalist writing a story about me would have known."

"I may have overstated my research a bit."

"I've been gathering that," he said as he unstrapped himself from the parachute.

The field they landed in was empty. Sofia could see the lights of a small town in the distance. In the low light, she could make out a road.

He reached out his hand to help her regain her balance. As she took it, an explosion of pain shook through her arm. She tried her best to hide it, but it was no use.

"I think your shoulder is dislocated," Cal said. "If we don't put it back in place soon, it'll swell and get worse."

"Would there be a doctor in the town?"

"You shouldn't wait that long. I can do it."

"Is it going to be painful?"

"Excruciatingly."

"Shit."

"Do you trust me?"

"Asks the guy who is obsessed with fairness and truth."

"So is that a yes?"

"Yes, that's a yes."

"I can't say the same about you, can I?" he said as he examined her shoulder.

"No," she said, too ashamed of herself to even meet his eyes. "I honestly thought you were going to leave me on the plane."

"I would never leave you to die."

"You had just found out that I've been lying to you since we first met. I wouldn't have been surprised if you did."

"So you admit it then? It was all just lies?"

"That's not what I meant."

"Hold still for a minute," Cal said as he reached out and grabbed her wrist over the top of the handcuffs. He studied her arm, placing his hand directly under her armpit, beneath the shoulder joint. She clenched her teeth as he felt out the joint. Even the slightest touch was brutal.

"Are you ready?"

"Not really."

"Too damn bad," Cal said, using the strength of his hands to rotate the joint, then snapped it back into place with a sickening pop.

Sofia's whole body jolted as the shock coursed through her. She trembled from the aftershock of pain. Cal's hands lingered on her skin. His firm touch turned gentle and comforting as another wave of pain crested through her.

She tried to look strong as he watched her.

"I'm fine."

"If you say that a few more times, maybe you'll start believing it."

She glared at him.

After she gathered herself, they began to walk across the field toward a nearby tar road. The beginning light of the morning sun started to peek over the brush. Cal kept his eyes on the horizon, scanning tree lines and utility poles for movement as they approached the road.

"Are you going to turn me in to the police?"

"What do you think?"

"I have no idea," she said as she looked down at her handcuffs. There were dark, bloody lines from where the metal cut into her wrists from the force of the canopy deploying.

"I thought you might have learned something about my character during the time we've spent together," Cal said. "But I guess it was all just a lie to get me to open up to you so you could lure Harold to his death."

"I tried to stop it."

"But it didn't matter in the end, did it? Harold would still be alive right now if not for you."

She didn't say anything.

She knew he was right.

For a few minutes, the only sound was their feet on the asphalt. With every step, she thought about apologizing. She tried to find a way to show him that not everything she said or did had been a lie. Part of the woman he saw was real, but he didn't want to hear it.

If he decides to turn me in to the police, I'll accept my fate.

After a few minutes, Cal stopped.

"Do you see something up ahead?" she asked.

"No," he said as he reached out and grabbed her hands. "But I have to do something."

The calluses on his fingers were rough against her skin. He found the cold metal of the handcuffs. He inserted the key and unlocked them.

"I'll help you get to the town," he said. "Then we'll both go our separate ways."

"Where will you go?"

"I have a friend who lives on the coast near Savannah. I'm going to reach out to him and continue the investigation."

"Will you stop me if I want to come with you?"

"Why would you want that?"

"I could ask the same thing about you. Harold is dead. You could call in the military and stop all this if you wanted to."

"Nahla is getting more and more violent," Cal stated. "Even if we don't know where they are going, I might be able to help in some way. I have to try."

"And I'd like to help you."

"I can't trust you."

"You can't," she said. "That's true, but I'd still be able to help you."

"I'm giving you the opportunity to start a new life and put what happened with the Valhner brothers behind you," Cal said, with a confused glance. "If you come with me, I can't promise your safety."

"Then it seems that you've not yet learned anything about *my* character during the time we've spent together," she said with a tight-lipped smile.

"And whose fault is that? I don't even know who you really are."

She considered trying to argue with him. She wanted to explain how much she respected him. She wanted him to understand how much of her true self she'd shared with him.

He doesn't care. If I want him to let me help him, I have to make a logical argument.

"I've spent time with Nahla, and I've seen how her team operates. I have knowledge about her that no one else does. That kind of information has to be useful to you."

"Like what?"

"I'm not entirely sure."

"Very helpful."

"She tried to kill us, Cal. She must be worried about the information I have. Let's work together and figure out what to do next."

Cal still didn't look convinced.

"Twenty-four hours, Cal. That's all I'm asking. Let me tell your story."

"I think I'm having déjà vu."

"I want to see the man behind the headlines," she said as she winked at him. Sofia swore she could see a flash of kindness in his eyes.

"If you lie to me again, I'm leaving you."

"One more day?" she said with a smile.

"One more day," Cal repeated, finally giving her a slight smile. "But I still have to give precedence to my current case."

"I wouldn't have it any other way."

CHAPTER 39

———

The old cargo plane hummed with the steady drone of its engines, a far cry from Harold's luxurious jet. The interior was stark and utilitarian, painted in dull shades of grey, with rivets and bolts visible along the walls.

Tariq was hunched over his laptop screens, parsing through live drone footage of Harold's downed plane. The fractured remains of the jet were scattered over a wide area, pieces of luxury and greed reduced to smoldering ruins, another symbol of the old world order brought to its knees.

Nahla's satisfaction was fleeting.

Between the debris, she saw military vehicles surrounding the crash.

This just got more complex.

Even worse, she was now concerned about how much information Sofia had been able to share. Nahla kept thinking over her previous interactions, reassuring herself that Sofia didn't know enough information to cause problems. This was the kind of mistake she couldn't afford to make. There were only a few hours between Sofia running from the party until they'd been able to take down her plane.

A lot can happen in three hours.

"It's time to change our plans," Nahla said as she approached her cousin.

"What's wrong?"

"In the event that Harold's employers know more information than we had anticipated. We need to take some additional precautions. We should relocate our third key sooner than originally planned."

"I don't think—"

"That wasn't a question, Tariq."

He nodded, his shoulders sagging slightly. Despite the years of planning, she still saw the traces of weakness, the hesitation that she feared could jeopardize everything.

No. I have to stop thinking like this.

She exhaled slowly, trying to bury the anxiety beneath the surface. This was her past rearing its ugly head, not her present. She thought about how much she had changed over the years, how different a woman she was now compared to the one who used to walk the streets of Khartoum with Uncle Hashim.

Tariq has changed too. I must trust him.

She reached out, placing a hand on his shoulder, feeling the tension there.

"I'm sorry," she said. "I know you understand the stakes. I simply think that we must be more cautious. We cannot allow things to fall apart when we are this close. In the event they capture one of us, I'd like to be prepared."

"Let us pray that never happens," he stated.

She nodded, not letting herself dwell on the potential consequences.

"Where do you have in mind?"

"Not here," she said, glancing around at the other team members on the plane. Most of them were fiercely loyal to the cause, but this wasn't the place to take chances. "We'll speak on it once we arrive."

She let her mind wander over each of the words that were ingrained in her mind. They were the very same words she'd recalled in that dirty alleyway.

Liberty. Party. Boat. Airport. Dress. Dance...

The words that she'd come to know as deeply as she knew the back of her own hand.

They were a part of her.

Therein lay the risk.

What if something happens to me?

Their plan was in motion, and there would no longer be a way to stop it.

Soon her seed phrase would become even more powerful. Imbued in these words was so much more than the keys to her bitcoin, but the memories of that dark, lonely time in her life.

But she was alone no more.

Nahla looked over her team. If something happened to her, they must be able to continue. The plan must be completed. Nothing overlooked. Nothing forgotten.

"No longer do we operate in secret," she said to the men surrounding her. "Years of work end today. But it's in these final stages that we'll face the most resistance."

She held their gaze, doing her best to mask the doubt stirring beneath her calm exterior.

"'We must all hang together, or assuredly we shall all hang separately.'"

"Ma'am," a soldier approached, his boots clanking on the metal floor. "I have good news and bad news."

Nahla's eyes narrowed.

"We received information that a credit card associated with Harold was used to rent a car. Its last transaction was made in a high-end boutique in DC yesterday evening. This gives us reason to believe one of the targets survived the drone attack."

She felt the anxiety come crashing back in.

"The good news better be *really* good."

"We were able to get the license plate number, and we know which direction they're headed."

"Assemble a team immediately."

The soldier nodded, then relayed the orders. Nahla watched him go, her mind racing.

This was it.

The final push.

CHAPTER 40

C al reached down and ran his fingers over his rib as they drove down the coastline. He was certain he'd cracked a rib on the plane. The jagged bone pushed into his lungs every time he took a breath.

The ocean moved in the background like an ever-pulsating life form as Cal focused on the road in front of them, the black asphalt winding its way through the quiet morning air.

Had it been wise to use Harold's credit card?

Cal's entire profession was based on the ability to track information flowing through the public Bitcoin timechain, but that was nothing compared to the kind of mass surveillance that existed in the fiat financial system.

Bankers built profiles on their customers using transaction data. They used algorithms and AI tools to analyze what kind of things you were likely to do with your money, even going as far as declining your card if you didn't act in accordance with their policies.

It was the antithesis of the financial freedom that Bitcoin offered. He felt dirty using the credit system that surveilled its users and farmed out their data to the highest bidder. But today, using Harold's credit card was a calculated risk. They were able to eat, buy clothes, and rent a car. After all, Nahla thought them dead. And they were rapidly putting miles between themselves and civilization as they drove toward the coastline.

I need to get out of my head and think about the problem in front of me.

A problem dressed in jeans and a green shirt.

Sofia crossed her legs and gazed out the window.

"How do you know this guy?" she asked.

"I helped him set up this facility a few years back."

"It's very rural," she said, toying with the diamond necklace she'd decided to keep despite the change of clothing.

Cal looked down at the golden Rolex Submariner still hanging on his wrist. It reminded him of Harold. He saw the flash of fear in the grey man's eyes as he was ripped into the night sky.

He blinked hard, clearing his mind.

"René is a bit of a recluse."

"I understand the urge to get away from people more every year."

"But you're such a social person," Cal said. "Was that a lie, too?"

"Just because I'm good at getting people to open up to me doesn't mean that I like to be around them all the time."

"People can be exhausting," Cal said. "For example, I recently became close with someone only to realize our entire relationship had been a lie."

Sofia bit her lip. Cal noticed a sadness in her eyes that wasn't there before the penthouse.

She didn't say anything.

The two of them sat in silence as they drove through a quaint town, the paint on their houses weathered by the salty air. The car passed a long, brick building with shattered windows and ivy crawling up the walls. An old textile mill. Its smokestack leaned over a collapsed loading dock, where rusted rollers lay unused. A sagging chain-link fence surrounded it, its warning signs faded and torn.

Living in New York City, Cal often forgot just how deeply neglected rural America had become. Industries that once formed the backbone of a thriving nation now rotted, day by day. People in towns like this blamed the rich men of Wall Street and Washington. And they were right to. But most never grasped the real root of the decay.

This was yet another casualty of a fiat currency system. It manufactured prosperity for the rich while draining wealth from everyone else. The US dollar's global dominance enriched those in politics and finance, but it also made American manufacturing less competitive. It gutted the working class.

Stealing from the rich will never be enough to fix all wealth disparity. You have to attack the root of the problem.

"What are you thinking about?" Sofia asked.

"What was it like?" Cal asked, deciding she probably had little interest in hearing more about the broken financial system.

"What was *what* like?"

"Killing the Valhner brothers."

She looked at him. For a moment, he thought she wasn't going to respond at all. He watched a darkness come over her.

"Do you want to know the truth?"

"That would certainly be a nice change of pace."

"Can you promise not to judge me too harshly?"

"No."

"I don't know what you want me to say then," she began. "That it was terrible and wrong? That I regret it like you regretted killing Max?"

"Do you?"

"I don't regret it at all."

"Not even a little?"

"At first, I didn't want to hurt them. I thought I was above the idea of revenge. I thought I should resist the urge to use violence to solve my problems. I thought I wanted closure."

"Did you get it?"

"I did," she said. "The second I looked into James' eyes, I realized I'd been lying to myself. I was transported back to the mattress in Khartoum. I could feel their hands on me again."

Cal watched as she stared off into the distance, her pupils wide.

"Each time I cut them, a little bit of my pain went away. There was so much adrenaline that it still seems foggy. It didn't even feel real until the moment I saw both of their corpses hanging over the horns of the bull of Bowling Green. A part of me thought it was just some fucked-up dream."

She sat there. The same beautiful woman who charmed him with her tantalizing smile. The same one he'd swung around on the dance floor. She transformed in front of him with each word spoken. He didn't know who this person was. That smile may have been beautiful, but it was capable of more darkness than he'd ever imagined.

A part of it scared him.

And if he was honest with himself, a part of it excited him.

"And you don't regret it at all?" Cal asked.

"I knew you wouldn't understand."

"I know intimately what committing violence does to a person," Cal said. "It's never the right choice."

"Do you see this shit?" Sofia asked as she pulled back her hair and exposed the faint scarring that surrounded her ear. "What would have happened if Nahla hadn't rushed me to a hospital to reattach it?"

Cal said nothing.

"I'm not the only woman they harassed," she continued.

"What do you mean?"

"I'm a journalist, Cal. I dig. Those two assholes physically abused multiple other women I tracked down. They told one of their interns they'd kill her if she went to the authorities."

"Damn."

"So I won't be having any of your high and mighty bullshit. I set those women free the second their hearts stopped beating. I only wish they could have shared the experience of sawing off James' ear in the same way he did mine."

"I'm sorry for what happened to you."

"Not as sorry as they are."

They passed another small ocean cottage in a town that had seen its best days a few decades earlier.

"I refuse to let myself be controlled by anyone anymore," Sofia continued. "Not by the Valhner brothers.

Not Nahla. *Not you.* I need to be better. I need to *do* better. I can never get back to who I was beforehand, but at least I can act as a force for good."

"Is that why you're still here?"

"No, it's because I *love* getting shot at and jumping out of planes."

Cal glared at her.

"I'm here because I feel like helping you could undo some of the things I regret."

"I don't know if I can live up to that," Cal said.

"You're a good person."

"I'm not sure if I agree with you."

"Are you serious?"

"I killed Max."

"And you deeply regret it."

"Regret means nothing. An innocent man is dead because of me."

"It was a mistake."

"Doesn't change what happened."

"We are trying to track down Nahla because you want to save people's lives," she said. "The lives of people you probably dislike. Yet you *still* put yourself in danger to do it. You can't convince me that you aren't a good person."

"I'm guilty of murder, Sofia. I'm not the beacon of hope you're making me out to be."

Cal turned the car, moving onto a smaller road as they came closer to the sea. The morning air was eerily still.

"Killing Max isn't why you feel guilty."

"How the hell do you know what I feel?"

"As your freshly-assigned military therapist, it's my job to understand your motivations."

Cal glared at her.

"Killing someone doesn't inherently make you a bad person. The reason you feel conflicted is that you didn't think for yourself."

"I'm sure you've been telling yourself that a lot over these last couple of days."

"You feel this guilt because you acted in a way that didn't align with your beliefs. You should have ignored Colonel Blackwell and protected Max."

"It's the military, Sofia. They literally train us *not* to do that."

"You claim that the anti-authoritarian aspects of Bitcoin attracted you, but you killed Max because an authority figure commanded you to do so. The entire system programmed you to follow commands, and now you sit here and criticize your individual actions."

"I'm the one who pulled the trigger. Me."

"You blame our broken financial systems for inequality. Isn't the same true here? The system made you kill Max. You should give yourself some grace."

"I killed Max. That's all there is to it."

"I've seen the sadness and regret in your eyes. I've listened to the way you've spoken about what happened. You had good intentions."

"Words are worthless," Cal said. "Actions are all that matter."

"Right, because shutting up about your feelings has worked wonders for you. Language is powerful, Cal. Words have inspired armies and brought peace to entire civilizations. I can tell by the way you speak that there is goodness inside of you."

"This is why I hate journalists," Cal said. "You're

all constantly prying into people's personal lives and twisting their words to fit your narrative."

"I'm so sorry," Sofia said. "How dare I have the gall to tell you that I think you're a good person?"

Cal stopped responding.

The car crested over a rolling hill as they descended toward the ocean. A thick fog wrapped around their vehicle, swallowing the headlights and muffling the world outside. Cal slowed down as the lighthouse came into view. A fleet of windmills sat motionless in the ocean behind it, barely visible over the fog that loomed over the placid waters.

They got out of the car and approached the old building. For a brief moment, Cal felt like he was transported back in time. He knocked on the old wooden door.

No response.

He waited for a minute, then another. There was nothing but the silence of the surrounding fog.

Sofia looked into his eyes in the same way she had on the plane.

Did I lead us all the way out here for nothing?

They had no backup plan.

No alternative.

"Maybe he isn't here," she said.

"Someone has to keep watch on the windmills."

"They aren't even spinning."

He knocked once more before hearing the sound of quiet footsteps behind them.

CHAPTER 41

S ofia spun around.

A thin man approached from one of the bluffs to the side of the lighthouse. His skin was weathered and tanned as though he had spent much of his time at sea. His wild white hair and beard framed a pair of sharp, intelligent eyes.

"Hello René," Cal said.

A slow smile spread across the man's face. Sofia finally let out a breath of relief.

"Come in, come in," he said as he opened the large wooden door.

As soon as Sofia stepped into the lighthouse, it felt like she had changed time periods. The centuries of weathering on the exterior were completely absent indoors. They stepped through the doorway into a comfortable home.

René hung up his jacket and continued inside. The circular bottom area of the lighthouse had been renovated into a nautical-themed living space. Ship wheels, model boats, and old maps adorned the walls. The large windows would have offered a breathtaking view of the ocean had it not been for the looming fog.

"I'm sorry to intrude like this, René," Cal said. "But we needed somewhere off the beaten path to slow down and think."

"I've never been one for the beaten path," René replied, casting a kind smile toward Sofia.

"We are in the middle of an investigation," Cal began as he stepped into the living space. "I'm hoping to have your help thinking through the next steps."

"Really, Cal?" René said. "You bring a beautiful young woman into my home and don't even introduce me to her?"

The old man caught her attention and gave her a playful wink.

"You'll have to forgive him. He's not very happy with me currently," she said as she reached out her hand. "My name is Sofia."

"It's a pleasure to meet you, Sofia," René said. "Cal's personality can be pretty abrasive sometimes, but he's a good guy underneath it all."

"I've been trying to tell him the same thing," Sofia said. "Although I think the word I used was 'asshole' instead of 'abrasive.'"

"Let me take your coat, dear," René said. Sofia obliged. As she did, René's eyes drifted down toward her wrists. Her shirt didn't hide the cuts from the handcuffs.

"You're hurt," René stated, his face immediately shifting into genuine concern.

"I'll be fine."

"You don't look fine," René said. "Please make yourself comfortable. I'll fetch some tea."

Cal didn't hesitate to find a spot on the couch with a vantage point out the window, allowing him to watch if anyone had followed them.

He never did seem able to turn those protective instincts off.

Sofia carefully lowered herself onto the soft cushions of the couch. Her shoulder still throbbed in pain from Cal putting it back into its socket.

"How do the two of you know each other?" Sofia asked.

"He didn't tell you?" René said with a warm twinkle in his eye.

"We got caught up in…. other things," Cal said.

"I can't blame the man for relishing in a good conversation with a beautiful woman," René replied as he found a couple of mugs and began to boil the tea.

"Cal told me he had an eccentric friend who lived on the outskirts of town. I had no idea that meant that you lived in a lighthouse and operated a wind farm."

"Not just any wind farm, my dear. I operate a Bitcoin mining facility."

"Of course you do," Sofia said as she looked at the windmills peeking out over the fog, their blades still static.

"Cal and I met when I began operations," René said. "I'd sold my previous businesses, hoping to get away from the craziness of the rest of the world and live out my retirement years as a self-sufficient old man by the sea."

"René had a long career in procuring energy from the ocean," Cal said.

"What does that mean?"

"I used to look over these very same waves and wonder how much we didn't yet know about the sea," René said. "When I was a boy, I hoped humanity might learn to harness the endless powers of the oceans. I spent my entire career making that happen."

"You grew up here?"

"In the town you drove past on the way," René said as he poured some warm water over the tea leaves. "I used to walk to this lighthouse with my parents on the weekends and look over the ocean."

"The most unique aspect of Bitcoin mining is that it can be done in remote places," Cal said. "Typically, power plants need to be close to cities since it's challenging to transport electricity across long distances."

"Why does Bitcoin require mining at all?"

An engine roared somewhere in the distance. Cal's brow furrowed as he looked out into the fog, a brief flash of concern in his eyes.

"Most people think that Bitcoin was a singular invention," Cal said. "But that couldn't be further from the truth. Cryptographers tried and failed to create an internet-native money for twenty-five years before Satoshi succeeded."

"What does that have to do with ocean energy?"

"Satoshi's brilliance wasn't a singular invention, but a combination of many interrelated ideas that allowed for humans to have digital scarcity. One of those ideas was using something called 'proof of work' for securing the Bitcoin network. It served as a way to tether our physical reality with the digital world."

"I don't understand."

"Basically, it means that miners receive some bitcoin

for helping to secure the network," René said, interrupting Cal's explanation and setting a warm tea in front of her.

She held the steaming cup up to her nose. It had a distinctive smell, like a bonfire next to the ocean.

"What is this?"

"Lapsang tea," René said. "It was the favorite of the British Royal Navy."

"It's fantastic," she said as she took a sip.

"It's harvested from the Wuyi Mountains of southeastern China. It used to be popular among pirates because the smoky scent was used to disguise opium shipments. I've got years' worth of it down in my store room."

"Where do you get it from?" Sofia asked as she began to feel the subtle effects of caffeine invigorating her body.

"Are we talking about tea or Bitcoin mining?" Cal asked, looking annoyed as René derailed their conversation.

"Lighten up, Cal," René said. "A man can have multiple interests."

"I don't think he agrees with you," Sofia said. "He basically never shuts up about Bitcoin and how money works."

René chuckled.

"May I continue?" Cal asked. "Or shall we learn more about maritime history?"

"Please go on," René said as he took a seat in the living room alongside them. "Be sure to include every boring detail for the lady. I'm sure she'll appreciate that."

Sofia smiled at René as she took another sip of the Lapsang.

"Bitcoin created an incentive to capture energy in rural towns," Cal stated. "Humanity can now harvest stranded energy from some of the most remote regions of the ocean and ease demand in more populated areas."

"That's how I got connected with Cal," René said. "This technology allows me to continue my life's mission and give back to the city I grew up in. The ocean provides power for the townspeople, and I mine bitcoin when they don't need as much energy."

"Interesting," Sofia said. "Between the money from mining bitcoin and selling your electricity to the nearby town, you must make a lot of money operating this place."

"You misunderstand me, young lady. This is the place where I fell in love with the beauty of the ocean. These people deserve to know the power that the sea provides them. No one in the town has to pay for electricity. Humans of the past used to worship the sea. The sea is the great frontier of energy abundance. Today, with technology, we can leverage that power more than ever before."

Cal smiled from behind René, enjoying watching Sofia get to meet this character.

"Bitcoin mining is like the bottom-feeder fish in the ocean," René said. "It consumes the stranded energy that might otherwise go to waste."

"How so?" Sofia asked.

"Bottom-feeder fish eat decaying material that falls to the bottom of the ocean. Dead plant matter, fallen leaves, animal carcasses. They eat all of it."

"Gross."

"It might be off-putting, but it's critical for the ecosystem. They turn this wasted energy into food for themselves. These bottom feeders serve as prey for the larger animals in the ecosystem, ensuring no energy goes to waste."

Sofia looked out the window of the lighthouse and over the calm ocean waves.

"A huge amount of energy in areas like this one is completely wasted. People use a lot of energy when they are home at night, but none when they are sleeping. But instead of wasting it, it can be used for Bitcoin mining. Helping to secure the wealth of every single person that uses the network."

Sofia smiled. It was clear how Cal and René became friends. Their passion was infectious.

I still can't help but be skeptical.

"Bottom feeders of the ocean are often misunderstood as being unappealing scavengers, but they're essential to a thriving ecosystem. The same is true of mining. People often criticize it for its energy use without recognizing its role in balancing energy markets."

"Great imagery," Sofia said. "Nothing sells a financial revolution like rotting seaweed and fish guts."

René chuckled.

"I appreciate both of your enthusiasm for the topic," Sofia continued. "But I'd like to remind you that Nahla is using the network to violently transfer wealth from the rich to the poor."

"Wait," René said. "Who is Nahla?"

CHAPTER 42

The resort was beautiful in the mid-morning sun. The warm air was filled with the scent of blooming flowers. Spanish moss hung from the branches and swayed in the soft breeze, casting intricate shadows on the gravel path beneath their feet.

"I just got confirmation the military found Harold's body," Tariq stated as he approached Nahla in the sunken gardens.

A wave of relief crashed through Nahla as she remembered the spiteful smile Harold flashed at her on the trading room floor.

"What of Cal and Sofia?"

"Our team has a location. They will arrive shortly."

I may have made a mistake, but I will not allow it to continue. It's time for additional precautions.

They continued down the gravel path. The entrance to the garden appeared, framed by a pair of weathered stone pillars. They seemed to stand as silent guardians to the history that filled this estate. A history defined by some of the wealthiest people in the history of the

United States. Out of all the symbolism she'd embedded into her plan, this one would be the most poignant.

One of the greatest atrocities to human freedom happened on the grounds where tourists now walked past, oblivious. This location was as important to American history as the Battles of Lexington and Concord, but it wasn't mentioned in any school textbooks. So few people understand what once happened here.

I'm going to change that.

Bees buzzed between flowers as they meandered along the winding paths of the garden. The air was filled with the scent of jasmine and lavender.

"How much farther?" Tariq asked, his tone impatient.

"Just a little," Nahla replied. "We're nearly out of sight."

They'd moved beyond the edges of the garden, into the trees that surrounded the resort. Sunlight filtered through the leaves, casting fractal patterns on the forest floor. Nahla heard the sound of waves crashing against the shore growing louder with each step.

"Let's see it," Nahla said, her voice steady and determined.

Tariq pulled out the titanium sheet with the twelve words etched into the metal. She grabbed it from him, running her fingertips over the words. *Simplistic yet indestructible.* These twelve words would outlive the man-made structures that peppered the estate grounds.

She walked up to a tree with a small hole a few feet overhead. Reaching up, she dropped the metal sheet inside. It made a few soft thuds as it fell deep into the core of the hollowed tree.

"You'll have to chop down the tree to retrieve it," Tariq said.

"Good," Nahla said. "It's a contingency plan. Nothing more. We must be equipped to handle any potential outcome."

"Let us hope it never comes to that."

"'To be prepared for war is one of the most effective means of preserving peace.'"

They both stood there for a moment, looking up at the tree. Neither said what they were surely thinking.

If either one of us dies with our keys memorized, the other must be able to continue our vision.

The two of them continued, walking toward the gently crashing waves of the ocean. She thought of the seed phrase now buried inside the tree and hoped that it would be lost to time. She hoped neither of them would ever need to return to this spot again. Even if someone did stumble upon it, they would have no idea of the magnitude of their discovery. The twelve-word seed phrase held no significance on its own. Two of the three private keys were required to move any of their funds.

"Have you destroyed the copies?" Nahla asked, turning to Tariq.

"Every single one. It only exists up here now," he said as he tapped on his temple. "And yours?"

She imagined Hashim sliding that sheet of paper across the table toward her. She remembered choking down the metal capsule.

"A physical copy hasn't existed since I left Khartoum," she said. "I couldn't forget it if I tried."

She recalled the hopeful look on Hashim's face as he handed her the twelve words, so excited he'd found a tool to escape their tyrannical government. If only he could see where they were now.

Did he fully grasp the change this technology would bring about?

No longer did you have to be a part of the Silicon Valley elite to have access to the best-performing financial asset the world had ever seen. Sovereign wealth funds and international oil tycoons could save their wealth in Bitcoin as easily as a poor girl from Sudan.

What would Hashim have thought about the way Nahla used it now?

Would he have supported taking from the wealthy and giving to the poor?

I'll never get to ask him.

"Hashim would be proud of you," Tariq said, his voice softening. "You've come so far."

She was transported back to Khartoum. Nahla smelled the military man's sweat as he smashed the gun into her face. She saw Hashim's warm blood flowing through the cracks of their dusty apartment floor. She saw the look on Tariq's face as he stood in the hallway, his eyes wide with fear.

"*We've* come so far, cousin."

CHAPTER 43

C al glanced at the walls of the lighthouse. He saw the remnants of the beautiful life René had made for himself. Pictures with his now-grown children and late wife lined the walls. Pieces of artwork from his time sailing around the globe were scattered among them.

What might Nahla think of René?

She acted as though all wealthy people were evil, but that so clearly wasn't true. René may have withdrawn from the world, but even still, he used his resources to help the townspeople nearby.

Cal wondered what kind of lies she told herself to justify killing Jonathan. He wondered if they were the same lies she told herself to justify bringing down Harold's plane.

I wish people could see that it's the monetary systems that are broken, rather than harboring disdain for everyone better off than you.

"Where are they going next?" René asked.

"We don't know," Cal said.

"And where is it happening?"

"We don't know that either."

"What *do* you know?"

"Every place that Nahla has selected so far has been synonymous with our failed financial system."

"Fort Knox is located in Kentucky," René stated. "The US government has been holding something like 5,000 tons of gold there since the 1930s."

"Allegedly," Cal said.

"Allegedly?" Sofia asked.

"No one from the public has seen it in years," Cal continued. "Many people think they've sold it."

"What do you think?"

"I think it illustrates why gold is an inferior monetary system to Bitcoin," Cal said. "If countries held reserves in Bitcoin, it'd be nearly impossible to lie about their finances. Any transfer between governments would be visible to everyone. Fully auditable. In real time."

"And there's no way to do that with gold?" Sofia asked.

"People have tried putting gold on a blockchain," Cal said. "But it's kind of a gimmick."

"That's a strong statement."

"Gold's flaws are why fiat money was needed in the first place," Cal continued. "You can't divide it easily. Digital gold tokens just recreate the same problem that exists with fiat currencies. You're relying on some vault or custodian not to sell your gold. That's not trustless."

"Isn't gold what backs the US dollar?" Sofia asked.

"That hasn't been the case since I was a young man," René stated, between sips of his Lapsang. "President Nixon took the USA off the gold standard in 1971."

"And the country has been deteriorating financially ever since," Cal said with a knowing smile.

"America's economic deterioration started around the same time," René said. "I feel terrible for my children. They can barely afford to get the kind of home I was once able to at their age. It's no wonder there is so much animosity between generations."

"What is the US dollar backed by then?" Sofia asked.

"Nothing," René said.

"That's not entirely true," Cal replied. "It's backed by violence."

Sofia looked at Cal skeptically.

"The US government forces other countries into using the US dollar for trade if they want the protection of our military. You will be thrown into prison if you do not pay your taxes in US dollars. The entire system is predicated on violence."

"Gold is so beautiful, though," Sofia said as she placed her hand on her diamond necklace, its chains molded out of the pure yellow metal. "And you can't touch a bitcoin, it's not physical."

"I can't argue with its beauty," Cal said as he looked at Sofia's necklace, resisting the urge to let his eyes linger on her chest. "But it being physical is a negative, not a positive."

"How so?"

"You can't send gold to any place in the entire world instantaneously," Cal said. "A person can't smuggle meaningful amounts of gold across borders, unless they... get creative."

"He means shoving it up your rectum," René said as he chuckled. "The old-fashioned way."

"This doesn't make sense, though," Sofia said. "Kentucky is hundreds of miles away."

"What's the problem with that?" René asked.

"Nahla was heading somewhere on the Atlantic," she continued. "One of her men mentioned flying back into Jacksonville."

"The drone that attacked our plane couldn't have been piloted from that far away," Cal agreed. "And one of Nahla's men mentioned taking hostages to the beach."

A knowing smile slowly spread across René's face.

CHAPTER 44

———

Sofia looked out one of the large windows that framed the fog-covered Atlantic coast. The breeze gently rustled the curtains, bringing with it the salty scent of the sea.

I hope the fog clears.

She shouldn't have felt so anxious. Nahla surely thought them dead. But something still ate at her, something out there beyond the suffocating mist that shrouded her view of the ocean.

"For the person who taught me so much about Bitcoin and monetary history, I'm shocked you haven't figured it out yet, Cal," René said. "It's a landmark frequently associated with Bitcoin."

"Wait," Sofia said. "Cal got some finance trivia wrong? I need a minute. My entire worldview is crumbling."

Cal laughed.

"A landmark associated with Bitcoin?" Sofia asked. "I didn't know anything like that existed."

"This one is quite old," René said. "It was established in the 1880s."

"Then how can it be associated with a new form of money?"

"When Cal and I first met, he told me that Bitcoin was designed to fix a very specific problem. This landmark is where that problem was born."

"The Federal Reserve," Cal said, a slow understanding spreading across his face.

"That doesn't make any sense," Sofia said. "We just drove past the Federal Reserve building in Washington, DC. Nahla would have to backtrack."

"That's where the Federal Reserve is *now*," René said. "Not where it was created."

Sofia gazed out into the fog, past René's driveway and the road that connected him with the town beyond.

For a second, she swore she saw movement.

"I know Nahla's final location," René said, with a grim look on his face. "Jekyll Island."

CHAPTER 45

———

T he early afternoon sun cast jagged shadows over the driftwood trees on Jekyll Island's beach. Their salt-bleached branches looked like a skeletal hand bursting out of the sand, grasping up toward the sky.

The waves of the Atlantic crashed against Nahla's feet. Cold and ceaseless. The tide erased her footprints and dragged debris back into the sea. Time devoured everything in the natural world.

Today, she intended to help it along.

The stage is set, the final act upon us.

Nahla walked up to them, bureaucrats, public officials, and modern-day oligarchs all tied up in front of her like the pigs they were, gagged and bound, awaiting judgment. None had taken her threats seriously. None had paid their dues to society. Yet each of them was happy to spend an exorbitant amount of money attending the penthouse party in DC.

They still wore their fancy outfits and jewelry from the party. Senator Rosewall's green suit was covered in sand.

"You sent your best and failed," she began, pacing in front of them. The tide came back in, splashing up toward their faces.

Senator Rosewall squirmed. Gone was the smug superiority Nahla remembered from the halls of the United Nations.

"Because you commit your acts of treason from behind lavish office desks, it divorces you from the pain you've brought to so many others. Rather than do your own bidding, you hired Harold to intimidate me. You stopped me from bringing forth incriminating information about al-Bashir. You caused immeasurable pain to millions of people. Today, you will understand their pain as intimately as the people whose lives you've stolen."

Nahla saw Senator Rosewall's emerald necklace lying in the sand. Ripped from the woman's neck in the powerful surf.

"Harold is dead," Nahla continued. "And in a few minutes, so too will the rest of the team he was working with. No one is coming to save you, senator."

The tide crashed in again, even higher this time. The saltwater flooded into their nostrils. They splashed and fought, gasping for breath after the waves pulled back out.

Nahla watched the senator's emerald necklace get pulled into the sea.

She smiled.

Fuck your status symbols.

"I first planned to kill you in the courtyard of the Jekyll Island Club resort," Nahla said, thinking back to the location where she and Tariq hid their third private key. "But there were servants and staff. Dinner parties and desserts. It was your kind of place. Not mine."

She paced back and forth in front of them. Each of them gasping for breath, preparing for the next crashing wave.

"The sand of the beach reminds me of the carefree young girl who once lived in Sudan, before greedy people like you sacrificed my country for financial gain. It reminds me of the shore where I watched men with machetes take my parents' lives. It reminds me of what I used to be. Just another piece of collateral damage. A voiceless victim."

Another wave crashed into them, submerging each of their faces underwater.

Through the sea foam, Nahla gazed into their eyes. The only thing she saw was frailty. These people may once have been rich and powerful, but today they would cower before her.

"I asked not for violence," she said as the surf receded. "But violence chose me. This is what I am. 'If there must be trouble, let it be in my day, that my child may have peace.'"

They gasped for breath, desperately attempting to fill their lungs with air before the next waves crashed over them. But Nahla had no intention of letting them die yet.

She had more intriguing plans.

Overhead, the white, barren branches of driftwood trees loomed over them.

Nooses hung from its limbs.

CHAPTER 46

———

"What is Jekyll Island?" Sofia asked.

Cal noticed how she took on that same inquisitive look he'd seen directed at him so often when they'd first met. No matter how many other lies she'd told him, there was truth in her actions.

She is a journalist to her core.

"Today it's a tourist attraction," René said. "But it was once a private club for the richest of the rich who went there to discuss the future of humanity. One of those discussions in particular, I suspect Nahla would find interesting."

"What was the topic of conversation?" Sofia asked.

"Creating a central bank, secretly, so the American public could not stop them."

"Why would the American people want to stop them?"

"Thomas Jefferson and Andrew Jackson warned that central banking would lead to inflation and crony capitalism," René said. "People back then actually used to care about what the men who built this country believed in."

"You sound like Nahla," Sofia said to René.

"What does that mean?"

"She's got a thing for quoting the Founding Fathers."

"Can't blame her," Cal said. "They were visionaries."

"You sound like her, too, sometimes," Sofia said. "The two of you are much more similar than I think you realize."

"I don't care if we see the world the same way," Cal said. "Violence is not the way to create the change you want to see in the world."

"Agree to disagree," Sofia said with a tight-lipped smile. "If the American people didn't want the Federal Reserve to happen, then how did it pass?"

"During that meeting on Jekyll Island, they secretly crafted the plans to develop the Federal Reserve Act," René said. "It was passed while Congress was on Christmas break, to ensure less opposition."

"Interesting," Sofia said as she leaned forward to grab her tea from the coffee table. "Do you—"

She winced in pain. Cal watched her try to hide it, but her shoulder spasmed while she extended her arm, spilling her Lapsang over her shirt.

"Shit."

"Are you okay?" René asked as he began to stand.

"I keep forgetting my shoulder isn't back to normal," Sofia said. "Could you please point me toward your bathroom?"

René pointed down the hallway. Sofia stepped away.

"I like her," René said, with a sly smile on his face.

"I thought you might."

"What's the story between you two?"

"You heard how crazy of a day we've been through," Cal said. "It's been exhausting—"

"That's not what I mean," René said. "The two of you couldn't take your eyes off of each other since you've been here."

"She's dangerous, René. I know she looks beautiful and innocent, but there is more to her than meets the eye."

"I may be getting old, but I'm not blind. That look in your eyes has nothing to do with danger."

The memory of dancing with Sofia in the Watergate passed through Cal's mind. The way she looked up at him while they danced. The feeling of his hands on her waist.

"It's a physical reaction to a beautiful woman, nothing more."

"And what about the way she looks at you?" René asked.

"She's a journalist. She gets paid to charm and get close to people. It's her profession."

"So she's writing a story about you?"

"Something like that."

"I hate to be the one to break this to you, but most people are bored to death when you start talking about Bitcoin and economic history."

"And?"

"She's still here and seems genuinely curious. That speaks volumes."

"Back when we were in the penthouse, I thought there might have been something more between us. But it was all lies."

René leaned forward, his eyes looking even more serious than when they explained the details of discovering the corpses of the Valhner brothers.

"Please take the advice of an old man who wishes more than anything he could go back in time and be less stubborn with the people he cared about."

"What advice is that?"

"The hardest part of sailing isn't catching the wind, it's knowing when to adjust your sails."

"What did I miss?" Sofia asked as she returned.

"Nothing really," René said. "I'm explaining to Cal how lucky he is to have the company of such a beautiful woman."

"Real subtle," Cal said.

Sofia blushed for a brief moment before cleaning up some of the tea that had dripped onto the floor.

"So," Sofia said after she finished up. "Where were we... Jekyll Island... Federal Reserve?"

René looked at Cal and raised his eyebrows.

"Here's the first thing you need to know about the Federal Reserve," Cal said. "It isn't federal, and it holds no reserves."

Sofia smiled. It was the same infectious smile that caused him to open up to her on the plane.

Could it be that this isn't just a tactic to get me to open up? Is her interest genuine?

"Bitcoin is a decentralized system with no central authority. The Federal Reserve is the exact opposite," Cal said. "A small group of people control how much money is created and which banks get access to it. Politicians often blame price gouging for inflation, but this is a lie that distracts people from seeing the root cause of this phenomenon."

"What about all the greedy companies that keep raising their prices?"

"I'm sure some of Harold's friends are to blame for that," Cal said. "But price increases are the symptom, not the underlying disease."

"What's the disease?"

"Central banks like the Federal Reserve print money to pay for things the governments have promised their people. Because more dollars now chase the same amount of goods, each dollar is worth less. Businesses aren't arbitrarily raising prices. They're adjusting to a weaker currency. That's why necessities like housing, food, and energy rise first."

"I've heard so many people claim otherwise," Sofia said.

"You underestimate the extent to which governments lie to their people," Cal said.

"People your age may be surprised," René said. "But my generation has watched this political theater play out time and time again. Politicians make promises they can only pay for by printing more money. Meanwhile, my children struggle to afford the things we once took for granted. Homes are out of reach unless you earn a high salary. College education requires a lifetime of debt slavery. Even with a good job, social security takes money from twenty-year-olds and funnels it to the older generations."

"Why doesn't a politician stop it?" Sofia asked.

"Unfortunately, it's not that easy."

"Why not? Just stop making more money. Stop making life more expensive for people, and stop what the Federal Reserve is doing."

"It's political suicide," René said. "The government has made promises and is indebted to its citizens. If they stop, all social security will end, all government bonds will default, and the entire global financial system will collapse."

"Perhaps that's not the worst thing," Sofia said. "I don't care if a bunch of rich older people lose their money."

"I used to feel that way," Cal said. "But the aftermath would be violent. I believe there is a more peaceful way."

"Always with the non-violent approach," Sofia said.

"One of us has to be an ethical human being."

Sofia glared at him.

René said nothing.

"You couldn't ask for more symbolism than Jekyll Island," Cal said. "The Federal Reserve is a system created by the wealthiest people in the world that leeches the power away from the lower classes. It fits the bill."

As the wind picked up, Cal looked out over the peaceful waves of the Atlantic and saw windmill blades slowly begin to rotate over the ocean.

The fog started to clear.

He could nearly make out the houses of the small town in which René grew up. Two large black SUVs sat parked in the distance. Cal saw a dark figure with a gun running between a tree and René's shed.

"We need to move," Cal shouted. "Now."

CHAPTER 47

———

Sofia launched herself out of the comfort of the chair. The aches and pains from the parachute deployment felt distant as a wave of adrenaline coursed through her veins.

"We need to get downstairs," René shouted as he threw open a door that led beneath the lighthouse. Cal's posture immediately grew more rigid, his eyes scanning for threats.

Just as the journalist will never leave me, the soldier will never leave him.

They spiraled down the staircase, its construction looking so much more modern than the renovated lighthouse that stood overhead. Something exploded up above. The crash of breaking glass and wood was followed by the thunder of boots overhead.

René guided them through a set of concrete hallways, passing tons of emergency supplies. Shelves were lined with vacuum-sealed rations, jugs of purified water, solar battery packs, and ammunition.

Sofia heard their destination before she saw it.

It sounded like a muffled jet engine.

The room was lined with tall racks, each filled with rows of specialized computers, their fans spinning rapidly to cool the powerful hardware. The air was thick with heat amidst the loud, constant whir of the machines. Large cables snaked across the floor, linking the racks to high-capacity power sources. Thick ventilation ducts ran across the ceiling overhead.

"I wish I could have shown you my operation," René said to her.

"Next time," Sofia said.

René grabbed a set of keys off the far side of the wall and tossed them at Cal. "Take my boat. You'll be slower by sea, but we aren't far from Jekyll Island."

"What will you do?" Cal asked as he caught the keys.

"You cannot bargain with the tide," René said. "When it takes you, it takes you."

"What does that mean?"

"I'm going to buy you some time."

"You're going to get yourself killed."

"I'm an old man who's lived a good life," René said. "If putting myself in harm's way means I can keep the two of you safe, then so be it."

"René, please."

"If they catch up to us, they will gun us down before you get offshore. Go. Stop worrying about me."

René didn't wait for a response.

"Fair winds and following seas," he said as he walked toward the sound of the soldiers.

Cal grabbed Sofia by the wrist and pulled her toward the docks.

The boat roared to life, the powerful engine vibrating beneath her. They accelerated into the ocean.

Gunshots rang out as they reached the first windmill. Sofia closed her eyes. She tried with everything in her power to push the images of bullets ripping through René's chest from her mind.

She couldn't.

Another bout of gunfire popped behind them. She looked back, but the lighthouse was gradually fading from view.

Cal's eyes went distant.

The windmills loomed above them like sentinels over the waters. Each blade sliced through the dissipating fog. She wondered what would happen to the people of the town if no one ever tended them again.

"I think it's time," Cal said.

"For what?"

"To admit this isn't something we can do alone. Nahla's too prepared. We need help."

The boat crashed through more waves as they continued down the coastline.

"It's time to make a call."

CHAPTER 48

———

The shores of Jekyll Island transformed before Nahla's eyes.

No longer did tourists walk among the ocean-bleached driftwood trees. No longer were the bodies of wealthy bureaucrats tied up in the surf.

She now stood in front of a crowd. Hundreds of faces looked at her with expectation. Every action so far was designed to create more spectacle. She had their attention, now it was time to use it.

Every person here had different reasons.

Morbid curiosity.

Resentment.

Greed.

They were people who wanted a solution to the financial stresses of this unfair world. People who sensed that something was wrong with this country that had once stood as a bastion of freedom.

People prepared to watch a revolution.

She would give it to them.

Nahla looked into the eyes of the elites tied to chairs

in front of the bloodthirsty crowd. Their hair and clothing were soaking wet from hours subjected to the crashing waves.

Nahla redirected her gaze to the crowd before her.

"Welcome," Nahla began, her voice carrying over the hush of the crowd. "Each of the men and women in front of you is complicit in stealing from the poorest of society. Politicians. Bureaucrats. Businessmen."

She paused, letting the gravity of her words sink in. The afternoon sun hung low in the sky, stretching out the shadows of the driftwood trees across the sand.

"The United States of America profits from war," Nahla continued, her voice steady. "Countries like mine have been pillaged because of the decisions of those who you see in front of you."

Nahla watched as the crowd grew. Their act of donating bitcoin to random addresses had been more impactful than she'd even imagined. She'd created intrigue.

The stage is set. Now I must simply deliver.

"Most American citizens couldn't point out Sudan on a map. They have no idea they are profiting from our suffering. But it's not the American people who are at fault. It is the system."

She spoke to the wealthy people tied up in front of her.

"Each one of *you* is a cog in that system. Each one of *you* profited from that system. Unfortunately, killing you alone will not be enough. Revolutions fail every year. People cut the head off of the hydra, not realizing that two more will always grow in its absence. If one truly wants to bring down the beast, they must starve it to death. They must destroy its power at the root."

She turned back to the crowd, the sun reflecting off the calm waters of the Atlantic Ocean.

"At the root of their power is the money."

She looked across the Atlantic and, for a moment, saw Hashim's smiling face like a mirage.

"Today, I present you with the opportunity to take what is rightfully yours. To fulfill the responsibility bestowed upon every American citizen by this country's founders. 'The duty of a true patriot is to protect his country from its government.'"

The time is now. This is for you, Uncle.

CHAPTER 49

———

The shores of Jekyll Island were silent, save for the voice of an angry woman. A voice Cal recognized immediately. A voice he last heard ordering his death.

What do you have planned, Nahla? How does this end?

Cal and Sofia parked René's boat at a nearby resort before moving down the beach toward the signs of commotion.

Nahla's words echoed through the twisted white trunks of the driftwood trees. The shoreline was covered with them, the closest one looking like the ribcage of a massive beached whale. Men with guns were scattered throughout the crowd. Even though Nahla's soldiers would be on high alert, there was enough people for them to blend in.

Cal took note of the areas that offered cover. If a firefight escalated, the driftwood trees would offer little protection. He felt that familiar tension in his gut. The sharp mental clarity only danger could bring. He hated himself for thinking the next thing that came to his mind, but he couldn't stop himself.

I'm enjoying this. I don't want this to end.

A part of him lay dormant during his civilian life, waiting for moments like this one.

"Today we bring about change," Nahla yelled over the massive crowd.

Nahla won over public opinion by stealing from the rich and giving to the poor. Her actions may have been violent, but there wasn't any fear in the eyes of the crowd.

There was excitement.

Desire.

Frenzy.

"When fire consumes the forest, the fertile ashes of death imbue new life into the world. Today, we begin a controlled burn. Today, we ignite the spark of change by spilling the blood of the bourgeoisie."

The crowd was enthralled by her words. Cal and Sofia crept farther down the beach, drawing near to where so many of the ships and yachts had landed on the shoreline.

That's when Cal saw them.

Twelve people stood on chairs in the sands of the beach, a noose hung over each of their necks. He wondered how many of them were Harold's employers. He wondered how many of them even deserved saving. He pushed that thought out of his mind the second he looked at Sofia.

She's here because she believes in me. I must live up to that image.

"The parasites standing before you have acquired their wealth not from contributions to humanity, but by stealing from you. In all of human history, when the lower classes revolted, they were at a disadvantage. The rich have always controlled the banks, but a new age has risen."

The lowering sun caused the shadows of the driftwood trees to grow long and claw-like across the sands of the beach.

"Bitcoin allows us to transfer wealth in a way no bank can ban. Pure economic freedom. An open protocol anyone on Earth can use. Today we'll use that system to take their power."

Cal gritted his teeth. The economically empowering elements that attracted him to Bitcoin were the exact tools Nahla was leveraging for her plan.

Does Nahla even understand the damage she is doing?

A free and open network was the kind of technology that should bring about peace. It could allow the most disadvantaged in society the opportunity to escape the inflation that keeps them poor. It could allow young families to escape from war-torn countries.

That was not the message Nahla was spreading. If she succeeded, the world would further associate this technological tool of hope and abundance with violence.

I have to stop her.

"On these very sands, one of the worst atrocities to humankind took place. A secret hidden in plain sight from the American people. Thomas Jefferson believed banks were more dangerous than standing armies. He was correct. On these sands, our nation was sent down a path of debt slavery. On these sands, the ultimate tool of government control was born. Right here on Jekyll Island, six of the richest men in the United States of America decided that money could no longer be left in the hands of the individual."

Cal and Sofia slipped behind one of the yachts, wading out in the water behind some of the boats parked along the shore.

"This history echoes through the present," Nahla continued, pacing in front of the people strapped to chairs. Cal felt the tension in the air, moving through the crowd like a cold, calculating cancer. "The wealthy continue to gain power through this system. The poor continue to lose it."

The crowd erupted in a wave of fury.

The powder keg was primed.

How does Nahla intend to use their outrage?

"This is the reason why I am here today on these shores. Money is at the root of their power, so we are going to take it."

Nahla placed her hand on one of the driftwood trees, looking up at its leafless limbs.

"Each passing wave goes by unnoticed. But slowly, the branches of this tree are worn away. The United States is the same. The spirit of this country has been gradually eroded by the ruling elites."

Cal looked at the line of boats Nahla's team had arrived in. Some of them were speedboats. Others looked like military vessels and yachts.

"Today, I present you a way out of this inescapable black hole of economic control. Let the waves crash. Let the fires burn down the underbrush. Today I offer the poor of this country a new beginning."

Then Cal noticed something curious.

A boat he recognized was docked farther down the beach.

The Castillo Tax.

CHAPTER 50

———

The inside of *The Castillo Tax* was in disarray. Empty glasses littered the bar. One of the leather couches had been overturned, its cushions partially pushed back like an afterthought. The portrait of Rafael Castillo hung askew. Someone had scrawled **"KILL THE BOURGEOISIE"** in thick black marker across his face.

Sofia heard Nahla's voice yelling outside the yacht.

Her instincts screamed at her to run, but with each quiet footfall, she followed Cal farther into the boat.

There was something magnetic about him. Something that allowed her to tap into a kind of bravery she didn't know she had. He had more than just a calming presence and intelligent eyes. There was hope in the way he looked at her, a quiet promise that life could get better, that *she* could be better.

Every lie she told him felt like a tear in the fabric of who she was. Each deception split her into fragments, each thread pulling her in a different direction, each a different truth to manage. It was exhausting. But the moment she turned on Nahla, all those parts of her realigned.

Is that the way Cal always feels? What is it like to have such a concrete sense of self?

She had spent so long navigating half-truths and bending reality to fit her needs. But standing beside Cal, it all felt so hollow. There was a beauty in the way he lived his life. A beauty in the simplicity of truth. A beauty in acting in alignment with your beliefs. She wondered if it was possible for her to ever be that way, too.

Cal stopped as they approached the captain's quarters and turned toward her, gesturing for her to stay quiet as Nahla's words reached them.

"You've indebted an entire country. No longer will these injustices go unnoticed. No longer will weak people like you control our world. 'Rebellion to tyrants is obedience to God.'"

Something moved in front of them.

Footsteps.

Sofia's heart stopped as Mike rounded the corner. She froze, unsure of what to do with herself as she looked at the big man.

Cal sprang forward, surprising him before he realized what was happening. In a single move, Cal tackled him to the ground. Mike fumbled for the gun holstered to his waist.

Cal was too fast.

He slammed him into the deck, pinning him to the ground.

Cal knelt on his sternum as his gun rattled across the tile.

Mike grabbed for his knife instead. His hand reached the blade, but Cal pinned it to the ground, slamming his free elbow into the bridge of Mike's nose.

Then he did it again.

And again.

Blood spattered across the floor. Mike dropped the knife, desperately trying to block the elbows Cal rained down.

Sofia's heart raced. She became acutely aware of how badly things could go if Cal lost this exchange. She imagined Mike killing Cal. Overpowering her. She imagined Nahla capturing her, parading her in front of the crowd and hanging her corpse upon one of the driftwood trees. Sofia shook the images from her mind, forcing herself into action. She fought the urge to run and lunged for the knife.

It trembled in her hands.

Fortunately, she didn't need to use it.

Cal's eyes were distant and emotionless. He was once again the calculating soldier molded by his years of training. She watched as the veins on Mike's neck bulged, his face bright red before he lost consciousness.

Cal relented.

"Find something to tie him up with," Cal whispered, his voice so much more composed than the emotions that rattled around inside of her.

She nodded, frantically searching around the yacht for rope or a restraint. She came across a roll of duct tape in one of the cabinets. She handed it to Cal, connecting with his eyes for a long moment. She thought back to what took place in the stairwell of the penthouse. Wondering how harshly he judged her for wanting to take that man's life.

Should I have felt more guilty for wanting to kill that man?

She didn't.

She knew that look in a man's eyes. She'd seen it in James Valhner's face as he cut off her ear. She saw it again in Mike's eyes as he launched himself toward Cal. He would have killed them without a second thought. These men didn't deserve kindness.

Cal restrained Mike while Sofia bound his arms and legs.

"He'll wake up in a few minutes," Cal said. "He'll be disoriented, but he'll be fine."

"He would have killed you," Sofia said, as she set the knife down.

"This again?" he asked, his eyes narrowing. "What was all that talk in the car about?"

"I meant it," she said as she saw a flash of distrust in his eyes, like she'd given him another reminder of her moral inferiority. She felt so exposed beneath their weight.

"Words are worthless," Cal said. "Actions are all that matter. If you want to be better, you must simply *act* better."

"And what if you weren't here with me?" she asked. "I couldn't have restrained him, Cal. Do you really expect me *not* to kill him if it means I might lose my own life?"

Saying it out loud made her feel weak beside him, but it was true.

"Good thing I was here."

Sofia finished restraining Mike in silence, securing the tape over his mouth, hands, and arms.

"We need to move," Cal said as he looked out across the waves of the ocean.

"What about the military?"

"I don't know how much longer they'll take," he said. "If we don't act now, more lives will be lost."

A part of her wanted to do nothing. To stay safe and wait for the military to come and watch from a distance, but the icy blue of Cal's eyes awakened something inside of her. He made her feel so self-conscious about her own morality. It was a new feeling for her.

Surprisingly, she found herself inspired, ready for a challenge.

"Just tell me what you need me to do."

CHAPTER 51

———

Nahla looked up at the twisted branches of the driftwood trees above them, each reaching up toward the sky like gnarled fingers clawing their way out of the earth.

Nooses hung down from their bleached white limbs, each attached to a politician's neck.

"Senator Rosewall," Nahla began, her voice carrying over the murmuring crowd. "Our festivities begin with you."

The senator closed her eyes as she balanced on the chair, a single footstep away from death.

Or maybe a push.

"I used to be so naive," Nahla said, pacing in front of the senator. "I thought this country's laws and legal systems would unearth the truth. If America's Founding Fathers could see how you've profited at the expense of others, you would have been tarred and feathered."

Nahla fought to keep her voice calm, but the rage simmering beneath it was unmistakable. The crowd watched in silence.

"My home country of Sudan has long been one of the most resource-rich in the world. For thousands of years, people in this region fed themselves from the Nile's bounty and our fertile soil."

Senator Rosewall had been such an imposing figure in the UN building, but she looked so small and frail now.

"Of course, the poor Sudanese people desperately needed help from First World countries like yours. How else would we bring industry to our country if not for our savior, the rich senator?" Nahla mocked, bowing down in feigned reverence. "But the real reason for your political support wasn't kindness, was it, senator?"

Nahla stared into her eyes, making sure she understood the pain she'd caused.

"Gold," Nahla said. "So much pain and suffering for my people over a shiny yellow rock."

She stepped closer to Senator Rosewall, her eyes never leaving the senator's face. "You ignored my pleas about Omar al-Bashir not because of ignorance, but because of *greed*. You owned massive shares of the gold mines in Sudan, and new political leadership would have put that at risk. Omar al-Bashir committed a genocide of my people, and you silenced my attempts to bring him down because it was good for your bank account."

The crowd grew more frenzied.

They wanted blood.

She wanted to give it to them.

"We act like democracy exists, like this system serves its people. However, Senator Rosewall made herself wealthy at the expense of the lower class. She does this without fear, without repercussions."

The senator looked down at her again, finally connecting with Nahla's eyes. She soaked it in. She only wished all the people of her country could feel the same vindication she did at this moment.

"You come back to the United States and parade your virtue around the rest of the First World, pretending that you are bringing socioeconomic power to us poor, needy Africans while you profit from our downfall."

Nahla sprang forward, slamming her elbow into the senator's abdomen. She watched her writhe as she tried not to fall off the chair to her death.

"Do you know how many children have died in those gold mines?"

The senator said nothing.

"We have a once-in-a-lifetime opportunity. The financial system is changing, and with it, the source of power for people like you. We have this single moment in history to take advantage of this change."

Nahla paused, taking in the crowd's energy and the raw fear in the eyes of those tethered to the trees. She then spoke as plainly as possible into the crowd and their raised cameras.

"I have compiled a list of the billionaires who have profited most from the plunder of the poor. Politicians. Global leaders. Businessmen. Their personal information has been published on the Bitcoin timechain. Alongside each of the names is the number of bitcoin each of them owes for their sins to be forgiven."

Nahla stepped closer to the senator.

"We do not want their fake government paper. We do not want their stocks and bonds. These things can be confiscated. These things can be frozen by the system. For the first time in human history, poor people finally have a financial tool that the wealthy elites cannot stop."

The crowd roared.

"'*We the people*' was a phrase that once held so much power on the shores of America, but it no longer strikes fear into the bones of the ruling class it once did. '*We the people*' will not allow such evils to continue."

Nahla stepped forward. In one swift movement, she kicked the chair from beneath Senator Rosewall. The rope snapped, and her feet desperately writhed in the air a couple of feet above the ground.

"The power is in the hands of the people once more. The rich will pay these reparations, or their lives will be forfeit. '*Death or taxes.*'"

Nahla looked into one of the cameras, imagining the wealthy people squirming as they watched from the comfort of their private jets. She wondered if they had any idea what was coming for them now that the masses they ruled over had a financial incentive to kill them.

"'*We the people*' demand our retribution."

CHAPTER 52

———

C al jumped off the yacht and back into the blue
waters of the Atlantic. His waterlogged clothes
clung to his body as he waded closer to Nahla.
The crowd grew more frenzied, and no one noticed as he rushed past them. He slipped by a soldier
with a gun, but the man was too caught up in Nahla's
speech to notice him.

I might die today.

People always thought soldiers struggled to adapt
to civilian life because of the trauma they faced on
the battlefield. That wasn't the case for Cal. The real
struggle he faced was how damn boring civilian life
was in comparison. The thrill of the last twenty-four
hours made him feel alive.

He looked at the far end of the beach, wondering
how long until reinforcements arrived.

Colonel Blackwell hadn't seemed concerned when
Cal made the call, but there was nothing else he could
do to speed them up. There was only one thing he

could control right now. Time. Delaying Nahla might be enough to save a few lives.

He crept behind the boats along the coastline.

"I speak now to the citizens of this country," Nahla said, looking out over the growing crowd of people along the beach. The countless phones and cameras live-streamed her words to the world. "Fear is the foundation of governments' control, so today I ask you to be brave."

Silence hung over the crowd.

"You've seen the riches we've already distributed across the world. You've seen their inability to stop us. I now offer these riches to *you*."

The driftwood trees, bleached and skeletal, jutted out from the sand like eerie sentinels. Cal moved past another one.

"Their wealth is not mine to take. It's *yours*."

Cal watched as Nahla stood commandingly in front of the crowd. The way she spoke reminded him so much of Max. They both had a passionate vision. He just wished they'd used it for something better.

"Some wealthy elites whose names are on my list will run. Some will hire security details. Some will barricade themselves inside their homes. If so, I ask that you provide them with... *encouragement*. Surround their mansions. Swarm their private jets. No bullet-proof glass or armored guard can stand in the way of an idea whose time has come."

Cal's stomach dropped.

There is no stopping this.

"Everyone who publicly supports our cause will inherit their wealth," Nahla said. "A new age begins today. The bourgeoisie will crumble as the lower class rises once more."

As much as Cal resented Nahla, he couldn't fault her plan. Instead of placing the list of people in the hands of the media or sharing it on social networks, they paid to embed it as a transaction on the Bitcoin network. The list was now stored on every Bitcoin node in the entire world.

Every continent.

Every country.

There were even nodes orbiting the Earth in space that now contained the list of names. The only way to destroy it would be to simultaneously erase millions of nodes across the entire network. Even in a world-wide blackout, Bitcoin would survive so long as a single computer came back online. It was a system so resilient that Cal believed it would outlast monuments like the Statue of Liberty.

The yacht's horn roared to life, a deafening blare that shattered the tension.

Cal sprinted.

Everyone on the beach looked toward the boat. Away from Nahla. Away from him.

Nahla barked some orders at a few of the men who surrounded her, pointing toward the yacht. They all ran off. He could only hope that Sofia was able to get out of there in time as four large, weapon-laden men barreled into the rear of the ship.

He couldn't let his thoughts linger on her. Not now. She played her part, now he must play his. He only had seconds before the men could get there and remove the chair that Sofia jammed against the yacht's horn. He flew past two security guards, their heads turned away toward the blaring horn.

Thirty more feet.

He dodged through the crowd. He wove between the driftwood trees and around the people standing on chairs, each of them awaiting their death. Their eyes were wide with terror, faces pale under the dimming light.

There was only sand between him and her.

Fifteen feet.

The crowd continued to look toward the yacht, but he could see in front of him, in front of Nahla. Something was happening in the crowd.

Is someone else moving toward her?

Ten feet.

The images of all the corpses Nahla left in her wake came racing through Cal's mind. There was no telling how much more violence she could unleash on the world if he failed. He thought of René, sacrificing himself to let him get the opportunity to stop her.

I will not let his sacrifice be in vain.

Then Cal saw him.

Mike.

His face was covered in blood from the fight on the yacht. There were fresh knife cuts through the electrical tape wrapped around his wrists and ankles.

He pointed a gun at Cal.

Then he fired.

CHAPTER 53

———

The gunshot rang out across the shore.

Perched on the roof of the yacht, Sofia had a clear view of the beach erupting into chaos. Her heart plummeted as she witnessed the last thing she wanted to see.

She watched blood erupt as the bullet passed through Cal.

She watched him collapse into the sand.

She watched as chaos exploded around him.

Something inside her ripped apart. All hope and optimism left. Her consciousness collapsed into the same numb and distant place she had gone to in al-Bashir's mansion.

More gunshots echoed from farther up the beach. She dove behind the radar dome mounted on the roof of the yacht, shielding herself from the gunfire. She became acutely aware of each movement she made on the fiberglass roof of the yacht. She heard the vibrations of a deep male voice from somewhere below.

Another peppering of gunshots rang out from farther up the shore.

Her ears rang.

Men in dark uniforms and tactical armor moved methodically down the shoreline. Military trucks slowly followed behind them down the beach.

She saw it happen again in her mind.

Cal sprinted toward Nahla.

Mike pulled up his gun and shot him.

This is my fault. I was the one who restrained him.

Another deep voice echoed from below.

She couldn't wait for them to find her. Sofia jumped to her feet, but on the slippery roof that was a harder task than she'd expected. She tripped, nearly crashing down into the shallow ocean water below. She caught her balance against one of the metal guard rails. Pain shot through her injured shoulder.

Get your shit together or you are going to die.

She dropped to the lower deck.

The fall was hard on her feet and knees, but it felt so distant from her now. Cal was dead. She would be too if she didn't get herself off this boat.

She had a plan, a half-assed one, but it was something. She would rush toward the military, doing whatever it took to get under their protection.

She sprinted toward the back of the yacht, attempting to keep her footfalls as quiet as possible. The air was thick with the scent of salt and fear.

Her heart stopped.

A man with a gun stood in front of her, looking out toward the beach.

Boots pounded on the wood of the yacht behind her.

Sofia jumped into the hallway and out of their line of sight. She moved into the galley, the same storage closets that she and Cal had seen when they'd talked to the crew in Vizcaya.

She threw open the door.

The putrid smell almost made her vomit on the spot. A dead woman. A plastic bag was wrapped over her bloodied head. She was crammed into the already tight closet alongside brooms and cleaning supplies.

Rafael Castillo's wife.

"She ran this way," said a voice from the rear of the yacht.

Sofia forced herself alongside the dead woman, jamming the door closed behind her and squeezing against the body. Just in time. The boots approached the spot where she had been standing.

Sofia held her breath.

The woman's weight shifted. The corpse fell on top of her. The dead woman's body was heavy against her chest and neck. The plastic bag that they'd used to kill Mrs. Castillo was now compressed against Sofia's face.

At that moment, as Sofia stared at the poor woman's battered face, she wished Cal had killed Mike.

Cal's moral code failed. It made the world a worse place by saving the evil person who took this woman's life. Mike deserves to be dead. Cal deserves to be alive.

She pushed those thoughts down.

She tried to breathe in.

The inhale forced the plastic to cover her nose and mouth. Suffocating, she could feel the woman's blood on the other side of the plastic bag against her face and eyes.

She couldn't make out the muffled words of the soldiers outside the door. She kept steady, not daring to adjust the plastic. They might hear her.

How long can I go without air?

She closed her eyes.

When she was tied to the bed in Khartoum, she focused on her breath. One after the other. Forcing her consciousness to a place far away from the present moment. She couldn't do that now. There was no breath to control, and the heartbeats that raced inside her chest only made her want to gasp for air.

Slowly, the footsteps passed.

She kept waiting.

Gunshots echoed in the background.

Her head grew light, and she feared she would pass out if she waited any longer. She took a chance, readjusting Rafael's wife's head as she took a desperate gasp of air. The smell of blood flooded her nose.

The corpse's leg slipped. Its weight shifted, and the body slammed into the door.

It swung open.

Shit.

No time.

No thinking.

She sprinted, not even looking back to see if Nahla's men saw her. There was no more time for caution, or she would end up like Mrs. Castillo.

It didn't matter how high up she was or how shallow the water might be. Broken ankles or shattered kneecaps were a small price to pay for keeping one's life. She ran toward the railing. Without looking down at the waters below, she threw herself over the edge.

She didn't fall.

A hand reached out, grasping onto the back of her shirt as she threw herself over the railing. She felt the fabric of her shirt stretch as her momentum pulled her crashing back to the yacht. Her ribs crushed against the railing.

"Got you, bitch."

CHAPTER 54

———

A bullet whizzed past Nahla's head. She hit the ground, crawling on her hands and knees behind one of the driftwood trees. The knotted roots of the sun-bleached wood offered minimal cover.

How could Cal be here?

There was no time to think about how her team had failed. She needed to get to safety. She popped her head out again. Another bullet zinged by, kicking up sand near her face.

No time to think.

Run.

The sand was soft, slowing her movements, but she still had the legs she'd built when she was young, running across the desert. She darted past the remains of a fallen tree. One of her bodyguards fell beside her.

A bullet ripped a chunk out of his neck. Blood splattered over her face.

She ran.

Another bout of machine gun fire sounded farther up the beach, followed by the cries of one of her wounded men.

Did he bring an army with him?

She turned back toward the beach. The spectacle she'd orchestrated for years unraveled in moments. Her men scattered, some fleeing by boat, others running inland.

From a distance, she watched one loyal soldier go from chair to chair, kicking each one out from under the feet of the condemned. Methodically, he ensured none of the twelve people escaped justice. The last moments of their lives were spent desperately kicking the air.

No matter how chaotic this became, at least they've been punished.

She looked away from the beach and locked eyes with a group of her soldiers taking cover where the trees met the sand. She sprinted toward them and ducked down.

Another burst of gunfire peppered the sand.

"It's a SEAL team," said the largest of the men between hard, heaving breaths. The gruffness of his voice didn't match the boyishness of his face. "We need to get you to safety immediately, ma'am. Let's move farther upshore."

Bullets whizzed through the air, the sharp cracks of gunfire punctuating the chaos. Each gunshot broke her heart. She envisioned the rounds ripping through the bodies of her men. They were more than paid soldiers. They believed in her cause. Each fallen comrade was a blow to her resolve.

No longer am I the small, innocent girl I once was.

She'd started this war. These men died for the same ideals she outlined. She couldn't allow herself to fail, or their deaths would be in vain.

She ran with everything she had, dodging among the trees, the underbrush tearing at her clothes. She tripped over a root, falling hard to the ground. Three gunshots erupted behind her, and one of her soldiers collapsed, a gaping hole where his left eye used to be.

They're in the woods, too.

She scrambled to her feet.

They pushed forward, weaving between the trees, their movements frantic. Nahla's adrenaline was through the roof. With each step, she wondered if it might be her last.

She recited the seed words in her mind.

Liberty. Party. Boat...

This is exactly why they'd taken these precautions and kept him a safe distance away from the beach. If one of the stray bullets landed in her skull, Tariq could recover the seed phrase they'd hidden in the tree and move the bitcoin.

I've given my entire life for this. Please. Let me see it through.

They reached the clearing just as the helicopter's rotors began to spin. The powerful downdraft whipped up sand and loose leaves, creating a whirlwind around them.

She threw herself onto the metal floor of the helicopter.

It shot straight up into the sky, giving Nahla a bird's-eye view of the carnage below.

The sands were soaked in red with bodies strewn across the ground. They belonged to those who had come out to support her, to the men who had sacrificed their lives for the same cause as hers. A few boats moved out to sea, but the sheer number of bodies scattered on the shore made her stomach lurch more than the forces of the helicopter's violent ascent.

CHAPTER 55

——

The clouds in the sky swirled above Cal. The taste of salt filled his mouth, and the sand beneath him felt coarse and gritty.

Gunshots. Beach. Nahla.

He lifted his hand to feel the damage. As he pressed into his shoulder, the pain was blinding. Blood ran out of the wound, pooling in the sand by his side. He rolled onto his stomach, the sand sticking to his sweat-drenched skin. The sound of a machine gun rattled from up the shore of the beach.

I have to move.

He threw himself into motion, completely ignoring the blinding pain of the gunshot wound.

He looked down the shoreline toward *The Castillo Tax.*

The boat was moving out to sea.

On the far side of the beach, Cal spotted a convoy of Humvees grinding across the sand. Soldiers dismounted, weapons ready, fanning out in controlled bursts of motion.

He couldn't rely on them. Not yet.

He'd lived inside the layers of military bureaucracy. He knew what would happen next. Radio chatter, conflicting orders, chain of command. It could be minutes before they even understood what was happening, let alone moved to stop it. He needed to get to Sofia as fast as possible. Every wasted minute could mean terrible pain for her to endure.

Or death.

He placed one foot in front of the other and slowly was able to move away from the blood-soaked sands, each step sending jolts of pain through his entire torso.

Above him, twelve bodies hung from the trees. Each of their lifeless forms hung still despite the surrounding chaos. The popping of gunshots somewhere in the treeline reminded him to stay low. He fumbled toward the shore and hopped inside the nearest yacht. The adrenaline took his pain away. The primal part of him that reveled in the chaos came alive.

It wasn't a full-sized yacht, but he didn't need it to be.

It looked fast.

Fast was good.

He ran toward the wheel and looked out over the coastline. Off in the distance, he could see *The Castillo Tax* chopping across the waves. Was Sofia alright? She had to be. He wouldn't allow himself to think otherwise. The keys were in the ignition, and he looked around, readying himself to pursue them across the sea when he heard a noise from the back of the yacht.

Boots.

He ran downstairs into the bottom of the boat. One of the smaller rooms underneath looked like a makeshift bar. He couldn't discern how many men there were. He slunk deeper into the room, preparing himself in case one of them came downstairs.

The boat lurched into motion.

Do I dare move?

He waited.

In his mind, he raced over all of his failures, reliving the way Mike looked at him as he took aim and fired.

He'd failed to stop Nahla.

He'd failed to protect Sofia.

He couldn't help but think again about how much simpler his life would be if he'd killed Mike.

Sofia's blood is on my hands. My moral code could very well be the reason she dies. Is that truly worth it?

Each wave that crashed against the boat caused his shoulder to throb. The dull, persistent ache grew sharper the farther they moved out to sea. If he didn't do something about the bleeding, he'd pass out before he could get to Sofia. He scanned the small room, its shelves lined with bottles and scattered supplies.

No first aid kit.

No gauze.

He grabbed a bottle of vodka off the shelf, tossing its cork aside. He took a long gulp, letting the burn coat his throat before tipping the bottle over his shoulder. The pain was immediate.

The alcohol poured into his raw flesh like liquid fire. He imagined himself being burned alive. He imagined someone shoving a hot poker straight into the bullet hole and twisting. He bit down on the collar of his shirt to stop himself from crying out.

He swayed for a moment, the world blurring at the edges, but he forced his focus back. A handful of dirty rags lay on the bar. There wasn't a better option. He wadded them up and pressed them into the wound, and they immediately turned deep red.

Slow the bleeding. That's the priority.

Next, he reached for a roll of electrical tape. It wasn't ideal, but neither was passing out in the bottom of this boat and leaving Sofia to die. He cut the tape with the straight razor from Harold's plane, clumsily wrapping it around his shoulder to bind the bar rags over the wound. He looped it over and over until the pressure was enough to stop the bleeding.

Crude, but functional.

His arm dangled uselessly.

He staggered up to one of the port side windows, looking off to where the men on the ship were taking him. He expected to see more sea, but there was something else off in the distance.

It grew larger and larger with each crashing wave.

He'd misunderstood.

They were not going out to sea. They were not escaping farther up the coast.

In front of them, adorned with black pirate flags, was a massive cargo ship.

CHAPTER 56

The *Castillo Tax* rocked back and forth as it carried Sofia out to sea.

How am I back in handcuffs again already?

The cold metal dug into her wrists, aggravating the still-fresh cuts from the parachute.

The popping of gunfire came from the shore. She may have been farther away from the gunfight, but she was also getting farther away from anyone who could help her.

"Who is she?" one of the soldiers asked.

Do none of them recognize me?

"Speak, girl."

"My name is Elizabeth," she said, attempting to flaunt a smile and use her charm. Something that would normally have been second nature was more challenging now that her life depended on it.

The image of Cal being shot in the head ran through her mind again. She pushed it down. She couldn't afford to let her emotions get the best of her at this moment.

Focus. Think.

"I was trying to warn you," she said.

Both of the men looked at each other, exchanging skeptical glances.

"I'm a journalist following Nahla's work," she began. "I've spent most of my career in war-torn countries in Africa. I've seen firsthand the kind of pain caused by the USA's financial manipulation. What you are doing is inspiring. I'm writing a story about you."

It worked once, why not try it again?

"Why did you interrupt Nahla's speech with the yacht horn?" the man asked, his eyes narrowing with suspicion.

There was no one to save her now. Her only hope was left in her hands. She had to do anything in her power to keep that spark of hope alive.

"I climbed to the top of the boat to have a better vantage point of the beach. I saw the SEAL teams approaching. No one else noticed. So I rang the horn to try and warn all of you to give you more time to act."

Both men looked skeptical, but their gazes softened.

Distant pops of gunfire rang from the distance, almost inaudible as they went deeper out into the ocean. Down below, she heard another pair of boots clanging against the floor of the yacht, running toward them.

"Please," she said. "I'm here to tell your story."

Another soldier came up from below deck, a phone pressed to his ear. He was older, with greying hair and a hardened face. The other soldiers turned and looked at the man like he was their superior.

"Those woods were covered with SEALs," he said. "I don't know how she could possibly have gotten out of there alive."

Sofia heard a male voice on the other end of the line.

"My unit alone just lost five men. We're still committed to the cause, but I need guarantees. Promise me their families will be taken care of."

The boat rocked harder as it pushed into deeper waters.

"I need assurance here and now," the soldier said. "We are all getting paid regardless of what happens to your cousin."

The voice on the phone continued to speak. The captain sat down and listened, his face like stone, but Sofia could see the tension in his shoulders.

"Fair enough," he said, and then hung up the phone.

"That bitch gave me a heart attack," the captain said to the other soldiers. "Tariq promises we'll get paid double. Triple if both of them survive."

Interesting.

The frustrated soldier looked at her.

"Why is she alive?"

"She's a journalist sympathetic to Nahla's cause," said the shorter man. "She claims she sounded the horn in an attempt to warn all of us."

"A lot of help that was," he said, looking even more skeptical than the others. "But it could be useful to have a hostage when the military catches up to us. Nahla might be able to use her for something."

Sofia's heart sank. She looked back toward the beach. With each crashing wave, they moved farther away from anyone who could save her.

My only hope is in the hands of a woman who has tried to kill me twice today.

CHAPTER 57

———

Nahla's breaths were short as the helicopter approached the cargo ship. Doubts raced through her mind as she failed to calm herself.

Cal ruined everything. This moment we'd worked so hard for is gone.

No.

Not everything.

Not yet.

Their message on the beach was a success. The list of billionaires was released to the public. The world saw what she'd done to the Valhner brothers, Rafael Castillo, and all the pompous politicians from the penthouse.

She'd ignited the powder keg.

An unstoppable spiral of incentives.

Even a single billionaire paying their bounty would show the world what was possible. The transparency of Bitcoin's timechain would shine, allowing anyone to watch as she distributed the wealth to her supporters. The more people saw it, the more people would gain confidence in her promises. She would inspire the lower classes of the world to take up arms against the elites.

Tariq may understand the technical details better than me, but I understand the power of incentives.

Nahla jumped out of the helicopter as soon as it touched down. One of her soldiers ran up to her, his face tense with urgency.

"Ma'am, many of our team members have returned to the ship. We need you—"

"No one needs *anything* from me until I speak with Tariq."

She continued toward the bridge, her boots clanging against the metal grates of the ship. The helicopter's rotors continued to wind down, creating a slow hum in the background.

She walked past their other drone. It sat ready for launch, a reminder of the one she used to take down Harold's jet.

None of this would have happened if I hadn't trusted Sofia.

Her soldiers were waiting for her in the cargo hold, but she had higher priorities. Tariq would need her key to sign the first round of transactions and distribute the bitcoin. If the world saw them send these first transactions, it would be clear their plan was still in motion, despite what transpired on the beach. They were now in a battle of public perception.

"Please, ma'am," said another one of her men, approaching cautiously. "There's something you need to see."

"The only thing I need to see right now is the inside of the bridge. The US military will be here in minutes."

"We've captured a woman stowing away in Castillo's yacht," the man yelled out. "She said her name is Elizabeth."

"I don't care, we have—"

"Ma'am," he cut in. "She's the one who interrupted you on the beach. We think it could be useful to have a hostage on board when the military arrives. She's a journalist writing a story—"

He continued speaking, but she didn't register the words. A journalist sounding a horn on the very same yacht Cal used as a distraction?

Could it be?

She stopped in her tracks, stepping close to the man. "What did she look like?"

"A thin woman with dark hair and olive skin."

"Bring her to me," Nahla said as a large smile spread across her face. "Tell Tariq to meet me on the front deck as soon as possible."

It took only moments for her men to drag Sofia to the deck. The sudden fear in her brown eyes made Nahla giddy.

They strapped her to a chair that butted up against the edge of the boat. The salty breeze ruffled her hair as she looked out at the vast expanse of ocean. Waves crashed against the hull of the ship below. For a moment, Nahla considered kicking the chair off the edge, letting Sofia drown in the waters with her hands tied behind her back.

I will not allow the ocean to steal your death away from me.

"You turned on me," Nahla said, looking into Sofia's eyes. Her pupils were wide with terrified focus.

"You lied to me."

"I did no such thing."

Nahla could barely hold back the rage. She was untethered on the beach, the fully realized expression of the woman she wanted to be when she left Khartoum.

That moment is gone. Taken.

"You said only deserving people would die," Sofia said.

"Every person I've killed deserved their death," Nahla replied. "Each of them acquired their wealth through the pillaging of others. Those who have profited from the systemic economic rape of the poor do not deserve to live."

"Cal was a good man," Sofia said. "He stole from no one."

The woman's eyes welled up with tears.

All Nahla saw was weakness.

The feeble will lash out against the strong for doing what is required.

"You used to be better than this," Sofia continued.

"I used to be *worse* than this," Nahla said as she brushed Sofia's hair aside and looked at the same ear that was severed on the night they first met. She remembered how small she felt as al-Bashir yelled commands at her. "I used to beg bureaucrats for permission. Now I demand change."

"You think you're better than these people, but you long for the same control they have."

"Can you blame me for savoring their fear?" Nahla said. "The people I hung acted as if they wanted what's best for this country, but their desires were selfish. 'We must guard against the impostures of pretended patriotism.'"

Nahla watched the fear growing in Sofia's eyes. She knew that fear. She'd seen it grow in Hashim when he lashed out against the brutish soldier.

A woman backed into a corner is dangerous.

"I see through your lies as easily as your soldiers see through your cause—"

Nahla slammed her fist into Sofia's face. The woman's confidence crumpled, and a small trickle of blood streamed down from her nose. A bruise formed on Sofia's cheekbone. Nahla imagined how satisfying it would be to shoot a hole through it.

Not yet.

Sofia spat out blood. Her eyes grew distant. Her spirit started to fracture.

Nahla took a pipe wrench from one of her soldiers.

"Let's have a little fun, shall we?"

CHAPTER 58

———

Cal watched as the yacht pulled up alongside the cargo ship. He listened carefully as the men cleared out. His makeshift bandage had stopped the bleeding, but his shoulder throbbed with pain.

He opened his phone.

No laptop. No proper setup. This would have to do.

He pulled up his tracking app. The Bitcoin price was surging upward with a continuous bid. Network fees were spiking to levels Cal hadn't seen in years.

Are people flooding into the Bitcoin network in hopes Nahla will send them money? Or are billionaires rushing to pay off their bounty?

He didn't know. The only thing Cal knew for certain was that word of Nahla's plan was spreading like wildfire.

He waited another minute, just to be sure everyone was off the yacht before moving. He took stock of the surroundings and found an armored vest. Cal checked the plate rating out of habit. Ceramic. It wouldn't stop everything, but it would hold up against small arms fire, and it matched the ones Nahla's soldiers wore on the beach. He slipped it on, hoping it could help him blend in.

Cal was briefly stationed on an aircraft carrier during his time overseas. He figured cargo ships were laid out in a similar manner. On military vessels, storage rooms were located in the rear of the ship.

I have to assume Sofia is there.

He climbed onto the roof of the yacht, using the rope ladder to pull himself up onto the deck of the cargo ship.

Two armed men passed him.

Cal stayed low, crouching behind empty storage containers as voices approached. While he waited, he read the branding on the side. In giant white letters, they each said *RC Enterprises.*

Nahla must have stolen the cargo ship from Rafael Castillo.

As soon as the men passed, Cal sprinted toward one of the rear hatches and climbed below.

He entered a sea of steel. Metal decks and railings surrounded what looked like the engine.

Cautiously, Cal continued deeper into the heart of the ship. The narrow corridors were a maze of pipes and wires. Each turn revealed similar-looking hallways. He picked up the pace, moving faster down the hallway toward the crew quarters.

He soon heard voices ahead, holding his breath as he listened.

Cal had no choice but to pass them if he wanted to get to the other side of the ship. Moving quickly, he tried to keep his footfalls as silent as possible. As he passed, he saw a group of Nahla's men looking at a computer. He recognized the Bitcoin wallet software on their screen, but he didn't linger despite his curiosity.

How many rich people have paid Nahla's ransom so far? How long until the government attempts to intervene?

Every step of the way, Cal had failed.

The only reason they found Nahla was because she had led them directly to her. Harold and René were dead. Their attempt to distract her on the beach hadn't stopped her from spreading her message of violence.

If I fail again, Sofia will die.

"Did you hear that?" said one of the men after Cal passed by. "Have others returned from the beach?"

A chair scraped against the ground as one of the soldiers stood.

Cal sprinted.

He raced toward the door at the end of the hallway, hoping with every shred of his being that there wasn't another group of soldiers behind it.

It was an empty bunk room. Despite being covered in gear and personal items, it didn't appear that anyone was currently there.

Footsteps followed.

He positioned himself at the edge of the doorway. He had to do this quietly. Tactically.

The soldier rounded the corner.

There was a second of confusion as the man looked down at Cal's vest, then looked at the bandages holding his shoulder together. That was all the time Cal needed. He lunged toward the man.

Cal could sense he was untrained from the first second he grabbed him. A simple body lock trip was enough to take the man to the ground. The surprise of hitting the metal deck took the air out of the soldier's lungs. Cal fell down with him, pressing his entire body weight into the man's chest.

The soldier gasped for air.

Cal pressed the cloth of his vest over the man's mouth.

No breathing.

No screaming.

The soldier spasmed and tried to move in every different direction. Each attempt failed. Hyperventilation began. Cal could feel the last strands of the man's spirit leave his body. With one final burst of desperation, the man attempted to turn away and escape.

Cal gave him a moment of hope before violently sliding his arm underneath the man's chin, locking in the rear naked choke. Cal winced as the soldier rolled him over, putting pressure on the bullet wound in his shoulder.

It doesn't matter. It's over.

There was no gasping for air. There was no crushing of the soldier's windpipe. Cal cut off the blood flow to the man's brain with precision. In seconds, he was unconscious.

Cal pulled the limp body into a nearby bunk, then tied the man up and covered his mouth with duct tape, double-checking to make the restraints much more secure than they were with Mike.

He imagined Sofia judging him again for not taking the life of a man who would certainly have taken his.

She's wrong.

Sofia wasn't capable of physically restraining the soldiers, but Cal was. There was no turning off his military training even if he'd wanted to. He had optionality.

With optionality came the kind of responsibility an unskilled person would never understand. He'd vowed to protect people, even if they didn't deserve it. He chose mercy when it would have been easier to choose violence.

Sofia doesn't see herself in these people. I do.

Cal saw children scavenging in the rubble of Sarajevo after the siege. He witnessed fathers forced to do heinous things to provide scraps of food for their families. He knew the kind of rage Nahla and her men must feel toward the wealthy of the world.

I wish they could see there is a peaceful path. A way forward without death threats and public hangings of the wealthy.

In sparing their lives, he hoped some of them might one day find that a more optimistic path existed. His thoughts were broken by a peppering of muffled gunshots from down the hallway.

Those sounded suppressed.

A moment later, a small team of US Navy SEALs entered the room, their guns raised and pointed at Cal.

Cal fell to his knees and showed them the palms of his hands.

"We've located Captain Lamarck," the SEAL team member said into his radio.

Cal looked into the body cameras mounted on the soldiers' chests. Top brass were surely watching. He'd wondered how long it would take for the world's elites to demand the US military take action. Apparently, not long.

"Prepare yourself," the soldier said as he reached out a hand and helped Cal up to his feet. "Colonel Blackwell needs to speak with you."

CHAPTER 59

———

Sofia watched the sun lowering on the horizon. She imagined the fireworks that would light up the skies over Jekyll Island resort this evening. *I hope I get to see them before I die.*

Nahla paced the deck in front of her, holding the wrench loosely in her hand. Her eyes filled with rage. Tariq approached them with a laptop and a small calculator-like device in his hand. There was an undercurrent of fear in his eyes.

"I've already signed all the transactions with my key, but we need yours to finalize the send."

Nahla handed over a small device that looked similar to the one he had. Tariq plugged it in, and Sofia watched as transactions started moving across the screen.

"This is the first chunk," Tariq said. "To make sure all of our soldiers are paid for their sacrifice. We'll need to do another round shortly to pay out all of our supporters."

"How long will this take?"

"I'm using a batch signing strategy," Tariq said. "By precomputing them and taking advantage of multi-threading, I've—"

"I don't need the details," Nahla said. "How long?"

"Couple minutes," Tariq said, his speech growing increasingly fast. "Redistributing their bitcoin in smaller chunks will take much longer with the high-fee environment. Adding thousands of transactions to the mempool will take at least a few hours to be confirmed, and the US military has already boarded the ship."

"Breathe, Tariq," Nahla said. "We are in control."

"If we don't get it sent out immediately, our new followers may lose interest, and our movement will lose steam."

How many bitcoin have they acquired so far? Is it more than the Valhner brothers? More than Rafael Castillo?

"This is why we took precautions," Nahla said as she reached out her hand and placed it on his shoulder. "So we wouldn't have to stress."

"They've captured my technical team," Tariq said, still struggling to catch his breath. "What if they give up information? What if we can't do any more payouts? What if—"

"Stop," Nahla commanded. "I need you to think clearly, now more than ever."

Nahla's phone rang.

She rejected the call, choosing instead to speak to the soldiers who surrounded them.

"The US military thinks I want to talk to them," Nahla said. "It appears they've realized the predicament they find themselves in."

It doesn't matter if the entire US Navy swarms the ship. There is no way Nahla is letting me out of this alive.

Only a few hours ago, Sofia dreamt about returning to the version of herself that existed before al-Bashir, before the Valhner brothers. She remembered the optimistic woman who discovered herself in the canals of Venice, the young woman who believed that the right words and language could change the world.

That dream died the moment she watched the bullet rip through Cal. His eyes implored her to be better. The more she gazed into them, the more she believed in herself. But that hope was gone.

He would have kept fighting. He would do what's right no matter how dim things appeared.

"She's lying to you," Sofia shouted at Nahla's men. "The only way any of you survive is if you turn her in. She will sacrifice each one of you to save herself."

Nahla looked on, amused.

"You saw what she did on the beach," Sofia continued. "She ran away while your brothers died around her."

"You understand nothing," Nahla sneered. "They are here because they believe in this cause."

"Do you know how many men you lost on the beach? Have you checked with their families since you got back to the cargo ship? No... You heard I was here and came straight away to get revenge."

Then she connected with Tariq's eyes.

"I overheard what you said to your soldiers on the phone. You have the power to fix this. You have a choice."

"It doesn't matter how big an arsenal the military has," Tariq said, his voice shaking. "They can't brute force a private key."

"But they don't have to, do they?" Sofia asked. "They don't have to break fancy cryptography. They only have to break you."

Sofia couldn't help but recognize a flash of recognition from Nahla. A quick snarl that was gone a moment later. No matter how confident she appeared, there was a crack. Sofia felt it with every part of her journalistic instincts.

Perhaps I can force a misstep.

"Tell me, Tariq. Will you be loyal to Nahla while lying beneath a waterboard? Will you take her secrets to the grave?"

"Push her up against the edge of the ship," Nahla commanded the nearest soldier.

Sofia resisted.

It was futile.

Handcuffed to the chair, she looked out across the endless, cold blue of the Atlantic Ocean.

She imagined being pushed forward.

She imagined plunging into the cold waters while tied to the heavy metal chair, gasping in the saltwater of the Atlantic as she drowned in the darkness below.

She imagined death.

A part of her wanted it. She could escape from whatever pain Nahla was about to subject her to.

"Nahla turned this crusade into her own personal vendetta," Sofia yelled. "She only serves her own greed."

"Lies," Nahla whispered from behind her.

"She killed Senator Rosewall and Harold because they wronged her."

"Seems like you of all people could understand what that's like."

"We are not the same," Sofia said. "You do all of this under the guise of the greater good, but you're using these soldiers as a means to an end. It's not their end. It's yours."

"You know nothing of their motivations."

"But I know exactly what motivates *you*," Sofia said. "It's not freedom. It's power. You act like you are superior to the elites, but you get off on having power over them in the same way they once had power over you."

"'Happiness and moral duty are inseparably connected,'" Nahla said as the cold metal of the pipe wrench wrapped around Sofia's pinky.

The noise came alongside the pain.

A brutal, wet snap split the air, like a stick breaking underfoot in the silence of the night. Her finger broke in half. She tried with everything she had not to let Nahla see any weakness, but the yell erupted out of her.

A searing agony shot up her arm.

She considered begging for death.

She pushed the thought from her mind.

My life is over. I can't change that, but I will not give up. It doesn't matter if she tortures me or how much more pain I have to endure. I have to try. I have to create doubt and chaos.

Truth.

Lies.

It didn't matter. There was a crack in Nahla's psyche, and she had to exploit it.

"Tariq," Sofia pleaded, ignoring Nahla completely. "You've watched with a front-row seat as Nahla spiraled into insanity. She's going to get you killed. I know you have access to the private keys. You can stop this."

Tariq looked at her, confused, but the rage in Nahla's eyes was now an inferno.

No more torture. I'm going to die.

In a swift movement, Nahla drew and cocked her gun. The black metal barrel pointed directly at Sofia's forehead. A look of pure malice covered Nahla's face.

The woman who had once been her savior would now end her life.

Sofia closed her eyes.

She thought her life might flash before her eyes. She thought she might see memories of her career and childhood, but the only thing she imagined was the smile on Cal's face as he swung her around on the dance floor.

It was all bullshit. The hope he gave me was a lie.

"Nahla," Tariq said nervously. "You shouldn't do this. There must be another way."

"I wish that were true," Nahla said.

The anger in her voice was gone, replaced with something else entirely.

Something Sofia didn't expect.

Sorrow.

The gun fired.

CHAPTER 60

―――

Nahla watched as Sofia opened her eyes.

Blood streamed beneath the woman's feet, trailing from the gaping bullet wound in Tariq's forehead. Nahla collapsed beside her cousin's body. His lifeless eyes reminded her so much of his father's.

She wanted to sob uncontrollably.

She wanted to scream.

She wanted to kill every person on the ship.

Forgive me, Hashim. There was no other way.

Her phone rang again. This time she answered.

"My name is Colonel Blackwell," the voice said. "You're surrounded by—"

"Stop talking," Nahla said, wiping away the tears and looking out toward the boats that now surrounded the cargo ship. "There is no collection of words you can string together that will change what is to come. Does your team currently have snipers trained on me?"

"Yes."

"Tell them to watch closely."

She crouched over Tariq's body and grabbed the signing device from his hand.

"This is not a negotiation," Nahla said as she threw the device into the ocean below. It sank into the dark, churning waters below.

"Wealthy elites from around the world are liquidating their assets and moving them to the Bitcoin network under threat of death."

There was a gust of ocean air, carrying the scent of salt and gunpowder.

"All sent to addresses *only I* now control."

She let the gravity of her words sink in, savoring the silence that followed.

"Two of three keys are required to move the funds," she said. "The first key lives exclusively inside my mind."

A cool gust of ocean air pulled through her hair.

"Tariq memorized the second," Nahla said as she looked down at the gaping hole in the side of her cousin's face. "The third is in a location the two of us hid together."

The colonel was silent.

"In other words, Colonel, the only person capable of moving this bitcoin is *me*."

She looked down at Tariq's blood-splattered laptop. More bitcoin poured in as people paid their bounties, hundreds of times more than Rafael Castillo or the Valhner brothers, and it would only keep growing as the peasant class revolted against their overlords.

Military men poured out from the cargo bay onto the deck, clad in riot gear and carrying body shields. Coast Guard vessels formed a perimeter around the cargo ship. Armed men stood on every boat, their rifles aimed at Nahla, waiting for the order to shoot.

A command that would never come.

A command that *could* never come.

Nahla undid the straps of her bulletproof vest and let it fall to the ground. She smiled and outstretched her arms, ensuring her vitals were visible to all the guns trained on her.

There was nothing to impede their shot, no protection or human shields.

"Do you understand, Colonel? A collection of wealth greater than most nation-states resides exclusively inside my mind. If you kill me, it's forever gone."

CHAPTER 61

———

"Captain Lamarck," Colonel Blackwell said, his voice gruff.

"Sir," Cal responded. His hand twitched upward but stopped short of a full salute.

Old habits die hard.

He felt out of place in his bloodstained civilian clothes and duct tape-covered shoulder.

"I wasn't expecting you in person," Cal said, eyeing the colonel's service uniform, its seams strained over his gut. His chest was stacked with more ribbons than Cal thought a desk-bound officer deserved. His eyes settled on the Meritorious Service Medal near the top of the rack, awarded for their takedown of Max Aldrich.

A medal earned by killing a good man.

"If it was up to me, I would still be out playing the back nine," the colonel said. "I shot two under on the front, but my phone wouldn't stop ringing."

"I'm so sorry that my trying to stop a domestic terrorist inconvenienced your golf game."

"Great to see you too, Captain Lamarck. I forgot how... forward you are."

And I forgot how fat you are.

"I'm surprised you got here so fast," Cal said.

"I had a team in the area investigating Harold's crashed jet. When you called, we were able to mobilize quickly."

"How did you know I made it to the cargo ship?"

"One of our snipers watched you slip onto the boat. Why you felt the need to do that is beyond me. You've caused us to be flying blind."

"Nahla's men have taken Sofia hostage. I came to find her."

"Nahla's holding her captive."

As the colonel spoke, Cal flashed back into his memories of working with him. The cold and calculated answers, the disinterest in anything other than completing the job.

Sofia's life is the least of his concerns.

"Captive?" Cal asked. "Is she safe?"

"Mostly," the colonel said. "But Nahla is demanding we let her fly the helicopter back to the mainland."

"What did you say?"

"That's obviously not going to happen," Colonel Blackwell chuckled.

"What are you planning then?"

"Governments from around the world are urging me to do everything in our power to get the money back. It's not just the wealthy who have been stolen from. If these funds are lost, many jurisdictions lose massive volumes of tax dollars."

"Oh no, the poor state bureaucracies. How will they possibly survive?"

Cal noticed some of the other military men around the room growing uncomfortable with how candidly he spoke to the colonel. He wondered if he was once that submissive to the authorities back when he served.

"Have I done something to offend you, Captain?" Colonel Blackwell asked.

You mean besides ordering me to kill Max?

Cal held his tongue.

If he wanted to get Sofia out of here alive, he had to put his personal baggage behind him, no matter how badly he wanted to punch Colonel Blackwell in the face.

"I apologize, Colonel," Cal said. "How can I help?"

"You could reverse the transactions."

"Bitcoin transactions are irreversible."

"This is coming from the highest levels of government," Colonel Blackwell said. "Our resources are unlimited."

Cal looked into the eyes of the military men in the room. They were men accustomed to the unwavering power of the United States government behind them. Men who were not used to being told no.

"I don't think you understand what the word *irreversible* means, Colonel."

"We can bring in someone else if you are unable to solve this problem for me, Captain."

"This *problem* is not solvable. The SHA-256 hashing algorithm used to secure Bitcoin was literally designed by the US military to be unbreakable. This protocol allows anyone in the world to secure their savings with the same level of security used to protect nuclear codes."

"Could we force Bitcoin miners in the USA to censor transactions to Nahla's address?"

"Bitcoin blocks are mined globally," Cal said. "From massive hydroelectric power plants in China to tiny waterfalls in rural Africa, you can't stop them all."

"What about commanding US-based Bitcoin exchanges to blacklist transactions sent to Nahla?"

"That'll make things more challenging for the billionaires with violent protesters surrounding their homes," Cal said. "They'll have to wire money to jurisdictions outside the USA."

"Give me *something*," Colonel Blackwell said, his voice growing more frustrated. "What kind of negotiating power do we have?"

"The *only* way to move the funds is by getting Nahla's private keys."

"Then it appears our contingency plan is a go," Colonel Blackwell said to one of the soldiers.

"Contingency plan?"

"I see an obvious solution," Colonel Blackwell said. "We will forcefully extract the information."

Torture.

"I think Nahla has prepared for that scenario," Cal said. "I've analyzed the addresses they're using. They each begin with the letter three, which indicates that it's using the pay-to-script hash format. They likely have a multisignature wallet configured or some kind of smart contract based—"

"I'm certain she prepared for that scenario," Colonel Blackwell said. "But I didn't need your digital forensics to figure it out. Nahla killed her cousin to gain unilateral control over the funds."

"Damn."

"We're mobilizing a team to get close enough to tranquilize her. A non-lethal extraction op."

"Nahla's spiraling," Cal said. "You need to proceed carefully."

The Colonel said nothing.

"What about Sofia?" Cal asked.

"We'll try our best to keep her safe."

Try their best? Have I really come this far to watch Sofia die from afar?

"Sir, Sofia's sacrifice is the reason you are even here right now. Without her, Nahla would have finished her plan uninterrupted on the beach."

"We'll do what we can," the colonel said. "But returning those funds is a matter of national security."

"What if I help you?"

"How?"

"Nahla will speak with me."

"This isn't a digital forensics case, Captain."

Cal let out a slow breath.

Last chance.

"Nahla's team has tried to kill me three times today. I assure you that she'll be thrilled at the opportunity to have me within shooting distance again."

The colonel examined him for a long moment, looking at the bullet hole in his shoulder and the battering of bruises he'd gained over the last two days.

"She's not mentally stable," Cal continued. "The only thing I know for certain is that she would relish the opportunity to kill me after I helped to interrupt her plan on the beach."

"And you are willing to take on this risk?"

"Absolutely."

"We cannot arm you with anything lethal," Colonel Blackwell said.

"Could I carry the tranquilizer?"

The colonel nodded.

"Excuse me, sir," said one of the soldiers. "Even if Cal can get close to Nahla, we can't protect him if—"

Colonel Blackwell held up his hand to silence the soldier.

"Captain Lamarck understands the situation. The rest of you will be standing by if something goes awry."

Colonel Blackwell did his best to hide his tight-lipped smile.

He doesn't care if Nahla kills me. In fact, it might be convenient for him.

Around the room, soldiers moved with quiet efficiency, settling into position and preparing for what would come next. One of them stepped forward, securing a tranquilizer gun in a hidden holster on Cal's back and inserting a communication device into his ear.

A single thought kept circling through Cal's mind.

This is a terrible idea.

CHAPTER 62

———

The handcuffs dug into Sofia's wrists.
Each heartbeat sent a dull throb through her freshly broken finger, and the ache crawled up her arm.

"I can't believe I once respected you," she said to Nahla.

Nahla turned to her, eyes narrowed. "I can't believe a privileged little princess like yourself thinks she understands my motivations."

I will not cower for you. You will not break me.

"You just killed the only family you have left. You aren't the Nahla I knew. You're a shell of the woman who saved my life."

"Tariq made a promise larger than himself," Nahla said, her voice cold and detached. "So did I. He knew the stakes."

"The surprise across your soldiers' faces tells me otherwise."

"Our cause is more important than any individual life," Nahla said. "Someone like you could never understand."

"Nothing is worth killing the people you care about."

"'Always stand on principle, even if you stand alone.'"

"You stand alone because you killed your family. You have no principles."

"Spoken like someone who's never had a cause worth dying for," Nahla said. "You can't hide the fear in your eyes from me. Tell me, do you see it in mine?"

"I see a monster. You get off on inflicting pain on others."

"You see what you want to see. You paint me as evil because I've acted in a way your sheltered life disagrees with. You think that you understand pain because of one bad night in Khartoum. I grew up in the pain of that city."

Sofia said nothing.

Nahla sauntered around her in a circle, tossing the pipe wrench from hand to hand.

"You know what might speed up our negotiations?" Nahla said. "Another broken finger or two."

Sofia would never beg for death. She would stay strong up until the very end. She let her consciousness grow distant, dissociating to escape the pain.

There's no more reason for hope.

Then she saw Cal.

CHAPTER 63

"I thought you were dead," Nahla said as Cal approached. "Though I'm grateful for the opportunity to finish the job."

"Think you'll be able to handle killing me yourself?" Cal asked, his tone calm. "Or do you need your men to tie me to a chair first?"

"I could say the same about you," she said. "You've been unable to kill any of my men. You're lucky Mike is a terrible shot."

"I wasn't trying to kill your men."

"You two are pathetic. Soft and privileged Americans, oblivious to the violent realities of the real world."

"Is that how you convinced yourself to kill a good man?"

"Who are you talking about?"

"Harold's friend Jonathan."

"You must be joking."

"He used his wealth to help people," Cal said. "Have you lost your path so much that you'll kill anyone more successful than you?"

"Sacrifice is required to bring about real change."

Cal paused for a moment. Nahla watched as he reached up and adjusted one of his earbuds.

They're feeding him instructions, using my relationship with him to get information on me.

Nahla considered killing him right then. She imagined Colonel Blackwell's surprise when she blew a hole through his lapdog's head. Or maybe she'd make Cal watch as she broke another one of Sofia's fingers?

It was their fault she was interrupted on the beach. It was their fault Tariq was dead.

I offered them a chance at reducing the power of the financial elites. Why would they reject me?

Cal must have brainwashed Sofia. His military training removed his ability to think independently. He was a puppet of the system she vowed to destroy.

Nahla looked Cal over as he approached. Underneath a haphazard bandage job, she saw dried blood covering his arm. She saw the bruises and the beating his body had taken over the last forty-eight hours.

Her men stopped him to check for weapons.

"You don't need to do that," Cal said. He untucked his shirt and turned around, exposing the tranquilizer gun strapped to his back. "The US military commanded me to shoot you with it. I have no intention of following their orders."

One of her men grabbed it from him and handed it to her.

"Why are you telling me this?" Nahla asked as she tossed it into the ocean.

"Because I didn't come here for them. I came here for *her.* They don't care if you kill Sofia. I do."

Nahla looked at Sofia. There was a newfound hope in her gaze, like Cal would be some savior, negotiating her to safety.

Not a chance I'm letting them slip away from me after the damage they've caused me.

Cal brought his hand to his ear. She watched him listen to orders from the Colonel. He turned around and faced the military men at the far end of the ship before addressing them.

"I told you to prioritize Sofia's safety, Colonel," Cal said. "You ignored me. I'm now doing this on my terms."

He paused, listening. In the distance, Nahla could hear the Colonel shouting at him. Cal ripped the earpiece out of his ear and tossed it onto the ground.

"I'm not with them," he said, gesturing to the soldiers that lined the other side of the deck. His eyes found Sofia's. "I'm with *her.*"

Nahla saw the hope she'd been trying to extinguish flicker back into Sofia's eyes.

"I understand the desire to remove the gap between the rich and the poor," Cal continued. "I've watched the country I grew up in collapse. My family fled to America to start a new life. Many of the institutions here are broken, but there is still hope."

"Don't pretend like you understand me. You have no idea the life I've lived."

"It's true. I don't. But I wish you could see that there is a better way, a more peaceful way."

"The Founding Fathers of this country would be disgusted by people like you," Nahla said. "They tore down the system and created a better one. They risked their lives and the lives of their families to do so, and here you are refusing to use violence against those who deserve it."

"Even those men understood how much innovation could empower human freedom," Cal said. "The individual technologies may have changed since their time, but the principles hold true. The internet allowed for open communication across the entire planet. In the same way, Bitcoin will bring socioeconomic prosperity to every person who chooses to embrace it."

"You are naive if you think the rich will willingly let go of their advantage in this world."

"It's not their choice," Cal said. "No matter what games the politicians play with their money printers, poor people have access to a savings technology that can never be debased. They have an escape hatch."

Cal stepped closer to her and looked down at Tariq's body. She wondered what he must think of her. The woman who was willing to kill her own family to succeed.

"Bitcoin is a tool," Cal said. "In that tool, you see a way to enact violence. I see a peaceful financial protest. I see hope."

"You are deluded if you think the ruling class will not find a way to destroy your optimism."

"Wealthy people are not inherently evil. It's the systems that are broken."

"Lies."

Cal met Sofia's eyes before glancing at Tariq's blood pooled beneath her.

"You don't have to listen to me," Cal said. "You hold all the cards. You've killed Harold, René, and countless others. There is nothing left for me to do but beg for your forgiveness."

Is this an attempt to play into my ego?

"You've won," he continued. "It's over. All that's left is the legacy you leave. Every single one of those soldiers is wearing a body camera. What happens when the American people watch the video of your actions? Will they see you torturing an innocent person? Is your movement about nothing more than revenge?"

He's acting. Manipulating. He's no better than Sofia. Throwing the earpiece into the ocean was just for show.

The military wanted him to gain her trust. It was their only play if they wanted a chance to get her keys.

"Sofia betrayed me," Nahla said. "She's no better than the bankers and politicians I hung on the beach."

"Fuck you," Sofia yelled, her voice cutting through the tension.

"Please," Cal said once more, his tone desperate. "No more violence. Let her go."

Nahla stepped closer, looking Cal squarely in the eye. The imposing man who dispatched her soldiers, survived a plane crash, and took a bullet to the shoulder now begged in front of her.

He is weak.

She looked down at the gold Rolex on his wrist. He talked like he understood her goals, he talked like he understood where she came from, but it was all for show. He was rich, just like the rest of them.

"As a young girl, I dreamed of escaping Sudan to the United States of America," Nahla said as she stepped closer to Cal. "I studied the words of men willing to do whatever it took to bring about change. Thomas Jefferson asked if a few lives lost would matter in one hundred years. In two hundred years."

Cal clenched his jaw as she stepped closer.

"The answer is no," Nahla continued. "'The tree of liberty must be refreshed from time to time with the blood of patriots and tyrants.' It's time for that tree to flourish once more. She's going to die for her country, and—"

The words stopped in her throat as the cold metal of Cal's straight razor sliced through the front of her neck.

CHAPTER 64

———

Nahla's hands clutched at her throat, desperately attempting to stop the blood from pouring down her chest. Her soldiers watched as their leader collapsed to the ground.

Shock transformed into chaos.

Cal locked eyes with Sofia for a split second. So many questions floated within them. He wanted to run to her. He wanted to comfort her and tell her that everything was going to be alright.

There wasn't time.

One of Nahla's soldiers began to take aim at him. A bullet whizzed over Cal's shoulder. The soldier's head exploded into a cloud of red mist. Gunfire erupted behind him as the military began to fire.

Another soldier charged him and began to draw his weapon. Cal dodged to the side, grabbing the soldier's gun and redirecting it toward the ground. He felt the bullet reverberate through the barrel and slam into the deck.

The smell of gunpowder filled the air.

Cal drove his forehead into the bridge of the soldier's nose, then used his bulletproof vest to throw him to the ground. The air left the man's lungs as he slammed into the hard metal deck.

Another bullet flew inches in front of Cal's face. It slammed into the man's neck and shattered his jaw.

That was too close.

In seconds, the entire outburst of violence was over. He gathered himself and raced to Sofia. He fell to his knees and placed his hands on her shoulders, hoping that some physical touch would help comfort her.

"I'm so sorry."

"What did you just do, Cal?" Sofia asked, her voice shaking.

He wanted to hold her. He wanted her to understand how much guilt he carried for putting her in this position.

"It's over," he said as he touched the side of her face.

The fear in her eyes softened, but she couldn't stop shaking.

The sound of military boots grew closer. Colonel Blackwell lumbered toward them, a look of disgust on his face.

"I put my neck on the line for you," Colonel Blackwell yelled.

This time, it was Cal who stepped up close to him. No more looking at his toes and following orders. No more asking permission. He stared the man right in the eyes, unflinching.

"Go fuck yourself, Colonel."

Cal glanced at the soldiers' body cameras. He imagined the top brass going over the video of what he was about to say. He imagined speaking to the rich elites who would surely demand to see the video of the man who stopped them from getting their money.

"You're no better than Nahla," Cal said. "You justified collateral damage to accomplish your goals."

"I do what has to be done," he said, his face red with rage. "I swore the same oath you once took. Does that mean nothing to you anymore, Captain?"

"Who decides on that greater good? Because you certainly didn't ask me if I was willing to gamble with Sofia's life."

"We live in the real world," Colonel Blackwell said. "We can't always wait for circumstances to be perfect to take action."

"On that we agree," Cal said as he looked at Tariq's laptop. It sat open next to his limp body, blood splattered over its screen. Hundreds of ransom transactions had already been confirmed on the network, sent by the rich elites paying their bounty.

Cal looked at Sofia. He wondered if she would ever be able to understand what he'd done. He didn't care how the military or the media would judge him.

The only opinion I care about is hers.

"How are you going to retrieve the bitcoin?" Colonel Blackwell asked, growing more frustrated.

"I'm not."

Cal looked toward the shore of Jekyll Island, toward the country that was currently celebrating its Independence Day.

"I *command* you to find a way," the colonel said.

Cal's mind flashed to Max's face. He remembered the pit in his stomach that opened up the moment he pulled the trigger.

"What kind of man would I be if I followed the commands of my superiors and let you torture Nahla? What kind of man would I be if I put Sofia's life in jeopardy to serve a cause I don't believe in?"

"You'd be a man who served his country," Colonel Blackwell said. "You'd be a soldier who did his goddamn job."

He looked at Sofia.

A wave of euphoria crashed through him, like a piece of himself finally returned after years of being lost.

"Nahla would've given the bitcoin to killers, you would've given it back to the undeserving, and Sofia would've been left to die. So I made a choice."

"And now you will face the consequences," said Colonel Blackwell.

Cal looked down at the blood-covered computer as another transaction worth billions of dollars of bitcoin was received into Nahla's wallet.

"Every dollar the billionaires spend to pay off their ransom is a dollar moving out of the old system and into a new system. Bitcoin that will never move again. Not for the rest of time."

"So it's just… gone?" Colonel Blackwell said. "You've screwed everyone."

"False," Cal said. "By destroying the keys, I've made every remaining bitcoin more scarce. Its value is now permanently embedded into the network. A donation to everyone who chooses to use it for the rest of time."

"You defied direct orders. You broke the chain of command," Colonel Blackwell said. "What gives you the right to make this decision?"

"The American spirit wasn't born of bureaucracy. It was forged in rebellion," Cal stated. "This country is deteriorating because of men like you."

Colonel Blackwell scowled at him.

"Nahla's actions were wrong," Cal said. "But she was right to reject authority. This country was built by people who stood up to their superiors. Liberty is wasted if it's not used to make hard choices."

He connected with Sofia's soft brown eyes.

"And I choose her."

CHAPTER 65

The wind blew through Sofia's hair as she looked out across the side of the cargo ship. In the distance, she watched fireworks lighting up the sky as Americans celebrated their freedom.

As soon as Cal finished speaking, military men swarmed him. They slammed him into the deck, pressing his face against the cold metal. A lone medic broke from the group and approached her.

"Are you hurt?" the medic asked, his words barely registering through the fog of shock.

She didn't respond. She refused to take her eyes off Cal.

The medic searched the soldiers' bodies nearby, finding the key and unlocking her handcuffs.

"We need to put your finger back into place," he said as he helped her stand up from the chair. "You need to come with me—"

She pushed the man away and walked toward Cal.

"...obstruction of justice," she heard Colonel Blackwell yelling at Cal. "I'll do everything in my power to ensure you are locked up."

The colonel stopped shouting when he saw her approaching. His face switched in a second from the anger he was projecting at Cal to fake kindness.

"You've been through a great deal today, ma'am. Are you alright?"

Sofia looked over his immaculately pressed uniform.

"Hello, Colonel," she said, eyeing the polished brass of his insignia. "Those medals are quite impressive. How many of them did you get for standing around and watching while people like Cal saved lives?"

Colonel Blackwell's jaw tightened.

"Why don't you get out of my way and let me speak with the man who saved my life," Sofia said.

She walked up to Cal. There were so many questions in the way he looked at her, like he wanted to beg for forgiveness, like he was disappointed in everything that had happened today.

"Looks like it's my turn to be in handcuffs this time around," he said, the corner of his mouth twisting into a smile.

She started thinking of what she could say to convey her gratitude. Something kind. Something witty. She wondered what words could possibly repay him for sacrificing his own freedom so she could live.

So she stopped searching for them.

Instead, she kissed him.

She let herself fall into the warmth of his body, holding back tears of gratitude. The sound of fireworks and the pain of her finger faded away.

She felt something shift inside him as their lips met. Even with his hands bound behind him, their bodies pressed close. The heat of him in her arms felt like coming home. Her hands drifted down to his chest. The rough fabric of his shirt against her palms and the steady beat of his heart beneath her fingers grounded her.

Colonel Blackwell ripped them apart, pulling Cal away from her and walking him toward one of the military boats. It felt just as painful as Nahla's wrench around her finger.

"What's going to happen to him?" she asked, her voice breaking.

"Justice," Colonel Blackwell said.

CHAPTER 66

SIX WEEKS LATER

Cal looked out the window of his prison cell. He knew the Statue of Liberty and the Upper Bay were behind the horizon, but all he saw was grey, lifeless concrete. The Metropolitan Detention Center in Brooklyn was only a few miles from the raging bull of Wall Street and his apartment in Midtown. Being close to home only made things worse.

Eat.

Read.

Lift.

Sleep.

Every day the same routine. Every day the same thoughts.

I'm going to die here.

There was no trial date. There was no opportunity to explain himself. No hope of escape. His entire life was uprooted. Apartment ransacked. Bank accounts frozen.

Nahla was right.

The American spirit still lives on inside many of its citizens, but the institutions are broken. The court systems of the United States were as disjointed as the financial systems. This country was no longer the bastion of freedom it pretended to be.

He tried to keep his optimism alive, but it was harder with each passing day.

In the beginning, he felt depressed about his situation, but over time, that gave way to numbness. His mind shifted toward the same thing it always did when he needed more hope. Sofia. He tried not to dwell on her too much, but the image of her dancing in the penthouse was hard to release.

Will she understand what I did? Will anyone understand what I did?

The average person doesn't care if the financial system is designed to make them poor. Even when presented with a way to escape from the system, they'll come up with every excuse to not learn about it.

They would rather choose the pain they know over the pain they don't. They won't change. I was dumb to have tried.

He kept spiraling.

Circles and circles.

Spinning around the same ideas, he repeatedly justified his actions on the cargo ship. Most mornings, he couldn't tell if he'd actually slept or if he'd stared at the ceiling all night.

He let his thoughts drift.

Wander.

He felt himself changing.

Without a problem to solve, he could feel his mind begin to atrophy. The traits that had served him so well in the real world were now unraveling his sanity. He felt his grasp on reality growing looser.

I have to remember who I am. What I stand for. What I know.

Still, his mind raced.

He became anxious about things outside his control. He worried the events of Jekyll Island would justify more government intervention. He worried that Nahla's brutality would inspire a new wave of public executions.

Jealousy is a poison, one so toxic it's toppled empires and destroyed the dreams and desires of great men.

The moment he watched Nahla hang Senator Rosewall on the beach, he knew the kind of path she would lead the world down.

Violence.

Envy.

Theft.

There was a better way, a more cooperative way. A path that allowed people to transact and collaborate freely. A path with incentive alignment that moved humanity toward abundance.

Was this just another delusion? Am I lying to myself to justify my actions just like Nahla?

As he stared into the concrete prison wall, completely alone with his thoughts, he realized that this was his life now.

This was who he was becoming.

I need to start coming to terms with the fact that I'm a failure.

CHAPTER 67

TWO WEEKS LATER

The sound of keyboards clicking filled the room as Sofia walked through the media agency.

Magazine covers lined the walls of the hallway. They stirred something inside her. She was reminded of the young woman who wanted nothing more than to work at a place like this. When she was in Venice, she had no idea where this profession would take her. She dreamed that her words could inspire humanitarian aid and save lives. She imagined writing stories about war-torn countries like Sudan. She envisioned her words informing Americans of the atrocities happening overseas.

I never anticipated the government deceit I exposed would turn out to be my own.

She felt the weight of her story in her hand as she considered turning around and leaving. There was no telling what would happen if she continued. The only certainty was that it would be challenging.

As people walked by on the streets outside, she wondered how many of them knew about what happened on the shores of Jekyll Island.

How many of them even care?

Videos from the beach circulated on the internet. Thousands of wealthy people were threatened, and many paid their ransom. But when people realized that Nahla could no longer send that bitcoin to her supporters, the revolution lost steam.

The US military brushed the entire thing under the rug and actively suppressed all the videos.

"You're really going through with it then?" the editor asked as she stepped into his office.

"I have to," she replied. Her mind flashed to Cal and how confident his eyes always made her feel.

I think that's the thing that I miss the most.

She imagined him locked up in that cell, sacrificing his freedom to save her life. She dreamt that one day their paths might cross again, but she didn't let herself live in that dream. There had been so many emotions. So many thrills. Now that she was back in reality, she was beginning to realize that she might be forced to let go of him.

She placed her story on the editor's desk.

This chapter of her life was closing.

"Colonel Blackwell told me that keeping my mouth shut was what was best for the country," Sofia stated. "He thought there would be more public outrage if what happened on the ship leaked out to the rest of the world."

"Are you sure you want to go through with this?" the editor asked. He took off his glasses and looked up at her. His grey eyes reminded her of Harold's, although there was much more kindness behind them.

"I was given a second chance at life," Sofia said. "I'm not going to spend it in fear. The world deserves to know what happened."

"We've got a big team of lawyers, but I will not be able to defend you from the state department," the editor said. "If we publish this, you could see jail time. Are you comfortable with that risk?"

"Absolutely not," Sofia said. "But I'm going to do it anyway."

CHAPTER 68

FIVE WEEKS LATER

The prison guard stopped in front of Cal's cell and motioned for him to stand. The cold, grey walls and narrow cot had become so familiar. His daily routine had become normal.

He set down his book alongside the rest of his meager possessions and followed the guard.

They weaved through the hallway of the facility. Each step echoed off the concrete floors. The headache-inducing fluorescent lights were an ever-present reminder of how desperately he longed for the feeling of real sunlight on his skin.

The guard opened the door to the visitation room and gestured for Cal to enter. The moment he saw Sofia, life flooded back into him. He was back on the deck of the cargo ship, standing in front of all the military men. He could almost hear the music from the penthouse dance floor as he swung her around in his arms.

He may have to spend the rest of his life in this cage, but within seconds of seeing her smile, he knew that sacrifice was worth it. She wore a fitted white blouse that highlighted her sun-kissed complexion, and a knee-length navy skirt. Her face was relaxed.

"Always with the handcuffs," she said.

Cal was unable to place the emotion in her voice.

"You look more beautiful than I remember."

"And you sound desperate," she smiled. "Just as unkempt as the day I first met you."

"How have you been?" Cal asked as he leaned forward, wishing to be a couple of inches closer to her. The handcuffs caught, yanking his arms back into the cold metal of the table.

"The world is turning upside down because of what Nahla did, you've been locked up in here without a court case, and the first thing you ask about is *me*?"

He nodded.

She smiled.

"I've been writing a lot," Sofia said as she ran her hand through her hair.

Cal looked at her ear. It took him back to the moment in the penthouse where his entire world was flipped on its head. It reminded him of how much more depth there was to this woman.

A depth I may never get to explore.

He made a conscious effort to soak in as much of this moment as possible. He would surely replay it over in his head as soon as he got back to his cell.

"It's good to see you reclaiming your old life," he said. "Is it crazy out there?"

"There was chaos over the Fourth of July weekend,"

she said. "Personal security details or private security teams don't matter much when you have an angry mob at your doorstep. I can only imagine what might have happened if you hadn't stopped her."

"I only wish we could have acted more quickly."

"I was amazed you *acted* at all," Sofia said.

"What do you mean?"

"All the times you disagreed with me… all the times you judged me… What happened to non-violence above all else?"

"You."

She stared back at him.

He wanted so badly to be able to take her into his arms again.

"I was wrong," he said. "You showed me that. There was a singular solution. A *moral* solution. I knew what I had to do the moment I saw you tied to that chair. I saw it more clearly than I've ever seen anything in my life."

He waited for her to say something.

She didn't.

He watched her eyes slowly tear up as the two of them sat in silence.

"Why are you visiting me today?" he asked, cutting through the quiet.

"I've been busy," she said as she brushed away a tear.

"With what?"

She stood up abruptly.

Had I done something to offend her?

"Wait," Cal said. "Will you be coming back here to visit me again?"

"No."

A wave of anger crashed over him.

"Maybe I was reading into something that wasn't there," Cal said, no longer able to hold his tongue. "Maybe the side of you I saw wasn't real, but the things I feel for you are."

It looked like there was more that she wanted to say, but she was holding it back for some reason.

"I don't know how many years I'll be in here," Cal continued. "All I'm asking is that I'll be able to see you again. I'm a better man with you in my life, even if it's only for an hour of visitation once a month."

She walked toward the door and gave him a tight-lipped smile. There was so much sadness behind her eyes. So much unsaid.

"You misunderstood what I came here for today, Cal."

Then she left. Leaving Cal with a cold, empty table and a prison guard who looked at him with a judgmental gaze.

He began racing through the moments they'd spent together once more, thinking desperately about what he might have done wrong, thinking through everything she'd said to him during their time together over the Fourth of July.

The guard closed the door behind her before guiding him out of the room. The officer led him back toward his cell through the labyrinth of concrete and fluorescent lights that seemed to leach the life out of him.

Is this my life now?

Spending his time behind bars. Reading books. Dreaming of what it would be like when he was finally released. He knew he could bear that burden, no matter how long he was locked here.

He knew in his heart that he did the right thing.

Even if she doesn't feel the same about me, I'd still do it over and over again.

Even being in a room with her for a minute filled him with a kind of euphoria he hadn't felt in months.

I have to accept what it is that she wants, even if that means she doesn't want to be with me.

The guard turned.

Instead of taking him back to his quarters, he changed direction toward the release processing room. He stood there in a daze as the guard explained that the DA dropped the case.

They conducted Cal's exit interview.

They took off his handcuffs.

His mind was still back in his cell, imagining what kind of meal he was going to have that evening and where he would sit for dinner. The world felt out of focus as he exited the prison. He'd expected to feel an overwhelming wave of relief, but the only thing he felt was confusion. His eyes adjusted to the sunshine, its warmth a stark contrast to the cold, artificial light of the prison.

Sofia was the first thing he saw, her eyes red with tears, but this time there was a smile on her face.

He walked toward her, feeling as though he was floating.

"I'm so sorry," she said, her voice breaking. "Your lawyers made me swear not to talk when there were prison cameras around."

"But the way you acted in there," Cal said. "I thought something might have changed between us."

"Nothing changed," she said. "Has something changed with you?"

"No."

A slow smile spread across her face.

He kissed her, this time so grateful that his hands weren't stuck behind his back in handcuffs. He took his time, closing his eyes and relishing in the freedom that was her skin beneath his fingers. The warmth of her embrace felt better than the home he'd been dreaming about.

"Why did they let me out?"

"It's like I said before. I've been writing a lot."

"About what?"

"About *you*, Cal. I couldn't stay silent while you were locked away in that place. I barely ate. I barely slept. I had to do everything in my power to get you out."

"I don't understand."

"You used to say that words were worthless, that actions are all that matter. But that's not true. Words are powerful enough to shift the direction of countries, change the minds of people, and sometimes… free a deserving man from prison."

CHAPTER 69

———

Sofia watched the realization spread over Cal's face. There was no way she could ever fully repay him, but she had to try. She'd thought about him every second she wrote, channeling her life force into the words on the page.

I hope you can see that.

"There was public blowback after I published my piece," she said. "Colonel Blackwell was forced to step down."

"But my release... how did this happen? I didn't think my charges were ever going away."

"Technically, they still haven't," she said. "They dropped some of the more serious charges to save face after Colonel Blackwell's resignation."

She grabbed his hand and guided him toward the car that was parked outside the prison.

Its door opened.

Sofia watched Cal's eyes light up.

"I thought you were dead," Cal said.

"Just old," René replied, a slow smile covering his wind-weathered face.

"With all the gunshots, I didn't think—"

"My lighthouse is independent of power grids, and I've been preparing for a full government collapse for years. Did you think that I wasn't *exceedingly* well-armed?"

Cal reached out for a handshake, but René hugged him instead. In an instant, the Cal Sofia knew came rushing back.

"You're luckier than you know," René said. "Sofia's been working nonstop to get you released. She wrote a brilliant piece about what you went through on the Fourth of July weekend. It's become quite popular."

Sofia smiled and opened the door for him. He sat next to her in the back seat as René started the car.

"That's hard to believe," Cal said. "People find my work unbearably boring."

"I think you're underselling yourself," Sofia stated.

"I've been doing this for a long time," Cal said. "What happened with Nahla isn't going to change that."

"You might be surprised," René said as he threw the car into drive and exited the prisoner pickup. They rounded the corner, leaving the grounds of the correctional facility.

A crowd of people swarmed the car.

They held signs and banners celebrating his release.

THANK YOU, CAL

BITCOIN IS HOPE

FIX THE MONEY, FIX THE WORLD

Sofia watched the shock on his face.

That single moment was worth the sleepless nights.

"Why?" Cal asked, as people cheered.

"They were inspired by your story," she said. "You did the right thing in the face of power."

Cal waved at them and smiled, disbelief still covering his face. Their car left the detention center, and René drove them toward the city. They cruised through the Brooklyn-Queens Expressway toward lower Manhattan.

"You should read it," René said as he tossed a copy of the article into the back seat.

Cal read the title of her piece out loud.

"'*Blood of the Bourgeoisie.*'"

"Dramatic," Cal muttered. "Has a bit of a French Revolution vibe."

"I thought you of all people would appreciate the reference to financial disparity and class struggles."

Cal continued flipping through the piece.

Sofia anxiously chewed on her bottom lip. She'd turned in countless stories during her time as a journalist, but watching his eyes comb over the page made her more nervous than she'd ever been in the past.

"Max Aldrich, the Vizcaya Mansion, and the Penthouse party," he began. "It's all here."

She nodded.

"No, really," Cal said as he got to the part where she detailed her time in Khartoum. Flipping through the pages where she described James Valhner cutting her ear. "It's *all* here."

She gave him a tight-lipped smile and watched him realize the extent of what she had done.

"I had to convince her not to admit to a double homicide," René said from the front of the car. "I thought it might be best *not* to publicly explain how she tortured two men, no matter how much they deserved it."

"Probably wise," Cal said.

"I told the truth to the best of my ability," Sofia continued. "Regardless of the consequences."

She looked to the west and caught a glimpse of the Statue of Liberty standing proudly in the bay. She thought about the woman she was on the day she first met Cal.

I was selfish. I was scared. No more.

Cal skimmed through the pages, reading chunks aloud.

"'Cal believes Bitcoin was founded on the same ideals as the United States of America. But instead of relying on the fallibility of man, it creates liberty and freedom through uncensorable code.'"

The corner of his mouth turned up into a smile.

"'The existing financial systems expand the divide between the rich and poor,'" Cal continued reading. "'Nahla saw this as a problem that could only be fixed through violence. Cal saw a more optimistic path. A technological path. He believes we can build a more equitable system that gives power back to the people.'"

"Are you ready to admit that I was right?" René asked from the front seat.

"Right about what?" Cal asked.

"She was genuinely interested in what you were saying after all."

Cal chuckled.

Sofia watched as his eyes made their way down to the Bitcoin address at the bottom of the page.

"Does it look familiar?" she asked.

His eyebrows furrowed.

"I used the address from the business card you gave me in Harold's town car," she said. "It's like you said. Anyone in the world can send bitcoin to that address. No middleman. No asking for permission."

"You didn't have to do that," Cal said.

"It doesn't matter that the FBI had every bank account in your name frozen. Thousands of people have sent you donations after hearing your story to thank you for what you did."

Cal reached across the car seat and placed his hand on hers.

"We still have more fights ahead of us," she said. "But at least you're not behind bars."

She connected with his deep blue eyes. The same ones she'd looked into beside the Hudson River. The same ones she'd betrayed in the penthouse. The same ones that had saved her life on the Fourth of July. They looked different now, more open and more trusting than she'd ever seen them.

"What do you think?" Sofia asked.

Cal flipped through the story again, coming back to the beginning. "You actually did after all, huh?"

"What's that?"

"Told my story," Cal said as a smile slowly spread over his face.

She smiled back at him.

"Unfortunately, it's not over quite yet," Sofia said. "You still have a legal battle in front of you."

"About that," Cal began. "Would you be willing to help me again?"

"I'm not sure—"

"Twenty-four hours, Sofia. That's all I'm asking. Help me clear my name."

"I thought you hated reporters?"

"I think I can manage for just a bit longer."

"One more day?"

"One more day."

THE END

ACKNOWLEDGEMENTS

My name gets to be on the cover, but writing a book is a massive team sport.

First and foremost, I want to thank my wife, Erin. Outside of being my favorite person in the world and the mother of my child, she is also the best editor I could ever ask for. It is easy to write a great book when you live with a brilliant editor and get to dissect stories with her every single day.

To the rest of my family, thank you. Your constant support drives and inspires me. I sacrificed so much time to bring this story into the world, and I am grateful for your patience.

Special thanks to Meghan Feir Walker for bringing the final layer of polish that made me comfortable wrapping this project up. Thanks also to Ivicia Jandrevic and Henry Ralf for once again knocking it out of the park with brilliant cover and internal design. You are both amazing at your craft.

Thank you to my close group of college friends. I'm frequently reminded of just how fortunate we are to have such a tight group to hang out with at this point in our lives and I never take you for granted.

Shout out to all the guys I train BJJ with. Practicing fighting with you is one of the few things that keeps me (somewhat) sane.

A huge thank you to the many beta readers and others who gave me early feedback or helped answer my endless questions. This book was rough in its early stages, and you powered through, giving me insights that were critical to getting it to the next level.

In no particular order: Ben Schmidt, David Branscum, Sadoshi, Brian Brookshire, David Burns, Doolan Wesley, Boyd Cohen, Zachary Armzallag, Kevin Perez, Devin Rose, and Colleen (The Bitcoin Gal).

In addition, thank you to my friends in the Bitcoin community. Writing a novel and spending thousands of hours on your own can feel isolating. Writing one on a topic that most people consider taboo is even more so. Having your support meant the world to me.

And lastly, a thank you to Satoshi Nakamoto. If it was not already clear, the network you created has fundamentally shaped my worldview and continually reminds me how profoundly optimistic technology can be for humanity.

ABOUT THE AUTHOR

Michael R. Sullivan is an author, software engineer, and family man.

Outside of writing code and stories, Michael is passionate (i.e. obsessed) about education and self growth. He is a musician, chess player, Brazilian Jiu Jitsu instructor, and health/fitness enthusiast fascinated with the idea of life-long learning across multiple domains.

———

GET IN TOUCH

If you'd like to hear more about the topic and ideas that make up the backbone of this book, or if you would like to see what I am up to.

FOLLOW ME ON X:
@SullyMichaelvan

CHECK OUT MY WEBSITE:
michaelrsullivan.com

OR GET IN TOUCH VIA EMAIL:
michaelrsullivan1@gmail.com

READ MORE

I wrote this book because I believe Bitcoin is one of the most important ideas in the world today. As the financial disparities grow and the ideas that America was founded on slowly melt away from underneath us, I couldn't help but to invest as much of my time as possible in spreading this message.

But there is another idea that I believe is equally important: *Embracing your disadvantages.*

My first novel *The Final Flaw* explores this deeply.

It follows Cal and Sofia's son, Charlie, in the future.

Here is a brief synopsis:

OUR FLAWS DEFINE US, WHAT HAPPENS WHEN THEY ARE GONE?

In the near future, genetic defects will soon be a thing of the past.

Every child is born using The Template, a revolutionary invention ensuring health and happiness. Its success brought about Mendelium, the largest technology company in the world, which now controls humanity's genetic future via a board of directors.

Charlie Lamarck, an engineer with Tourette's syndrome, is working to create a better life for future generations when he's suddenly thrust into a position of power by Gerhard Geller, the eccentric CEO who has taken a liking to him—perhaps too quickly.

Charlie's differences have brought success into his life, and he's skeptical of a world without flaws. Now, he faces a choice.

Should Charlie work to change the future, or will he be part of the last generation shaped by their own genetic disadvantages?

Compelling, genuine, timely, and unforgettable: The Final Flaw is a gripping exploration into our differences and what makes us unique as human beings. This thought-provoking novel underlines the positives of neurological diversity and paints an all-too-realistic future of the corporatization of genetic technologies.